THE V. I. P.

Books by
Elleston Trevor

Elleston Trevor

The V.I.P.

AN ENSIGN NOVEL

Ensign edition published in MCMLXXIV by
World Distributors (Manchester) Ltd
12 Lever Street, Manchester M60 1TS

First published in Great Britain by
William Heinemann Ltd.

Copyright © MCMLIX by Elleston Trevor

Made and printed in Great Britain by
C. Nicholls & Company Ltd.
The Philips Park Press, Manchester

SBN 7235 5222 3

TO JONNI

CHAPTER I

The big shapes kept dropping out of the sky. Since dark a thin rain had started, and it swirled past the lamps where bowsers were refuelling aircraft below the terrace.

Louise watched from the terrace. When she saw lights flickering again above the buildings she pressed the scarf against the side of her face where the rain blew, and watched the aircraft's approach. Its lights flickered with precise regularity and it came in directly towards the Terminal, so that to her eyes it seemed to hover nearly motionless, a floating firework of three coloured lights in the black sky. It seemed impossible that a machine as perfectly controlled as this had ever gone skating across the ground here to burn itself out, the screams dying away long before the flames. One did not think of it, unless perhaps someone loved were on the approaching aircraft, and then, just for an instant. . . . But Louise did not think of it. The man she was here to meet was a stranger.

The lights floated lower towards those on the ground. This was Flight 27 from Vienna, a few minutes late because of diminishing visibility. Mr. Turocz should be on board.

The landing-lights came on and felt for the ground with grey fingers. She could hear the engines now. She waited without moving, a little apart from the other people. In her macintosh pocket her hand crumbled and sifted the remains of the biscuit. If Mr. Turocz weren't on this flight she would buy more biscuits and have more coffee. Until he came she might as well be at Central Terminal as any-where else. Inside the hall it was warm and she could watch people: the displaced persons wandering out of their element. Even those with big houses and many friends were displaced for a time, here, a few things in a bag and a ticket in their hand, their eyes touched by the half-admitted thoughts of what it had been like when they had left, and what it would be like when they arrived. A traveller makes a permanent shift of ground, however slight; and nothing will be quite the same when he goes home again.

The long grey beams of light came sweeping through the haze, their tips touching along the ground and finding the runway. Below the terrace a truck went jogging along the line of lamps. Voices called from among the bowsers. Suddenly the aircraft was down and its lights mingled with all the others, so that Louise lost sight of it as a separate shape; it had surrendered its identity. The crumbs had become powdered in her pocket, clogging her nails. People were moving along the terrace and she followed them to the big swing-doors. The announcement was coming over the loud-speakers. Their footsteps were quiet across the floor, muted under the vast acoustic ceiling.

Mr. Turocz was not on this flight. There had been one possibility: a small dark man with worried eyes, papers spilling from his hands and pockets as he tried to contain the bewilderment of being here, so far away from where-ever he had been before: but when she spoke to him he answered in German, and his eyes were already flitting away from her face into the bewildering spaces of the hall, looking for escape. She went back to the refreshment counter and asked for more biscuits and some coffee.

Her friend the immigration man saw her there. "No luck yet?"

"No," she said. "I couldn't have missed him, could I?"

He did not look at her, but watched everyone else, perhaps from habit. "If you did, we wouldn't have. I'm going off now, but I've asked them to get a message up to you if he comes through."

"Thank you."

"I'd say you've had it."

She nodded, not to argue. "Will you have some coffee with me?" She didn't know his name, but he had been helpful to her on previous missions.

He gave a brief shake of his head, a man used to the minimum gestures. "I've no time. If you want to give it up, let me run you as far as civilisation. Earls Court, isn't it?"

"I'll wait a bit longer, I think." She couldn't remember ever having told him where she lived.

He left her and she watched him go down the hall, a tall, neat figure with a quick walk. It was probably he who had checked the little German through, leaving him littered with his spilled papers and no more certain of his true identity than they were. But the papers must have been in order: the man himself must go on searching for his own place in the pattern of things.

She stirred her coffee as an excuse for movement. On the wall the huge figureless clock showed nearly eleven. The board indicated two more flights in from Vienna before midnight. She would see them in, and then go.

The stocky man in uniform had come back for another tea. She judged him to be a chauffeur. There had been two of them, solid and smart in blue macintoshes and peaked caps, making her picture a long, smooth, many-cylindered car in which they would sit efficiently as they

3

sent it through the streets. She could not see the second man now.

Perhaps before leaving at midnight she ought to ring Unic House, in case there were a message about Mr. Turocz. He might have been detained in Vienna: might even have been turned back, to be lost again in the labyrinth of his own country. In that case there would be no message at Unic House or anywhere else. But she would telephone. He might still have his freedom.

She put the last two biscuits into her pocket, for nibbling on the terrace when she went outside again. Along the counter, a man was talking to the chauffeur, saying something about his friend being taken ill. She watched them go up the stairs and turn right, in the direction of the men's lavatories.

The loud-speakers announced the Alitalia Flight 34 from Rome. There were fewer people now in the enormous hall; it was assuming the deserted aspect a late hour brings to meeting-places. She felt loneliness coming back and she remembered that her flat was empty at this moment, and that the people she worked with at Unic would be strangers again tomorrow, as they had been today. Everyone was a stranger. That was why she didn't mind being here in this huge impersonal building where strangers were shuffled and dealt, turned face upwards under the lights and the scrutiny of indifferent eyes, to be shuffled and dealt again and dismissed, their names in the books, nothing more than their names and the details that didn't describe them except as movable units. Even the big clocks here had no figures; their thin hands felt over their own blind faces and failed, hour after hour, to find identity.

"Your change."

"Oh. Thank you."

4

She went up the stairs and out to the terrace. The rain touched her face, webby and cool. A soft dying scream sounded below the terrace where the plane from Rome had swung and halted. She went to the parapet and watched the people coming down the steps from the cabin, uncertain of their feet, hitching their collars higher, one of them stopping and waiting for another. Two small children stood patiently, unsteadily, as if tumbled out of their beds before it was morning. The grown-ups would take care of them. There was nothing the grown-ups didn't know or couldn't do. Their young feet splashed through shallow puddles; their hands were lifted to find the bigger hands, the guiding ones, the hands of the all-knowing people who were so sure in everything they did.

Luggage came dropping from the aircraft through the hatches and on to the trucks like chocolates spilling from a box. The crew walked together towards the bright buildings, anonymous in their uniforms. Already fuel was going into the aircraft.

Watching, Louise experienced the sudden feeling that here was another stage in her life. It wasn't a new sensation; she had stood in places before and admitted it, becoming in a few seconds aware that although there was no journey or job completed and no exact future planned, this moment found her at a point in her life where she could realise herself and set herself apart from all other people, from the past and the future, from all known things. Whatever had happened in her past, it made no difference now; whatever would happen to her, this moment was fixed in time. She stood on an island in time, isolated, the sequence of her life for these few seconds broken so that she could experience nothing but stillness, and remoteness, and calm.

She had told someone, once, a little of it: 'I feel as if I've been shunted into a siding, while everything else goes rushing past.' They had said it was an understandable feeling: she wanted a moment to take stock. 'No, I don't take stock. I don't work anything out. It's just that for a few minutes I seem to have time to realise that I exist—that I am me. Not that I've come from anywhere, or that I'm going anywhere. Just that I *am*.' They had said that it was very odd, then. She had never told anyone else, because she knew that it wasn't odd. It was very important, and right. She was prepared to be defiant about that; but there'd be no call for defiance, because she'd never tell anyone again.

She munched the other half of her biscuit, the rain soft on her face. The moment was over. She was Louise, working for Unic, waiting at the airport for Mr. Turocz, chilled now and sick of biscuits, watching the flicker of lights that were poised again over the buildings as another aircraft came into the circuit.

So that it was coincidence, nothing more, that as she moved forward into this new sequence of her life after the moment's pause, she was in fact exposed to great change.

The lights hovered, red, green, white, flicking on, off, on, off, their rhythm precise as the Swissair Flight 6 from Geneva arrived over London Airport and received permission to land.

It was nothing to do with Mr. Turocz. He would come—if he came—from Vienna. Flight 6 was from Geneva, and she stood here on the terrace to watch it come in, merely from idle interest. The rain was cool on her skin. The lights of the aircraft were now close enough to be reflected in her eyes, so that the first fragile contact was made between the people on board it, and herself.

6

An official car went out from the Passenger Building and stopped by the aircraft. In a moment another followed it. The door of the aircraft was opened and the steps were rolled into position. An officer stood at the bottom of the steps. A man came through the doorway.

In the Passenger Building there was no announcement on the loud-speakers that Flight 6 from Geneva had in fact landed.

Below the terrace a group of mechanics had formed, men in white overalls with their hands in their pockets. They stood and watched the party leaving the aircraft. There were three men in the party, and a woman. They were ushered into the cars and the doors were closed. Among the group of mechanics a man asked a question, but nobody answered. The first car moved off and the other followed.

A steward came down the steps from the aircraft and spoke to the officer. Forward in the aircraft, the baggage-doors opened. The truck was already waiting, with an official standing by.

A fuel-bowser swung past the tip of the port mainplane and halted. The group of mechanics broke up. The steward climbed the steps and vanished into the aircraft. The two cars were out of sight between the buildings.

At the main inquiry desk in the hall, the young woman spoke into the microphone.

Will those meeting unaccompanied children on Flight 19 from Berne please wait at Channel Four.

She hooked her microphone back. People were moving at the end of the hall past the arrival channels.

"Excuse me."

"Yes?"

A girl in a macintosh, her hands on the ledge. "Who were the passengers from Geneva, please?"

"Geneva? Which flight?" She reached for her book.

"It landed a few minutes ago."

The young woman opened her book. "I don't think it was on normal passenger schedule, was it?" The question sounded deliberate, as if time must be gained.

"No. It was a V.I.P. and his party. I was on the terrace, and——"

"I see." She reached for another book and studied it. "I'm afraid there's no record." She closed the book and looked at the girl.

"Oh."

"You're not meeting Flight 19 from Berne? It's just landed."

"No. I'm here to meet someone from Vienna——"

"The next flight in from Vienna is at——"

"Yes, I know. He's not come yet. But I was on the terrace when the plane landed from Geneva. I'm sure——"

"There was a mistake, I think, on the arrivals board." She turned her head and the girl followed her gaze. There had been notice of Flight 6 from Geneva, scheduled to land at 23.05 hours. It was no longer there. Against the other recent arrivals was the word 'In'. They had not been removed. Only Flight 6 had been removed.

"It's very important," the girl in the macintosh said. "I work at Unic, in the Slavakian Section."

8

"I'm sorry I can't help you."

Children were coming in from Channel Four. Their voices were piping, as thin as the cries of birds, as they met the people who were waiting for them.

"If—if a V.I.P. has arrived from Geneva, will they have taken him to the Commandant Suite?"

"That would be the routine."

"It's in the Passenger Building, isn't it? In this block?"

"The Commandant Suite?" It was deliberate.

"Yes."

"It's in this building. Are you expecting a V.I.P.?" Her eyes were cool. It didn't look an expensive macintosh.

"No. But I recognised——"

The young woman waited, and then said: "You thought you recognised someone?"

"I expect I was mistaken." It was the girl's turn to be evasive. Nobody could trust anyone else, even enough to mention the name of the man who had arrived in London.

"You say you work with Unic? If you have any official identification . . ."

"I'm sure I was mistaken. Thank you."

"I'm sorry I can't be of any help to you."

"Thank you."

The girl in the macintosh went away towards the telephones.

At this hour the headquarters of United Nations International Communications looked like a battleship lit over-all, a blaze of light among the darker buildings in Aldersgrove. Transmission continued throughout the night.

Czinitri was alone in the Programme Organiser's office, Slavakian Section. He answered the telephone. He did not give his name.

"This is Louise. Is that Kristov?"

"Yes. Can't you sleep?"

"I'm at London Airport."

"Why?"

"I have to meet someone."

"He is lucky, then."

"Kristov, is Tony there?"

"No. I will not tell him you are meeting gentlemen at the airport. I swear upon the Sacred Microphone that I will say nothing of this to——"

"This is important, Kristov. I haven't much time. Is there a message for me?"

"From whom?"

"The P.O. Anyone. Please find out. Hurry."

Czinitri shrugged and rested the receiver, going out into the staircase hall. There was nothing on the board. The P.O. was down in the studio, and, anyway, if she had left a message for little Louise she would have done it efficiently. The whole of Unic House and London Airport would have heard about it in triplicate.

He went back to the telephone and drooped his thin scarecrow body over it.

"There is no message."

"Oh. Thank you."

He started to say something, but she had rung off.

Ten minutes before the Swissair Flight 6 from Geneva had touched down at London Airport Central, two chauffeurs had reported at the Commandant Suite. The only other people in attendance were airport officials.

Outside the building a black limousine was parked. Its rear window was of smoked glass and the silk blinds were drawn down over the rear quarter-lights.

The young woman in the inquiry desk opened the little gate and asked the Swiss child to come inside. She spoke to him softly in French, saying that she would very quickly find out how he had come to miss the others, and that the people who were meeting him would be told at once that he was here. To prove her great powers, she unhooked her microphone and repeated, quite unnecessarily, an announcement in English that she had given out a few minutes before.

Flight 9 from Nice has been a little delayed due to weather conditions, but will arrive at 23.25 hours, that is in ten minutes from now.

Her hope that the boy spoke no English was realised. His eyes had grown enormous with drama. She then lifted one of her telephones and set about the business of having him rescued.

When she had made the call she found the girl in the macintosh writing a note on the pad at the counter. From where she stood, the young woman could see only that the message was being written in neither English nor French. As the girl had told her that she worked in the Slavakian section at Unic, she thought it was possibly in that language.

"Have you an envelope, please?"

"Of course."

The girl folded the paper, took a key from her pocket and put it into the envelope with the paper. On the envelope she wrote the name 'Mr. Turocz'.

She spoke quickly and seriously. "Your immigration officers will be sending a message up here for me when this passenger arrives. I shan't be here. Would you make certain he gets this envelope?"

"I will. From Vienna, you said?"

"Yes. He speaks no English and he'll be quite lost here, without this envelope."

"I understand."

"If there's any trouble—if he hasn't any money or there's a query at Immigration—would you please ring Unic House and ask personally for Miss Thorne, Programme Organiser." She took the pad again and began writing. "Aldersgrove 2266 is the number. Extension 5. Miss Thorne, personally—nobody else."

"She's sure to be there?"

"Yes, all night."

"I'll see to it for you."

"I'm sorry to give you all this trouble, but it's very important to this man."

"It's no trouble. I'm here to help." For the first time she smiled, but it gave her face no warmth.

"Thank you."

As the girl turned away, the child opened the little gate to follow, excited to be found again. The young woman spoke to him quickly in French and the girl turned back—"I'm sorry?"

"It's all right. He thought you'd come to meet him."

The girl looked down at the child. "Is he lost?"

"Well, let's say he's in my filing-system for the moment."

"Then he doesn't need to worry." She blew the child a quick kiss and went away down the long polished floor. By the time she reached the exit doors she was running.

The car from the Foreign Office had left Whitehall with little enough time in which to reach London Airport and meet the Geneva flight landing at five minutes past eleven; but the warning had been short and the two Civil Servants had not been easy to locate at this hour.

Stross had been at a party in Hampstead and Crowther had been helping to build a new arch for a model railway lay-out at his friend's flat in Bayswater. Stross was not exactly showing the drink, but the party had been going for three hours, and the top layer had been dissolved away from all the deeper layers of inhibition that had quietly encased his soul over the years, so that now he seemed in some danger of expressing emotions that were almost human as he sat beside Crowther in the back of the car.

"And Margaret?"

They talked of their wives. Margaret was well.

The driver sped them along Constitution Hill, his neck stiff with deference, his ears dutifully deaf.

"They've started work, I believe." The extension to the pavilion at Lord's would be ready by the summer. The two men looked out of the windows, carried along upon light conversation and discreetly-upholstered seats. Their last driver had been dismissed for phoning the newspapers the moment he had discharged his passengers at Gatwick when President Bensuta had arrived from Venezuela. No one was remotely interested in President Bensuta, and only one paper had used the information as a fill-in on page four: but urgent directives had circulated at the Foreign Office within twenty-four hours. It might have been serious.

Tonight, it would be very serious. Fleet Street would change the headlines and clear the front page, and the barricades along the Danube might well go down.

"Less talent, I'd say, than Olivier. As Hamlet, possibly, but not Macbeth!"

"He'll extend his range, with the right producer, don't worry."

The arch was designed to span three main lines and the new siding. Robert was like a schoolboy about it. There was something odd about Robert, when you thought about it. A splendid chap, but . . . a bit odd. No eye for—well, women, and that sort of thing.

The car took them through Kensington and slowed, meeting traffic. The theatres were out, and restaurants filling.

Mab, her name was. Mab Someone. Terribly fond of Pernod. And all that talk about Whistler. Was it all put on? It didn't matter. She was so attractive that you didn't mind listening. You could enjoy the wicked privilege of standing close to her while she drank Pernod and talked about Whistler, and you didn't have the impression that she noticed you were studying her bare shoulders and the soft shadows where her dress began. Or did she notice, really? Was that what it was all for—the dull talk, so that you could just stand and look and think, and worry the dream, half-determined with the next drink to attempt an assignation for next week?

"Take the Citroën. Years ahead of its time. How can we hope to compete?"

"I expect you're right."

Soft shadows. If only . . .

They said Robert's mother had wrapped him in cotton wool. Perhaps it accounted for . . .

The other car hit them as the lights changed to green—a grinding of metal, a swerve—and they were stationary with the front wheels locked into the kerb. Someone began hooting. Stross and Crowther leaned forward. Their driver was getting out.

"I did my best, but he must be blind." He shut the door and began talking to the other driver, whose car was hooked into his own, the front bumpers caught fast.

"Damn," said Stross. Crowther looked at his watch.

"It wasn't his fault."

"That's not the thing. We're pushed for time as it is." Stross climbed out of the car and looked round for a policeman. He couldn't see one. Crowther climbed out, too. Stross was always trying to take the initiative.

Crowther told the driver to get the cars unlocked and press on to the airport. The driver nodded and got into the car, but the other man leaned in at the window, still arguing. A medley of hooting had struck up. Stross said: "If we can get a police-car along, they'd take us there."

A saloon was standing at the kerb, directly in front of them. Two men were coming towards them, to offer help. Crowther was trying to prise the other driver away from the window so that his own man could pull the car free.

"We're on urgent business. Please take my card. We can sort this out tomorrow——"

"Where was his signal? If he'd given a signal, I'd have had a chance to miss him!"

"Look, I've asked someone to find a policeman. We must get this car free while we're waiting——"

"I'm not moving mine. And you're not moving yours. You'd better find your witnesses, if you ask me. You'll need 'em."

"Here's my official card. Now please——"

"Official, are you? So'm I—a British citizen. Now don't try coming the acid——"

"If we can help you . . ."

Crowther stood on the running-board of the other car, trying to see a helmet. He stood like a pale statue in the bedlam of hooting.

"We're making for London Airport, ourselves. We could drop you off, anywhere in that direction . . ."

Stross turned his head. "What?"

The two men from the saloon were offering assistance.

"Crowther!"

"Yes?"

"Wait a minute."

"I can't help that," the other driver was shouting. "I don't move this car till the p'lice have been and measured up!"

"Where did you say you were going?"

"London Airport. I heard you say you were on urgent business, so I thought I'd mention it."

"I see."

A throng was collecting on the pavement. Crowther could feel the drizzle soaking into his collar. He joined Stross.

The motorist was saying: "If we can give you a lift, I'd be glad to go. We're a little short of time, actually."

"Yes, of course. It's good of you."

Crowther looked round at the mêlée. There were plenty of taxis here, but they were all engaged and their drivers angry, hooting without pause. It was the after-theatre rush hour.

"All right?" Stross murmured. Crowther nodded.

"The quickest way." Stross's damned initiative had done it again: they'd got a lift. He said to their driver: "You'll have to deal with this. Bring me a report in the morning, and don't stand any nonsense from that fellow."

They followed the motorist and his companion. The car was a new one, and looked fast. As it drove away, they looked at their watches in the same instant; but neither spoke. The car turned off the main road to the right, accelerating with dash. The motorist spoke over his shoulder:

"We'll nip down here and cut out the traffic."

"You know the way?"

"Lord yes!"

His companion rested an arm along the back of his seat, grinning pleasantly to Stross and Crowther. "He works at the airport. Does this trip twice a day. You'll be all right."

Stross sat back. "Splendid." His head felt muzzy. They shouldn't drag a chap out of a party on business. Did they take one for a machine?

Crowther was looking at his watch again and Stross wished the man would sit back and relax. They were in luck. If they didn't arrive in time it would be no one's fault, except that fool driver's, and he was an act of God.

The car swerved again on its soft springs, now running along a road parallel with the one they had started from. The man knew his way, certainly.

Stross began talking to Crowther about the accident, trying to make him sit back and compose himself. His pale face was tight across the eyes. Crowther took too much notice of life. Everything was vitally important to him. No wonder he lived on Placidex. He had to.

A meat-van was backing across the street. The motorist put his brakes on, changed down and swung left, taking a narrow turning and speeding up again.

"Obstacle race," he said cheerfully.

Crowther sat at the edge of the seat, his wrists crossed, the watch-face uppermost.

"Have a pill," Stross murmured.

"What?"

"Nothing."

The car took another turning, and stopped. Crowther had to put his hands against the back of the passenger's seat to stop himself pitching forward. Stross was surprised to see actual fear on his face.

"Got it wrong," the motorist said. "Sorry."

The street was deserted.

Stross saw Crowther lean back, as if retreating from the men in front. He looked at Stross with the face of a lost child.

The motorist's friend said: "Try left. That should get us to the Parade."

The driver moved the car forward, crawling in low gear and craning his neck to make out the name of the street. "We've by-passed the Parade already."

The aura of fear that was spreading from Crowther touched Stross and he tried to clear his head. He felt angry with Crowther. The man was no earthly good in a crisis.

He leaned forward. "If you'll just drive on until we see a taxi, we'll have to take it."

"Endervell Street," said the driver. "Where the devil's that?"

"Where we are now," his friend said, and grinned.

"Look here," Crowther began with a brave squeak, but Stross said:

"I must impress it on you that we have to be at the airport as soon as possible."

The driver nodded, only half attentive. "I'm doing my best, old man." His friend was fishing a map-book from the pocket in the door.

"What was it?"

"Endervell."

"Dead-Endervell, eh? Don't worry, we'll make it."

The car stopped again. This street, too, was deserted. The hour was late and the drizzle worsening. Crowther sat stiffly, staring his watch-face out.

"I'm damned if I can find Endervell Street," said the man with the map.

The driver started off again. "I'll keep going. We might find a taxi even if we don't find the way."

"If you please," Stross said.

"It's most important," Crowther nodded.

The driver turned his head. "It's fairly important that I get there myself. I happen to work there and I happen to be late. Since we're trying to do you a good turn I suggest you sit back and——"

"Take it easy, Jack," his friend said. He shot a friendly wink to Crowther. "It's always the same when you lose your way. Gets you upset."

In the next street they saw a taxi and Stross leaned forward, knocking against Crowther's knee. "Can you stop that cab?"

"You really want to?" asked the passenger.

"Please. If you please."

The driver nodded and accelerated, passing the taxi and drawing ahead, then slowing, waving it down. The other man looked at Crowther. "It's not a good idea, to change horses in mid-stream. Is it?"

Stross said sharply: "We'll get out here."

"All I mean is, it won't be so fast, along the arterial."

The driver was still slowing, and said to his companion: "Nip out and grab the taxi, and make sure."

"Right."

The saloon stopped. The lights of the taxi winked in the driving-mirror. The man dropped the map on the seat and snapped the door open, trotting along the road to talk to the taxi-driver.

Stross said: "You've been most kind. It was unfortunate."

"Thank you," Crowther said pertly. "Thank you so much." Stross opened the door and stepped out. Crowther followed. As he slammed the door shut the taxi grated into gear and turned out, passing the saloon, accelerating. Stross gave a shout and waved his hand but the taxi did not stop.

The motorist was getting out, and his friend came back to join them. "He was engaged," he said.

"But the flag wasn't down," said Stross. He was enraged. Beneath all the layers of inhibition that had formed round his soul over the years, rage churned: with Crowther, these men, himself. There was nothing of its heat in his voice. In bed, in his bath, in his marriage and in his every affair, wherever he was, at any instant of the day or the night, he was an official spokesman. "He wouldn't have stopped at all, if he'd been engaged."

The four men stood together in the drizzle, half-way along the deserted street, the name of which none of them knew.

Stross looked into the faces of the two men. They looked back at him. For the first time, in silence, they understood one another. The rain fell across their heads.

Crowther was staring at his watch. It showed a few minutes past eleven. They were still some miles from the airport. He looked up at Stross, wondering at the composure of his face.

Stross said: "Please take me to the nearest telephone."

The motorist nodded. He turned his head, saying to his friend: "We'll see if we can find a telephone."

"In this place, it won't be easy. We're in the back o' beyond." He gave a slow smile.

The rain pattered softly on the metal roof of the car.

Stross said: "On second thoughts, perhaps we'll walk."

He looked at Crowther and they began walking side by side along the empty street. Their footsteps echoed from the brick walls. They walked past black railings. Crowther's breathing was audible, painful. He walked faster than Stross and had to slow down and wait for him; and then his feet hurried again, taking him as if to the end of a leash held by Stross; then he felt its intangible tug and he slowed again.

At last he looked back over his shoulder as Stross knew he would.

"What are they doing?" Stross asked him, not moving his head.

"Nothing." The word burst softly out in relief.

They walked on, and came to the end of the street. For a moment Stross stopped and turned round, gazing down the bleak perspective of the roadway. The lamps made a series of bright pools along the wet surface. The car was still there and the two men were standing beside it as they had been before. They looked up the street at Stross and Crowther, their faces two anonymous pale blobs above the two dark coats.

"Come along," said Stross, and turned the corner.

CHAPTER III

The black limousine drove into the tunnel and the lights flickered along the cellulose, their reflections sliding down the domed back and vanishing like bubbles. Behind it came the taxi.

The lights were red at the main road. The taxi-driver said over his shoulder: "In case there's traffic, Miss, where are we going?"

"The West End," Louise told him. The taxi was a normal saloon without a division. She leaned forward with her hands on the seat-back in front of her, gazing through the windscreen at the limousine ahead of them. Not even the outline of heads was visible through the smoked glass of its rear window. But she knew he was in there, with the others. She had glimpsed his face again, once. His face had changed, since the photograph on her desk was taken; five years ago; but she had recognised him at once, as if her memory of him had also changed, little by little as each year had passed, so that she would know him immediately, today.

Her hands were gripped together on the seat-back, and no longer trembled. Her voice was less easy to compose.

The lights changed and the limousine turned right, and the taxi followed. The driver said: "Whereabouts, in the West End, Miss?"

"I don't know. A hotel."

"There's plenty of them. You see, if we lose track of him, when there's traffic——"

"Don't lose track of him." She saw his eyes flick upwards in the mirror to look at her. "It's very important, not to lose track of him."

"I'll do my best."

She offered her pathetic credentials again. "I'm at Unic. This is very urgent."

"Oh-ah." His eyes moved again in the mirror. She was able to flash a smile to him. Her excitement was now so intense that its force carried her along, clearing her head and brightening her eyes. She was under the influence of emotional benzedrine. It was in her veins, her voice, her fingers. The driver said again: "Well, I'll do my best, then."

"You must." She could command multitudes. The driver was a good man. He sat like an amiable bear and his voice was rough, a London voice.

"They—er—they know we're followin' them?"

"I don't expect so."

For half a mile he thought about this. "Better if we didn't show it, like? I mean, keep back a bit?" There was silence, but she must have heard him, for she was still leaning well forward, her chin on her hands as she gazed through the windscreen. "Eh, Miss?"

"I'm sorry?"

It was rum. Her eyes looked so bright, made her look a bit sort of out-of-herself. But it wasn't drink. There was no drink on her breath. "I said, is it all right, I mean us followin' them? I mean, you don't mind if they know?"

He watched her in the mirror. She was a pretty enough kid all right. A bit like Ma Jones's eldest, but older, of course.

"I don't expect they'll know," she said.

It wouldn't do to ask outright, who they were following. So long as they paid the fare, you just took them where

23

they said: that was your job. But it was clear as daylight, when you thought about it. Someone said there was a V.I.P. come through, soon after eleven. And this was a V.I.P. transport all right, no error. So it was some film-star. That was what made the kid's eyes bright like that, and her voice full o' Christmas candles. As long as she didn't start tearing her clothes off and yelling *Frankie!* or whatever it was, it'd be all right. You couldn't stand for that sort of thing, and keep your licence.

"He's turning right."

"Yes, Miss." Twenty-two years at the wheel, a veteran. But then, she was excited. You didn't mind.

The taxi swung to the right, after the limousine. A small green saloon slipped into the space between them.

"Don't lose them."

"We're all right. They're not goin' fast."

"We must get rid of that green one."

"He'll overtake 'em, like he did us. Don't you worry."

In half a mile the green car seemed to slacken speed. The limousine was drawing farther ahead. Twice the taxi tried to overtake the green car and come up on the limousine, but it was baulked.

"We mustn't lose them."

"Now you just leave it to me, Miss."

The green car was still slowing, minute by minute, and holding the crown of the road. The taxi flashed his lights but it made no difference. The limousine was a hundred yards in the lead. Bad luck at the traffic-lights could lose it now.

Louise put her hand on the driver's shoulder.

"Please," she said.

He flashed his lights again, and then pipped the horn; but the green car stayed in his path, so he snicked into

24

third and checked his mirror and pulled well out with the throttle down. For a long time the green car kept alongside, accelerating with him, so that the taxi-driver was forced to follow the path he had chosen, on the wrong side of the road. Then the car dropped back suddenly, giving way.

"That was delib'rate, you know. That was plain delib'rate!"

"Was it?"

"I'll say it was!"

They drew up on the limousine and went through the lights together on the amber. "We'd've lost him, see? We'd've lost him, then."

"We mustn't."

The driver took a glance at the lights in his mirror. The green car had tucked in behind them.

"Where did you say you worked, Miss?"

"At Unic."

You learned things. In twenty-two years, you learned things. You got sensitive. You remembered. There was that time when a copper jumped in and said: 'See if you can catch that Packard. You can put your foot down. Never mind the limit.' They'd gone six miles, right through Deptford and Greenwich, and the Packard had finished up on her side with the front through the railings. The letter was still at home, somewhere . . . 'A gallant contribution to the efforts of the Metropolitan Police in their vigilance against crime.' Something like that. Sir James Forsythe, Chief Commissioner. Milly had cried with pride, the silly thing. But you remembered.

The green car still tailed them.

"Must be excitin', at Unic, Miss. Broadcast all over the world, I expect, don't you?"

"Yes."

"Have to go careful, I expect. I mean, what with the cold war, and everythin'?"

"I find it an interesting job."

"I mean, you got to be careful what you say, I expect?"

"I find foreign languages very interesting."

He gave it up. In a way, he'd got his answer.

"Where are we now, please?"

"Eh? Brentford."

"But this isn't the way into the West End."

"Cert'nly it isn't. We turned off that route a long time back."

"Oh." Her voice was perplexed. He moved his head in a quick glance.

"All right, are we?" he said.

"Yes. I—I'm not sure of their actual destination."

The side-lights had gone from the mirror. Suddenly the green car was alongside them in a surge of acceleration and two men were looking in at them from a yard's distance. The taxi-driver lifted his foot and the other car went ahead, tucking in behind the limousine.

"Look, Miss, I'm quite prepared to follow that Daimler, but if there's going to be any funny stuff, I've got my licence to think about——"

"It's a police escort, that's all."

"Eh? Patrol cars are black."

"It's a special one."

"Don't tell me. You know how long I been drivin' taxis in London?"

The green car was slowing, moving over to the crown again. The taxi had to drop back.

The girl said: "There's nothing to worry about."

"I dunno so much." It was different when you had a

copper on board to take the responsibility. "This is delib'rate, you see. I don't mind havin' a go, but if I smash this lot up tryin' to get past——"

"You won't. You're too good a driver."

The green car still slowed. The limousine was drawing well ahead. "I'm sorry, Miss, but I didn't bargain for this. I mean you can't expect it, can you?"

Louise turned her face and spoke with a soft insistence. "Please. This is awfully important to me. It really is." That was all she said, but he had glanced at her for an instant and seen the start of tears.

He said nothing, but checked his mirror and took a sight past the near-side of the green car, slowing to drop back from it.

"Please."

He said: "I'm not goin' to stop. Just givin' myself some elbow-room." He checked his mirror once more and changed down, building up his speed until the lower ratio was letting the engine use all its power. Then he was committed, pulling out wide and coming up fast on the green car, getting alongside and giving it room, going past it and pulling in obliquely ahead of it with the street-island swishing by on the off-side with little enough to spare.

The limousine was fifty yards in front of them. He closed the gap. In his mirror were perched the lights of the green car.

"That was splendid," said Louise. The tears of frustration had gone.

"It's funny. If you'd offered me an extra quid, I wouldn't have done it. As it is, call me a mug."

They neared Isleworth, on the south side of the River.

"Is the clock on your dashboard right?"

"Eh? It might be a minute fast."

She leaned her chin on her hands, watching the dark rear window of the limousine. It was midnight. This fabulous day, that had only come to life less than an hour ago, was over now. He had changed so much: he was older by five years but so was she, so was all the world: it wasn't just the passage of time that had made his face so different, but the passage of thought. He looked so bitter, now.

"Where are we?"

"Eh? Richmond."

She looked back. The green car was with them. It didn't matter. It might really be a police escort, suspicious of them.

The road was narrower. They drove through an avenue, a tunnel of spring leaves, light green, rushing above their lamps. The limousine was slowing.

"Long way from the West End, this is."

There were big houses, here, among tall trees. A driveway opened on the left and the limousine turned into it.

"You want me to——" but he had to stamp on the brake as the green car swerved across his radiator, a hand waving him down. They stopped. A man got out of the green car, leaving his driver at the wheel.

Louise sat back. The man's silhouette was suddenly filled in by the glow of the sidelamp; then he became dark again. He stood by the window and said to the taxi-driver:

"I'm a police officer. Who is your passenger?"

The driver looked up into the man's face. "You want to watch your drivin', then, don't you?"

The man opened the rear door and looked in, snapping a torch on. Its wash of light dazzled Louise. She did not move, but clenched her eyes against the glare. It remained on her face until her eyes began to water; then the beam of the torch went down, sweeping round the inside of the car. The driver screwed his shoulders round. "I'll just see your credentials, if you don't mind."

The man moved his torch methodically across the foot-wells, then switched it off and stood back.

"You can proceed," he said. He threw the rear door shut. After the glare, Louise could see very little, but the man's footsteps were on the road, sounding away.

"The name of the house."

"Eh?"

"All I want is the name of the house."

He peered through the windscreen. The other car was moving again, turning into the driveway.

"Beacons."

"Thank you." She was shivering. "We can go now."

He put the gears in, and turned the car. As they drove back along the avenue, she looked for the name of it, and slowed the driver until they reached the cross-roads, and could see the name-plate. South Avenue.

"Back to the airport?"

"No. The nearest Tube station."

"Mortlake. But you won't get a train. It's gone midnight."

"Oh."

He drove slowly. "Where've you got to get to, then?"

"Unic House. No—Earls Court. I can phone from there."

"It's a good walk. You want me to take you?"

"How much will it cost?"

"I dunno, rightly." He looked at his meter. "There's thirty-two bob up to now. I can't pick up a fare, except at the airport an' Waterloo Terminus. On the other hand, Earls Court's not on my way back, see?"

She made no answer and he jerked his head to look at

her across the seat-squab. She sat staring. There was something about her face . . . "You all right, Miss?"

"What?" Her eyes struggled to recognise him.

He stopped the car. "You're all right, are you?"

The engine idled, its sound pointing the sense of intimacy in which they sat here, two strangers in the small space along a street that slept.

"Would you say he was a police officer?" she asked.

"Eh? That feller?" His face was squeezed in amusement. "Yeh. He's a police officer, an' I'm Danny Kaye."

She was quiet again. He said: "If it's all the same to you, Miss, we'll get on, eh?"

"I didn't ask you to stop."

"That's right, you didn't. But you look a bit worried. I thought p'r'aps . . ."

She shivered again, hunched in her cold macintosh, her hands out of sight. "I think I'm a little bit mad."

"It's a free country." But he looked nervous.

She was leaning forward, her whole body trying to explain this to herself as well as to him. "I've never been so close to anything as—as big as this. It's unnerving."

He nodded amiably. "I'll get you to Earls Court—never mind about the extra—an' you can have a good night's sleep, what's left of it."

"Don't you care?"

He hooked his left arm over the seat-squab. "Listen, Miss. In my job I come up against a lot of funny people. They want to go somewhere? I'll take 'em. But that's all. I don't get mixed up in anythin', see? It don't pay."

She sat back again. "Of course not."

"Don't think I mean any offence. If you want to follow a V.I.P. round the place, that's your business. But you can't blame his friends checkin' up on you. Course, if he'd been rough, I'd've clipped him—but he wasn't." He lifted his hand and laid it flat on the top of the seat, solemnly. "Take my advice, you'll go home an' go to bed."

"Yes." But she didn't seem fully aware of his presence. It gave him the odd feeling of being half invisible. He turned away from her and settled himself in the seat. She said: "Leinster Road, Number 15."

"That's by the Tube?"

"Yes. Quite near."

He took the Upper Richmond Road.

"It didn't occur to me, you know." She was leaning forward again, so that he could hear more easily. "I really thought it might be a police car. The green one. Then, when you said it wasn't, I was worried. But you must be right—they were friends of his, looking after him. An escort. It's very natural. So everything's all right."

She watched the side of his face, still needful of this stranger's reassurance.

"Don't you worry, Miss. Everything's right as rain."

She closed her eyes.

Shortly before half-past eleven a telephone call was made from the Commandant Suite at Central Terminal to Brown's Hotel. The manager himself was requested to come to the telephone.

"This is Sir Edmond Stross, speaking from London Airport."

"Oh yes, Sir Edmond. Good evening."

"You are expecting a distinguished person and his party, from abroad. Reservations have been made with you."

There was a brief pause. "I'm afraid I'm not able to discuss——"

"Quite so——"

31

"You'll understand, of course—on the telephone——"

"Yes. If this person arrives before I do, at your hotel, will you please say to him that representatives of the Foreign Office will present themselves there within a few moments of his own arrival. We have been delayed."

"I am making a note of this, Sir Edmond."

"Thank you. Will you please offer him our most respectful apologies. The delay was unavoidable."

"I'll see it, Sir Edmond."

"Thank you. Naturally, it's very important."

He rang off and met Crowther, who had been using another line. Crowther seemed excited. "They're taking immediate action."

"I hope so. Did you give them the number of the car?"

"Oh yes—and a description of the two men." He cast glances about him, to Stross's annoyance. Stross had no taste for drama. He held that affairs at diplomatic level should be conducted in a civilised manner.

"We must go," he said, and took Crowther out to the police car, saying to the officers: "If we can overtake the other car and reach the hotel first, it would meet approval at high level. You may accept my authority for the well-considered breach of the traffic regulations if necessary."

In the back of the police car, Crowther said anxiously: "But what reason? What *purpose* had they?"

"Nuisance value."

"I wish I could be sure of that."

"So do I."

Soon after midnight a B.E.A. passenger using the men's lavatory outside the restaurant in the main hall of Central Terminal heard moans from one of the cubicles, and the sound of vomiting. After hesitating a moment he rapped at the door, and managed to get an answer, though in a weak voice. He went to summon help.

A commissionaire opened the door of the cubicle, and that of another in the same lavatory. Two men were brought out, one unconscious, the other in a dazed state. Both were in their underclothes. Two bundles of clothing were found. Each man's throat was badly bruised and a resident staff nurse found indications of toxic malaise. At the request of the man who had first recovered, a telephone call was made to the night office of the Burlington Motor-Hire Service, of which the men were employees. The police were also informed.

Following these calls, the Burlington Motor-Hire Service contacted the operations-room of the Metropolitan Police through the emergency system and reported the theft of one of their cars: a Daimler limousine. Arrangements had earlier been made for this car to meet an important person arriving at London Airport. The two men found in the lavatory had been the chauffeur and escort.

Before half-past twelve, patrol cars were warned by radio to keep a look-out for the Daimler; but soon afterwards it was found parked in a street only a few minutes away from the night office of the hire company, abandoned but undamaged. Two officers of Scotland Yard took immediate charge of it, for by this time the pattern of these events was becoming clear.

At a few minutes after one o'clock a reporter telephoned the night desk of his newspaper, spoke personally to the night editor and gave him the first brief details of his story, which he claimed was big. The editor agreed, and called in his chief sub to re-make the front page of the next edition.

CHAPTER IV

Mr. Turocz's coat was as dark as the curtains behind him, so that when Louise came into the room it seemed that a face and two hands went floating into the air as he stood up. They hovered with a genie's deference.

She spoke to him in Slavakian, asking his name. He was eager to show his papers to prove his identity. They came crackling out of his pockets: he was so like the little German at the airport. These were the hounded. She examined his papers briefly, knowing that he was proud of them. It was something, in his world, to possess identity.

"I am sorry," she said, "that I was not there to meet you."

"It was my fault. They held me for a time at Vienna, and I missed several planes." He stared at her with brown dazed eyes: he was in England, and here was an English woman talking to him in such bad Slavakian that for the first time in three years he wanted to laugh. It would be a strange sound and he was afraid of making it.

"I wonder," she asked, "if you could lend me five shillings?"

He touched his ear. "I am sorry. I am a little deaf."

She too wanted to laugh, because it had been a favourite joke in her family, a long time ago. When she had asked her father for more pocket-money, he had pretended to be a little deaf. This accident of touching off a memory dear to her made Mr. Turocz less of a stranger. She said: "No.

34

My Slavakian is poor." More carefully: "Please may I borrow five shillings?"

He covered most of his surprise, fumbling at once for money. He offered a bundle of creased notes which he prised from a special pocket in the lining of his waistcoat. He held it out to her in both hands, and instinctively she knew that this was his all. A great gem, or a handful of rice: here was his total estate. His eyes were like a dog's and she felt angry with him for his gratitude. Quickly she extracted a single pound note and held it up. "One pound. I will return it tomorrow. Please stay here. I will be only a few minutes."

She went down to the street, but the taxi had gone. The driver had told her not to worry. Two bob wouldn't break him. She had left him all she had, which was thirty shillings, and asked him to wait. If Mr. Turocz were not here she would rouse the porter. But now the taxi had gone.

Mr. Turocz was standing exactly as she had left him. She held out his pound note, but he stepped back, waggling his finger and his head. She insisted, explaining: "It was for a taxi, but he would not wait." Again he demurred, asking that she keep it until tomorrow. She touched his hand with the note, so that he had to accept it. "I have money at the office," she explained. "I had no money here." She turned away, for him to overcome his embarrassment that his help was not wanted. Taking off her macintosh she dropped it across the chair and bent to light the gasfire. The smell of Mr. Turocz was in the room: black tobacco and damp cloth.

Louise stood up. "Let me have your coat. It is wet."

He allowed her. "English rain." He made it sound another name for Paradise. He was smiling now, a dark face and white teeth, his eyes like his brother's. She draped his coat on the back of the chair and moved it nearer the fire.

"Your brother is very well, Mr. Turocz. He could not come to the airport. He had work with us. But he will call here for you, soon." The phrases were painful, and would sound even worse to his ears. "You do not speak English?"

"No. I have tried to learn, but it has to be done in secret, and a book in English is a passport to the labour camp."

"I understand."

Then in English he said: "Your tongue beautiful, yet is heart." His smile was eager for even false praise.

"That is very good," she nodded. "But it is not beautiful. It is very hard, yes. Please sit down, Mr. Turocz."

He accepted the arm-chair as a choice prize. They were all like this, when they arrived. They allowed their pride to creep from its shell later, though sometimes it was pricked in the dark and rushed forth suddenly like a bull from the *toril* gate.

His dark wet coat began steaming in the warmth. She perched on the stool, looking up at his face. "Your brother told me that you were coming. We could not tell any of the others. They must not know that you are here. When you go back, you will be interrogated, and asked if you have been talking to your ex-compatriots here. If you have talked to them, you will have to lie, and it will make it hard. You might reveal that you are lying, and they will send you to the camps. That is why we do not tell your friends here that you have come. They would be delighted to greet you, but it is best. You can talk to your brother, because you have come to see him, officially, and they will realise that."

He nodded, almost at each word. Sometimes as she

talked he dared to help her, when she misused an idiom and puzzled him. His smile came more often, reminding her of his brother at Unic. He asked her about his brother and they talked more freely, while on the chair his dark coat steamed; and after a while they didn't notice the steady gasp of the gas-fire that before had provided the only sound common to their strangeness.

She said that England had welcomed his friends, and had been privileged to offer them her nationality.

He said that England must now seem the fatherland to them with all its kindness. Then he changed it to 'motherland', and she laughed and said that all people had a favourite parent—and for an instant she was plunged into the black cold memory of the drone of planes and the staircase crumbling and her mother's face, her father's shout. To this day she had never been able to remember what he had shouted. She remembered only the voice of Mrs. Lattimer—'There, there, it might have been all of you, my lamb.'

"We listen to the broadcasts," said Mr. Turocz, who was not watching her face. "It is our great joy. Many times I have sat in the cupboard, with the door locked and the headphones on, and heard my brother's voice; and I have pretended he was there with me in the same house, as he was before. It is quite extraordinary—to hear his voice in my head. Sometimes it is painful not to answer him and share a joke——" He spread his empty hands, the pain in his eyes, his face smiling about the joke that had never been shared.

"You can answer him soon," she said.

"Yes. Yes." He looked towards the door, as if he could hear his brother coming. "I never thought I would see him again."

"You will see him soon."

He looked down at his folded hands, embarrassed by his own enormous need. "If I did not go back, it would be hard for my family. They would be made to suffer. When Andrey came away, it was easier." He failed to keep envy out of his voice, and seemed aware of it, for he added: "We are glad—we are all glad that at least one of our family came away."

"Perhaps everything will change, soon. It seems——"

"There is a lot of shooting, but the tanks . . ." He placed his thumbs together against his mouth.

She said in a moment, cautiously: "Another of your people arrived tonight, in London. Did you know?"

"What is his name?" But the question was innocent.

She folded her arms across her knees, looking down at her feet. She hadn't realised her shoes were soaked. "He used some other name, I expect." If he had known about the flight from Geneva they might have talked about it and she could have relieved her mind of the pressure; but he seemed not to know. In any case, she must be careful. Nobody from over there was safe, until they were questioned.

"I am not to be trusted. I understand." She looked up at him again. There was bitterness in his face and it reminded her of the man at the airport whose name she mustn't say aloud, though it was in her mind like a big signboard that she must stare at and not read aloud to anyone. The next word she spoke was hesitant, as if she were afraid that the name was on her tongue, despite her discipline.

"Of course we trust you." She disliked the habit she had got into, of saying 'we' for 'I', meaning 'we at Unic' or 'we of the free West'. An organisation like Unic could submerge your identity if you were not careful. Freedom could be pilfered from under your eyes, while you were made most conscious of it.

"I understand," he said.

"We have to be careful—for your sake. We know Andrey, who is splendid, but we have never seen his brother. You look like him and have his gestures—the way you put your thumbs t gether like that when you must stop yourself speaking of painful things—but if they wanted to send a man here to make trouble, he would come as your brother's brother——"

"Andrey will know me——"

"Of course." She felt inhospitable, having to withhold her trust, and she got up and found a half-bottle of sweet sherry to offer him, as if wine could atone for hard eyes. They sipped the sherry. "Has it been bad in your country?"

He said yes, it had been bad. "There are new laws, bad laws. The theft of an orange from a government store is punishable by death.. So is 'hooliganism'—which means calling a greeting in the morning to your neighbour across the street. But the punishment is nearly always reduced— or should I not say postponed? The offenders are sent to cut reeds along the Danube, for processing cellulose."

"Postponed? Why do they die?"

"They die of two things. Pneumonia, and the lack of the will to do otherwise." He sipped his wine with feigned relish. It was South African and badly chosen, and she knew from Andrey Turocz of the vineyards that had been theirs, five years ago. "But we listen," he said, "to your broadcasts. You can have no idea of what they mean. It is hope coming through the air." He smiled thinly. "Hope is a habit over there."

"Are the broadcasts accurate, when there is a chance of checking the facts?"

"In most instances, yes."

"In most . . . You see, our organisation is still new. We are feeling our way. We have been told that we fall short of the service you received previously from the B.B.C. Is that true?"

Mr. Turocz shrugged with his neck. "When we are thrown a life-line we do not complain that it is rough to the touch."

"You will be questioned at Unic House. We want to know how we can improve our service. We have no other means of finding out, except from you yourselves." She thought she heard a sound from the stairs outside, but it wasn't repeated. Seeing that she had turned her head to listen, he half rose from the chair and she looked back at him quickly. His face was white.

"What is it, Mr. Turocz?" She was alarmed.

"A mistake." He sank slowly down again. On a face so blanched, the apologetic smile had a clown's pathos. "I was stupid. I was forgetting this was England."

She filled his glass again. "I see. I thought I heard your brother coming. I am sorry."

The wine shivered in the glass.

"We—we are told," she said, "that our transmissions are jammed soon after we begin broadcasting."

"Yes." He had to wait. The word had been unsteady. "Yes. The jamming begins five or six minutes after you start transmitting. It always takes them a few minutes to find your new wave-length." He refused to do more than sip the wine. His colour was returning.

"We try to condense the important news into the first few minutes each evening. It is not always easy——" She stopped, and quickly put her hand on his sleeve. "It is all right. It is your brother, now." She had heard the sound again, and went quickly to the door, opening it.

A man's face flickered in the gloom, illumined by a match. Her nerves had been unsteadied by Mr. Turocz's fear, and she felt her fingers tighten on the edge of the door. It was a stranger's face.

"I didn't know which bell." He blew out the match.

Cool air moved in from the landing. "I am not expecting you," she said.

The man seemed puzzled. *"Parlez-vous français, Ma'm'selle?"*

For an instant she doubted reality. Her nerves had been strained, ever since the plane from Geneva had landed, and her talk with Mr. Turocz had not relieved them. Desperate for an escape from this dream that seemed suddenly to be upon her, she missed the obvious. The man spoke to her again in French, but she interrupted him as she understood. She had addressed him in the language she had been using to Mr. Turocz, not realising as she had stood there watching the apparition of this stranger's face in the matchlight that he had spoken in English about the bell.

"I'm sorry. Who are you, please?"

His face, lit from the room, lost its perplexity. "James Praggart." He found a card. "Reporter." She read the name of his newspaper. "Sorry to disturb you." He was looking into the room at Mr. Turocz.

The cool air made her shiver. "Will you come in?"

"Thank you."

Mr. Turocz remained standing. She said to him that the visitor was an English journalist, and that there was nothing to trouble him.

"A friend of mine, Mr. Turocz," she said to Praggart.

He wouldn't remember the name because she had pronounced it with full accent; and she had said that he was a friend so that Praggart should know Mr. Turocz had her allegiance. It might be important. "How can I help you?"

"I've just come from the airport." He had a round, smooth face and ginger hair, and stood with his hat dangling. "I'm trying to follow a story. A taxi-driver told me where I could find you, and——"

"I see." Her head was aching. She pressed her fingers to her temples. There was so much to beware of. "Will you sit down, Mr. Praggart? There's only the stool, I'm afraid."

Mr. Turocz asked if he should leave, but she made him take the chair again. "If Andrey is not here in a few minutes, we will telephone him." She turned to Praggart and said in English: "What else did the taxi-driver say?"

Carefully he said: "Well, it isn't only the taxi-driver. A few things have happened. But I believe you followed——"

"Would you like a drink?"

He looked startled by the deliberate interruption. She found another glass. "We shouldn't mention any particular name. You can't translate that name into English, can you? Call him the V.I.P." If Mr. Turocz understood, then he knew more English than he admitted, and was therefore not safe—possibly not even Andrey's brother.

"All right," Praggart said, with a shut face. "You followed the V.I.P. In my job, I have to ask people for anything they can tell me—anything they don't mind telling me."

"I followed his car to a place. The taxi-driver will have

told you where. Then I came back here. It's not much of a story."

"The police are in this, of course."

"Why?"

"Well——" He glanced at Turocz and gave him a quick smile in the international language of friendship. "You see, they think the V.I.P. has been abducted."

She should have telephoned before—the police and Unic. It was stupid to have waited so long. But they knew the house. She had followed the car there. It was all right.

"The thing is," said Praggart, "I want to find out all I can. I'm not in competition with the police, but when they find me on the job they'll try to shut everything down on me, because this is a pretty big affair."

Louise said to Mr. Turocz: "We talk of the police, only because of another matter, not to do with yourself."

He thanked her. He had been nurturing his fears again and she had noticed. The word 'police' was very similar in his own language, and he had been listening.

She told Praggart: "I don't know anything, I'm afraid. I recognised him at the airport, that's all."

"Why did you follow his car?"

"I work at Unic, in the Slavakian Section. That's partly why I know his face. There are photographs there. I felt I should know where he was to stay." Her other reason was not for the newspapers.

"You were the only person in this country to know where he'd gone, until the police caught up with things. The taxi-driver hasn't been told who the V.I.P. is. Nobody has. I was lucky—I got it through on the grape-vine from Switzerland." He offered a disarming smile.

People could be heard on the stairs outside and Praggart

added: "So you realise you're in a bit of a hornet's nest."
Louise looked at the door. "I'll print what you've given me, if I may. It's not much, but with pictures——"

The bell rang.

Mr. Turocz said: "It will be my brother?"

"Perhaps." She answered the door. There were two men who said they were from Scotland Yard. Turocz and Praggart were standing up as she came back with the officers.

One of them said: "Hello, Prag. Trust you."

The journalist grinned, finishing his drink. Poor Turocz was looking bedevilled. He knew a police officer when he saw one, in whatever country. He lived most of his life with their hard eyes and stiff mouths and short words.

"He doesn't speak English," Louise told them. "I am responsible for him."

They looked away from Turocz, and Louise saw him almost slump as if a spotlight had been freezing him into rigidity and was now switched off. She told him: "This has nothing to do with you. Have no fear."

"Would you mind," asked one of the officers, "translating that?"

"I told him not to worry. In his country they are hard pressed by the police."

"You can tell him we've checked on him at the airport, if you like."

"I'll leave it, I think. It might confuse him."

Her small room seemed to have shrunk still further, with the four men crowded in it as thick as dummies in a window.

"We won't disturb you for long, Miss Cameron."

She remembered they would have seen her name outside the door, on the bell-panel.

"We've been along to the house in Richmond, but there's a private family living there. The taxi-driver says that he didn't make a mistake, but we'd like your help. It wouldn't take long. Would you mind if we took you there in the car, just to make sure?"

Praggart had stepped back an inch, and tipped the fender on to its edge with a clatter. "Very sorry." He straightened it, and grinned gently at her. "Bit of a full house tonight. You must be fed-up."

"Miss Cameron?" They were waiting. Like Praggart, they didn't always manage to hide the fact that they were in a hurry.

"I—I've got to wait here for someone," she said. Had the reporter tipped the fender over deliberately for some reason? It had seemed so natural, but one suspected even innocence tonight. "Mr. Turocz's brother is coming."

"Can't you leave Mr. Turocz here to wait for him?"

"I suppose so." She tried to understand her own reluctance. If that weren't the right house, then they would never find the right one now. There was no point in going there. She was too late.

"We'd really appreciate your help."

"All right." She picked up her macintosh, but it was clammy. "I'll get a coat." She went into her bedroom, leaving the door open.

Praggart said: "Can I go along? I've got a car down there."

"We can't stop you. Your editor's had a call from us, so don't be surprised if there's a black-out."

"Never mind, I'm enjoying myself."

"Some people are lucky."

Louise came back in a coat. "I'm ready."

"Then we'll go."

She told Mr. Turocz: "I have to go out, but will be back very soon. Please wait here for Andrey. The wine is there."

He looked anxious. "I cannot help?"

"No," she smiled. "They are not arresting me. I will return soon. If you are hungry, please find something in the kitchen. You have travelled far today."

"You may need your key——"

"Oh yes."

He gave it to her, holding the envelope with her note in it. "I may keep this?"

"Of course."

It was another credential, more valuable than food.

She went down the stairs with the two officers and Praggart. In the hall of the block their footsteps echoed from the high stone walls. She walked between the officers. A light flashed, blinding her.

"My own chap," said Praggart. "I didn't bring him up-stairs."

The flash came again. They walked through the big doorway into the rain and the lamplight.

CHAPTER V

A bulletin was going out hourly from Aldersgrove.

This is Unic Radio. Then, for half a minute, the Slavakian Anthem. Time was short: jamming would start in a few minutes. Then: *Your King is in London. King Nikolas of Slavakia is known to have arrived last night in London from the Continent. With him was a selected party of advisers. It is believed here in official circles that King Nikolas intends to make important requests to the British Government, among which may well be a plea for non-military aid for his country at this crucial time. Previous rumours of a hunting accident in the Tyrol can be discounted.*

Kristov Czinitri and Professor Mejilinkov had been taking it in turns at the microphone since eight o'clock. It was now noon. As they looked through the big glass panel at the programme controller they could see the throng of faces in the background. Slavakian-born Britons and Slavakian nationals had besieged Unic House during the morning after seeing the first editions. Parties of a dozen were still being admitted, after screening at the security check, and were allowed to stand packed together in the ante-room and watch the announcers through the panel, as on Slavakian fête days. Their faces were like children's: hope lit their eyes, but they must not raise their voices in front of the grown-ups, for they were talking.

We are keeping in touch with these events. Further news will be broadcast as it comes in. In the meantime, tell your friends. King Nikolas has arrived in London, and there can be no conceivable doubt that he is here in the name of his people. Long live the King!

The Anthem was played again, now in its full six verses. It was not possible to tell whether jamming had already started; but the chief news was over.

The rumours were dead. They had varied, during the last three days, when the first shots were fired in the streets of Drovnik and the first banner with the king's name on it had been hoisted from a lamp-post opposite the Parliament building. Reports had been picked up from many sources, but their authenticity had been difficult to judge. On the principle that there is no smoke without fire, two main news-stories had been accepted in the European capitals: that ex-King Nikolas had met with a hunting accident and had sustained grave injuries; and that he had simply disappeared from the villa in Geneva where he and a few friends had been living for two years. People could take their choice, and even by contrived mental process could believe that he had disappeared from his villa—that is to say, gone off quietly for a hunting trip in the Tyrol—and had there met with an accident. Or conversely he had met with the accident and was subsequently hurried into a nursing home, the location of which was unknown—which amounted to a disappearance.

The few people versed in political propaganda had believed neither story. Revolution had broken out in Slavakia against the tyranny of its foreign dictatorship and the people were demanding a reinstatement of the monarchy: therefore it was an obvious move on the part of the present government to let it be known that however much the people wanted their king, he was not available. The king was a symbol, not a cause; but to captive minds a symbol is important. This one had been removed.

In London the Foreign Office had been ready to give its blessing to Unic's immediate suggestion that, whatever the ex-King had come for, his arrival should be made known to his people. In the streets and squares of Drovnik the banners could go up again. The symbol was alive. The cause could keep its name: Nikolas the Second.

Long live the King! These words had been heard only five times over Unic Radio in its programmes to Slavakia: at each Christmas, when the king had broadcast to his people from his exile in Spain, South America and Switzerland. Today there were hyacinths and crocuses in London parks and in the window-boxes along the great stone walls of Unic House, but there was the spirit of Christmas in the offices and studios. Together with the scent of spring bulbs it was in the air; with the light from the windows it was in the eyes.

In the underground canteen an acoustic ceiling spanned the walls across three thousand square feet of floor-space, but people had to raise their voices almost to a shout during the lunch-break, or go unheard.

Andrey Turocz was there, although he had been given two days' leave so that he could share them with his brother, Bjelik, and show him a little of London. Bjelik was down there too, smuggled in and incognito, sitting at the table that was a lake of spilled coffee as Andrey talked, his hands flying out and his eyes alive——

"You didn't know he was arriving?"

"I assure you——"

"But it's fantastic! On the same night—you, and the King! And they've given me two days' leave—did I tell you they've given me two days' leave?" He slapped Bjelik on the knee again—"Did I tell you?"

"Yes, yes, you told me, Andrey." Dear God, to sit here—sit anywhere—and say that name aloud, without first a glance over the shoulder. . . . "What would happen, Andrey, if I stood up now and bellowed *Nikolas!* If I did *that*?"

"You'd be told to sit down and shut up! There's a rule about too much noise here. People can't eat, in this country, unless it's as quiet as a grave——"

"You don't understand me——"

"Of course I understand you. They were in Drovnik long before I left. I haven't forgotten. That's why I came, isn't it?" He touched his brother's knee again, as if to reassure himself that he was still here, Bjelik here, looking older and with a pinched face, but here in London. "Does my father still hate me for leaving them? Does he?"

"It's some time since I've seen him."

"What do you mean?" The hand tightened.

"He was sent away last year——"

"Why wasn't I told?" The chair scraped, but he didn't know why he was getting up, staring so accusingly at his brother: there was nowhere to go, and it was not he who should accuse. "Why didn't you write——"

"Sit down, Andrey! We didn't tell you because your mother said you'd be bound to come home and try to find your father, and perhaps make trouble for all of us. Besides, it isn't easy for you now. You're British." It was said with a note of sympathy, and Andrey knew, from these few words, what they thought of him at home. He tried to protest——

"But I'm working for you all, here! Every day we keep you warned of events, and——" He stopped speaking, because his brother's eyes had lost their interest.

"I shouldn't have come away," Bjelik said slowly.

50

"When I left, two days ago, it didn't seem as if a revolution had begun. There were a few shots—a bunch of students painted his name—the King's name—on a sheet and waved it about. I would have stayed if I had known. I never saw the tanks. I heard about them in Vienna——"

Andrey sat with his shoulders hunched, his cuff touching the spilled pools of coffee where his face was reflected. "If it succeeded, Bjelik, and you put Nikolas back, what would I do?"

"What would *you* do? Aren't you comfortable here?"

"If I went home, how would people think of me?" He looked into his brother's face, his country's face.

"You're British. This is your home and these are your people——"

"I was born by the Duna." He was an exile and would always look like this with this nostalgia in his eyes, and would always think of himself as a second-class citizen, here in his new country.

"It was your own choice, Andrey. We do as we choose, and live where we like. After all, what does it matter what names we give ourselves and our countries and our kings? We're all people, aren't we? Haven't we all got faces and hands—does a Chinaman love in a different way or die in a different way from a Spaniard?" He smiled to his brother, who had become such a stranger in this short time. "The thing is to be free, Andrey." He looked round the restaurant at the other tables, at the bent heads and moving hands, where the talk flowed, a fierce waterfall of talk that was almost frightening to listen to. Wasn't there *anything* you couldn't talk about, here? It was profligate, this much freedom. It was like watching an orgy, and he felt a kind of drunkenness.

Andrey was asking: "What did my father do?"

"Whistled in the street. There are new laws . . ."

In the corner of the canteen Louise sat with Tony Messiter, who in his quiet way had managed to isolate their table. While she ate her meal he watched her, toying with toast and coffee, though whenever she looked at him he appeared to be gazing at the wall or at the other tables. He spoke little. She had been badgered most of the morning, for every newspaper carried the headlines and her picture: the scene in the block of flats, Louise walking out between the two police officers.

"If I'd known it would look like that," she said, "I'd have flung my hands up to cover my face."

"It would have looked worse. At least in this picture you're accepting arrest with dignity. Very English."

She didn't know if these tilts at Englishness were scathing or affectionate, if the gentle middle-aged American smile was benign or patronising. He hadn't been here more than a few months, and England was new to him. Perhaps he still had to decide about it.

"It's not very English for a girl to be marched out with no fresh make-up on between two policemen." She spooned the mousse without tasting it. "Oh, Lord, I was so stupid, Tony."

"You weren't to know he was being hi-jacked. They'll find him."

"They don't know where to start. We drew blank last night. I took them to the house, but he's not there. Something odd happened."

"Not very. They had to shake you off without doing anything outrageous. Until they saw your taxi, their operation was very smooth and right on schedule. At Richmond they decided to throw you off, so they drove into the grounds of that house, waited until you'd gone, then drove out again and went on their way. The driver would have said he'd made a mistake."

"I must have been too exhausted to think straight. I should have followed them into the drive."

"You had no reason," said Messiter. "Any more than you had reason to follow them from the airport."

She looked away too casually. "I thought I'd missed some message—I even rang through to here to ask. I couldn't believe he was arriving in London and we didn't know about it. It occurred to me he was here to make a broadcast to his people, or something." She had to turn her head back at last, because of his silence. "Well?"

"Well what, Louise?"

"Couldn't it have been that?"

"Oh, sure."

It was said of this American that he was high up in some un-named political service and that his work here as a programme organiser was a front. One could believe it. He was a man with his ear to the ground. He listened well: only after the passage of time, when one had half forgotten old conversations, did it become clear how well he listened, and remembered. Unic House was a voice— the first big radio station in the new Western network still under construction as a machine in political propaganda. Influenced by their mission, people here talked freely. A man who listened, as Messiter did, was unusual; so there were stories about him. It had occurred to few people that it might simply be his character that made him listen.

The only story that was generally accepted was that he was in love with Louise. Yet he had never touched her hand.

"I don't see that it matters," she said, "why I followed them. It would have been more to the point if I'd carried on, instead of losing them."

"You weren't to know." He left her to bring more coffee, and when he had sat down again he said: "You met him once, didn't you?" His tone was bland: but then his tone was always bland.

"Did I ever say that?"

"I seem to remember . . ."

She looked at the room and saw Kristov explaining something to the new girl in the Russian section. The Turocz brothers sat close together, one tapping the other's knee as they talked. Professor Mejilinkov was alone, reading his books. Where had these people been when she was over there, five years ago? They seemed so much a part of this building.

"Then I must have told you," she said to Messiter. "You couldn't really call it a meeting."

He waited, but had to ask: "What could you call it?"

"I was with a bunch of students out there in 1954. It was only a few months before they forced him to abdicate —that's why I remember him so well——"

"Of course."

"We were trailing round the museums. Balkan Art. There was a formal Press reception at the Palace in Drovnik, and we were allowed in, just to watch things—a whole tribe of pimply young rubber-necks, shuffling and whispering. . . ."

But she wished now that she had not begun to tell him. The voyage home had been miserable, humiliating. They had never stopped ragging her about what had happened.

"Then we saw him come in."

He watched the black curve of hair where it touched

her neck, and sketched her in his mind. Yesterday he had made two new sketches, quite good ones, and then burned them with all the others and written to his chief for a transfer, for private reasons. A spell in some outpost would be better than this masochism.

"Then what happened?" he asked.

"Why should anything happen?"

"He just went out again?"

"Of course not. He made a short speech and shook hands with some of the journalists—there was a Chinese woman there, very small and exquisite, out of place with all those tough-looking men. I remember wondering how she could have become a journalist. Then our leader— she was an art teacher, but we had to call her our leader on this trip—isn't that kind of thing ghastly——?"

"Too ghastly."

"She was formally introduced—because you couldn't pretend that a whole scrum of kids just weren't there, and we didn't look any more like journalists than the Chinese girl—she shook hands with him, I mean our leader did, and said that we were the youth of our country and had come all the way from England to enrich our minds in the treasure-houses of his ancient kingdom—she really used words like that, quite awful, considering they'd just completed a brand-new overhead railway through Drovnik and built a college of advanced science as a contribution to world atomic research—and he thanked her very simply. Wonderfully simply. And we breathed again."

For a long time he watched her face thoughtfully. "And then what happened?"

"That was all." He knew that it wasn't exactly a lie, but an intimation that if there were anything else, she would never tell him.

"It doesn't sound," he said, "like a reason for following him last night."

"Did I say it was a reason?"

"No."

She found her brief-case, and he knew he had gone too far, and said too much. He, the listener. So he said: "It was nice of you to lunch with me. I like being seen around with the Girl on Today's Front Page."

She smiled, knowing that he was choosing to sit here with her despite, and not because of, her little limelight. "Except when you're trying to winkle something out of me," she said, "I feel such . . . I feel so easy in your company."

Easy. He mustn't imagine, later, when he was alone, and thinking back on this hour, that it meant anything more than just that: easy.

"It's because my conversation is middle-aged, and comforting."

"You don't talk very much, Tony. Hardly at all."

"Then it's the way I listen."

"I don't talk much, either."

"You did," he said, "just now."

He got up to help her with the chair.

"Just now?" she said.

"The idyll. In Drovnik. When you fell in love."

"What a comic idea! I told you, nothing happened."

"Sometimes, when we're most in love, it doesn't."

There was no fresh news by seven in the evening, when the first main transmissions of the day began.

"It is ridiculous," Czinitri told his P.O. "We announce with solemnity that Nikolas is in London, without adding the small point that no one can find him."

"The police will find him." Miss Thorne wore a tweed suit and brogues and carried a spiritual Britannia's trident.

"Are they clairvoyant?"

"No. Efficient." She gathered her programme layouts and looked at the wall-clock. "Studio Three."

Loping along the corridors with her, he went on complaining. "So what do we give out, officially?"

"You've seen your script. As yet, the King has made no statement."

"Is that news?"

"It's accurate information."

They passed through the main vestibule, where people were crowded, waiting for their security-check.

Since middle day the rumours had varied from the plausible to the absurd. Only one scrap of information had been vouched for: that the police had received fourteen calls from people who declared they had seen the ex-King in the last few hours. Each line of search had been taken up, but everywhere they drew blank.

The Foreign Secretary, Mr. Clive Petrie, had spent more than two hours with the Prime Minister at Downing Street. There was no statement.

A policeman was posted at the doors of Unic House, where a small crowd had gathered, mostly émigrés from the Balkan countries. Two plain-clothes detectives were known to be inside the building.

The main transmissions had been running for half an hour when Louise came through the vestibule and stopped for a moment to talk to someone. The place was crowded. She was on her way out when she felt a hand on her arm.

"I was coming to see you." It was Praggart, the reporter. He seemed excited, and was trying not to show it. He spoke quietly, standing close to her in the throng of people. "Are you still on duty?"

"No. Released. What's happened?"

"Don't know, for certain." A rather breathless laugh brightened his round face. He still held her arm, looking at the faces near him and then lowering his voice again. "I think I can scoop the Street, though. Listen, at what distance do you think you could recognise him again?"

"Nik——?"

"Yes." His hand tightened to stop her. "Him."

They moved against the wall as someone edged past them.

"Have you——?" but he stopped her again.

"I think so. If it's right, I've got to pass it on to the police, pretty b. quick, obviously. But I'll be first there. Now—what distance? How far away, in good light?"

"I don't know——"

"Twenty-five yards?"

"I don't know——"

"Doesn't matter. We'll try it anyway."

"All right."

He began steering her carefully through the people. Some of them looked at them, wondering at the excitement in Praggart's face. "How do you look as if you haven't just found a fiver?"

"What?" Some of the words had been lost as they edged for the doors.

"Doesn't matter."

"How certain are you?"

"Don't know. It's up to you. I've never seen him. You have." They were outside at last. "Car's over there. I couldn't park it closer. Come on."

They hurried through the cool night air.

CHAPTER VI

She stood alone in the hall, and the feeling came over her, of being lost. It had come before, and she steeled herself to it, knowing that she could not defend herself but must endure it until it passed. She had grown used to thinking of it—as people do with their particular recurring ailments —as 'her' feeling, that must be like no one else's in the world, unexplainable to another person, private and incurable.

It was no more pleasant for its familiarity. While it lasted she was helpless, more alone than a traveller lost in the desert with only the shadows of vultures surrounding him on the sand. She was cut off from all known things, and her fear was not nameless: it was the fear of never being able to find them again.

The huge staircase rose into the shadows beside her, its stone pilasters tracing upwards from the carved stone column at its base; yet for all its solidity she was certain for an instant that it was crumbling, and she moved away from it, her shoes sounding brittle on the chequered tiles.

A high lamp cast light across the walls and winked on metal ornaments. A bronze tiger loped on its marble base, dust on its flattened head. A fern, rust-brown at the tips of its fronds, grew from a vase the size of a half-barrel in a corner, eking out its dark unwatered life, ugly and without purpose. Perhaps, if sunlight came in here by day . . . but sunlight was among things lost and she couldn't get back.

Three portraits showed wan faces from the gloom of sombre oils, one of them touched by a fringe of light that filtered through coloured glass above the door—and something moved and when she turned she saw another face, a fourth, alive and watching her—and the sharp sound of her breath made an echo among the walls.

The man said something but she didn't catch the words, which were not English. By gripping the pockets of her coat she fought down the shivering, and in a moment everything returned, and she was back.

"I didn't see you," she said.

"It's gloomy, in here." It was Slavakian, with a northern peasant's accent. He was standing in a recess beside the outer doors, a toothpick like a cigarette in his mouth. He had the attitude of a slack sentry and she knew without questioning her instinct that if she moved towards those doors he would stop her.

They stared at each other until she had the uneasy feeling that he was an animal and that there was no communication possible between them. There had to be speech again.

"Will Mr. Praggart be long?"

He sidled the toothpick to the other end of his mouth, reflectively. "He is in there."

"I know, but——"

Then Praggart came back. "Sorry I kept you waiting." It seemed to her that his voice had changed. His excitement was gone.

"Is it no good?" she asked.

"Oh, yes——"

"You've seen him?"

"Yes. We'll go in now." He waited by the inner door. He had not spoken quietly—the need for caution was over.

She didn't understand. "Through here," he said.

He followed her into a small ante-room, a brighter place, furnished with simple pieces. A few coals flickered in the hearth and there was brass about, but nothing shone.

Praggart passed her and opened a pair of narrow doors, beautifully carved and recessed into the panelling. The sound of voices came through to her.

"In here, please." There was no longer conspiracy between them. He had become a bored usher. From beyond the doors another man watched her, and stepped back to make way for her as she went into the room. The voices stopped and there was silence.

It was a drawing-room of great size. Firelight came from a hearth in which were settle seats and an untidy assortment of fire-dogs. Chandeliers, with many of their drops missing, blazed icily above the heads of the dark-clothed men who stood in groups, watching her, their faces turned to her and their bodies still. A woman was among them, but her face was as pale as theirs and her dress as dark; she stood out by virtue only of her burning red hair that was drawn back and pinned, its anger tamed.

Suddenly they began talking again and one by one turned away to resume their discussions. A man who had been in the woman's group now broke away and came up to Louise. Beside her, Praggart said: "Major Bell—Miss Cameron."

Major Bell offered his hand, bending his large body over her, scrutinising her face. "Good evening, Miss Cameron."

Praggart said: "I'll get off, now."

The Major nodded but did not look at him. Louise heard the doors close behind her. Sweat from Bell's hand was cool on her own and she passed its palm against her coat as she looked up at his face. His yellow eyes regarded her without expression for so long that she had the feeling of a few minutes ago return to her: that this was an animal with whom there could be no communication. A cat stared in this way, anonymous and unembarrassed.

"I would like to offer you a drink, Miss Cameron. I'm sure you're chilled from the journey."

She looked past him at the others. "Is this a party?"

"Oh, yes." His eyes became squeezed to glints in the fleshy face as he smiled, obviously delighted with the idea. "Quite a party . . ." He touched her arm. "Come and warm yourself by the fire—and what would you like? We have a good bar here."

"Nothing, thank you."

"Later, perhaps."

To remove his hand she turned a little and went towards the great hearth. The heat from the embers was so fierce that the groups of people stood well away from it. The voices were lowered to a murmur as she and Major Bell moved across the room, and she knew again that she was being watched.

"I'd be glad," she told the Major, "if you'd explain."

He smiled quickly again, the flaccid wrinkles leaving only a glint of eyes. She felt she was in the presence of electric tension—it emanated from his whole body. He breathed with a kind of nervous control made necessary by fear or rage or perhaps the need to listen with complete attention—not to any sound now audible but to a sound that might come, from anywhere.

"What did Praggart tell you?" he asked over-gently.

"Nothing definite, but it's obvious that I was brought here deliberately for some reason. I'd like to know why."

"I was hoping you'd want to meet a few of the people here." He couldn't trouble to disguise the lameness of this answer; his mind was only half engaged by her as he

62

looked about the room, as if perpetually counting the heads. He was waiting for something, and it was becoming clear that she too must wait.

The heat from the fire began to sting her legs through the stockings and she moved away, ignoring the Major and trying to find one single clue to her situation. The woman with red hair was looking at her, standing at the edge of a group; but she looked away without a sign in her eyes that she had seen more than a piece of furniture. As Louise began studying the people individually their number seemed to diminish: to a newcomer, a few people appear as a crowd at first. The man who had stepped away from the doors when she had come in was standing near them now, positioned like the one in the hall outside but less slack in his bearing, more of the sentry in his attitude. He looked at nobody.

The red-haired woman, thin in her black dress, was talking to two men, making a small party group except that there were no drinks in their hands. Beyond them, two men stood together, not talking; one smoked a cigarette in a holder and his head was lifted a little as he gazed upwards, taken with his own thoughts. Three other men were grouped by one of the massive curtains, and they talked softly and quickly, their hands restless, gesticulating. All were in dark suits, as anonymous as a conclave of business-men.

"Who is that woman?"

It was not Major Bell's voice, but as she turned, she saw him approaching her. Another man was standing near the hearth and she realised he must have come into the room by the small door near it. It had been his voice.

Major Bell said to her: "I'd like you to meet someone, if you'll allow . . ."

She followed him to the man, and Bell introduced them:

"Sir, may I present Miss Cameron . . . Miss Cameron, the ex-King Nikolas of Slavakia."

His face was white, strained, hollow with shadows and the flash of his eyes came from a kind of fever. It was all she could manage to face this withering scrutiny. She was naked in front of him, shivering.

"Delighted." His English was without accent. The tension in her nerves, singing for relief, came near to spilling a laugh from her—this young aged haunted face showed many things, but not delight. "You are Scottish?" he asked.

"English." She could hear her own voice and thought with a shock that she had been given a drug—the word was slurred.

"What are you doing here?"

"I don't know."

When he looked away to Major Bell she felt her body slacken like a snapped string. For a second she let her eyes close, and heard him saying in accents that flew like knives: "I would point out to you, Major, that I didn't abdicate. My title is intact." He left them with an impatient swing of his shoulders.

Bell's voice came to her as if from a distance. "He's very angry."

The fierce red of the fire swam against her face, hurting her eyes. "I'd like a drink, now."

"Of course. What can I——?"

"Brandy if you have it." She moved away from the heat, and found herself looking down at a giltwood Adam table, her eye unmindfully tracing the enrichments, using them for a focus while her nerves tried to relax. There was so much she knew, now, that was unknown before. Oh Lord, she said to the table, I feel like a drink . . .

"You're quite well, Miss Cameron?" The Major was back.

"Quite." She took the brandy and began sipping it.

"It must be some time since you saw him last?"

"Yes." The fumes nourished her nerves. A flame in the hearth burned in the bright curve of the glass. In a little while she would be able to think again.

"He's changed, of course," he said, sounding as if he wanted to excuse her for something.

"Yes." But she must begin to think. The questions were coming at her already, quick feathered darts picking for the bull's-eye. Bell said:

"I wouldn't have recognised him, as easily as you did."

"He looks ill. Old."

Not looking at him, she could hear the quick boyish smile in his voice. "He's not ill. That's rage."

The brandy ministered to her, giving her a little courage to endure this odd crisis that had caught her up. She was annoyed with herself for having displayed her nerves—'You're quite well, Miss Cameron?'—and asking for brandy. She was, after all, talking to a civilised Englishman in a house near the Thames; and there was no need to behave like a spinster in fright of rape. But Praggart had been English . . . had shown himself capable of a technique as smooth as a blade; and she was here now, shut in with strangers, alone.

"A little more . . . ?"

Her glass was empty. He took it from her. "No, thank you." He was surprised, disappointed, the good host whose best Courvoisier is refused. At another time she might have been persuaded.

"We haven't dined here, yet," he said. "Half an hour won't be too long to wait?"

"I didn't know I was staying. The invitation was rather informal—I suppose kidnapping has to be like that, or it wouldn't work."

For the first time he seemed really amused. "The idea is that you stay the night, Miss Cameron."

"I'm sorry, but I've got other plans."

"I have arranged everything," he said. He was watching the room again, waiting. The ex-King had come in, but Major Bell still waited, his head turning like a radar-finder, his ochre-coloured eyes touching a face and watching and passing on, leaving nobody out.

Louise said: "When I'm ready to go——"

"You are not going." It was said as an aside in the tone of an order to his dog, while he watched the faces in the room.

"When I'm ready to go, I'll make the attempt, on principle. I don't know how much you know about women. They can do an awful lot of damage if you get their goat —you understand the expression, to 'get someone's goat'? I'm not sure how English you are, under the stiff major's moustache, so let me know if my slang confuses you."

He spared her a glance. "You don't want to go."

"Why don't I?"

His head jerked the fraction of an inch. "Because he is here."

So this was how dangerous Bell was. He knew her mind. It was startling to realise that someone was thinking her own thoughts ahead of her. Before he had spoken she had believed that at some moment this evening she would make an attempt to leave, but Bell was right. She didn't want to go; and that was her reason. Praggart had known her mind,

66

too. The efficiency of the thing was chilling. A second abduction—her own—with no crowding in of strangers, no scuffle of feet on the pavement cut off by the click of the car door, no drugs, not even a spoken threat. Praggart had crooked his finger, and here she was.

She said: "If I'm staying the night, I'll have to ring my parents and let them know."

"They've been dead for ten years."

The yellow eyes frightened her at last.

Her anger and fear must be showing in her eyes, so she looked round the room, as he did, in case with a sudden glance he found her unready. "I'm on duty," she said, "before midnight. Perhaps you'll have a message sent to the studios for me—I don't want to let them down."

"You're next on duty at noon tomorrow. A note will be sent. You've caught the fashionable 'flu, and there'll be a doctor's confirmation. Your flat has been locked and I have the key for you. The cooker has been turned off, and everything is safe there." She knew he had interrupted his watch on the room and was looking at her, but kept her head turned away. "In your room here you'll find the few necessities for the night, and so on."

She detected pride in his voice and wondered if it were a weakness worth remembering. "You're brilliantly efficient."

"It's routine."

"You must have applied your talents to more important things, in the last war—and probably since."

"Nothing so important as this."

"My cooker?"

"It was a detail. In planning to blow up Parliament, one mustn't forget the matches."

He was observing the room again and for a moment she

made herself watch his face. It was a grown man's face, yet the image of the boy's was still in it; and though the hair was thinning at the brow, and the nose was drink-veined, and the flesh folded heavily round the eyes that watched so intently, it was possible to see this face at school, revealing its miniature moods, darkening in arrogance, breaking into the quick charming smile, sulking, hating, and staring just as it stared now at its enemies. Something in this face—and therefore in this man—would never grow up.

Louise tried to imagine an expression impossible for this face to wear. Not kindness: it was an eater's face, a giver's; nor fear: there was some of it in his eyes now; nor patience: a man who respects detail must have that—but trust . . . she couldn't imagine trust in those eyes. Would he trust even a dog, even his brother? Not with this face. It still had the image of its youth in it, but for one thing—trust. That had died with the boy.

She looked away. It would be stupid to feel pity for a man like this.

"I want to know why I was brought here," she said.

"To help us. You're safe here."

"I wasn't in any danger."

"No. We were. I don't imagine you'd tell us why you had orders to follow the ex-King's party from the airport, or why Turocz was sent for. Whatever the reason, there's no danger in it for us, all the time you're in our sight." He spoke haltingly, sparing her only a part of his mind while he watched the room.

"Shall I expect to see Mr. Turocz here, then?"

"No. They've questioned him at the Embassy. They have the right, officially. We use what rights we have, to save trouble. Excuse me." He left her abruptly and was across the room as she tried to see what had happened.

One of the men who had been in the group with the red-haired woman was now by the doors, talking to the drab little guard. Major Bell interrupted them and in a moment the guard opened one of the doors and looked outside. A face came against the light and hovered in the doorway and then the Major stepped back, allowing the man to leave the room. The guard shut the door and stood with his back to it again. To Louise it made a clear enough picture: the man had left the group and gone to the doors, wishing to go out; the guard had prevented him until Bell arrived to order the assistance of the guard in the ante-room—perhaps he was the man she had seen in the hall, the one with the toothpick. And it was he who had now been detailed to escort the prisoner.

That was the word for him: prisoner. It was the word for them all, here. This room, with its brocade curtains and gilt and ormolu and veneered parquetry, its firelight and rich carpeting, was a cell, and the house a prison. The atmosphere was heavy with the sense of captivity—voices had become hushed and faces were turned to watch the man go out, to watch Major Bell and judge his attitude in case it had changed and would reveal something, give them hope or new warning. The room had the close climate of a cage.

Louise realised that she must talk to someone to rid herself of the tension, and started towards the nearest group of people; but Bell had crossed the room and stood beside her again, his back turned to the wall and the hearth so that he could keep them in sight.

He spoke more quickly now, giving her his full attention as if this had to be said before he could return to his vigil. "We're trying to keep things civilised, here, for all the apparent barbarity of the situation. You are here against your will and I apologise—but you see, this is a very big issue. I don't think you need to be reminded of that, but I have to make things clear. You know perhaps better than I do, from your work at Unic, how many hundreds are dying out there at this moment, across the barricades. Whether the killing will stop or spread through the whole country depends a great deal on what happens in this house in the next few hours——" but he couldn't stand the strain of turning his whole mind away from its vigilance, even for these few seconds, and he was silent, oblivious to her.

If I stepped quietly back, she thought, and went to the door, the small door near the hearth, he wouldn't know I'd moved. There's a man—must be—on the other side of the door, and I'd be stopped, but it would give him a shock, and make him——

"The question of escape," he said suddenly like a distant machine-gun that had begun firing again, "is not worth considering. The position is this. My organisation had first felt it necessary to remove the ex-King from the world scene altogether, and then it was felt that, apart from the danger of his becoming a martyr following his death, he might prove more useful alive. We are working with that in mind. Someone is coming here to talk to him. But this is the point, Miss Cameron: he cannot be allowed his freedom. If it becomes impossible for us to keep him in our charge—here or anywhere else—he will have to be removed, that is to say, be killed."

He stopped again, turning the switch in his brain. Louise had been trying hard not to look at the ex-King since he had left them; but now she looked across the room and saw his face, the taut angle of his body, the tilt of his head as he listened to the man who was speaking to him. More than a mere prison, then: a condemned cell. She watched the ex-King as the Major spoke.

"There's a man here for the sole purpose of ensuring that he doesn't escape the house. Should anyone else escape, and summon help, then his duty is to kill him. I want you to get this quite clear in your mind. His life is partly in your hands. When you are alone in your room, or at a window, and it seems easy to make a run for it, remember that you'll be party to assassination."

Watching the drawn face with its feverish eyes, the set of the dark suit, the stillness of the hands, she realised only casually that the Major had left her. She did not look away from the ex-King: she was mesmerised, while nausea spread like a slow poison in her stomach, chilling her as she forced herself to reckon with his future . . . a bright knife, slipping into him for the sake of silence, or the cough of a gun, and the fall . . . and Miss Thorne would edit the announcement for Kristov Czinitri, who would settle himself in the chair and give his habitual glance upwards to the microphone before saying: *We have to report, with the most profound regret, that today . . .*

With all his grace of a man he was an animal, here, caged and at the disposal of the butcher. They would finish him as casually as if they were snapping a bird's neck for the market. The clock above the hearth would tick, and the firelight flicker, just as now, while the descendant of a dynasty would sprawl on the floor, humiliated. 'There's a man here for the sole purpose . . .' She looked away, at the other faces. Which man? Just one of the men in here, or was he somewhere else in the house, waiting, reading a newspaper, copying the habits of a human? The nausea was rising and would overwhelm her. She moved to the end of the hearth and put her arms on the great cold marble shelf above it, leaning her brow against its chill, and thinking: it's only because the room is elegant and we all seem civilised; it makes it more horrible. If he were in the doorway of a Drovnik street, waiting for a lull in the firing, ready to run for cover, you'd say his luck might go either way, alive this minute and dead the next. But here, with his shadow on silk curtains, the fall softened by the rugs . . .

Her head throbbed against the marble. Was anyone watching? Bell would be watching: he watched them all. He would be contemptuous of her, seeing how white her face was as she leaned here trying not to be sick. It should rouse her pride; but it didn't matter what Bell thought; he was a barbarian, however civilised he wanted things to look. He must have spent his life in unimaginable ways since something had warped him and left him twisted inside the urbane skin, but he ought to know that people must turn sick at the thought of things he had grown to stomach.

In the shelters ten years ago she had sat protected by warm bodies and kind eyes, cheerful voices—Mrs. Lattimer knitting with her deft confident fingers, her white hair shining: 'Don't you worry, my lamb, we're safe enough down here,' and Mr. Topson's shoes, always clean like his collar, his glasses polished like diamonds, very often a new book for her: 'A wonderful story, this is, a very wonderful story,' and the new clean pages coming open with glimpses of the coloured pictures showing suddenly, as gaudy as flowers in the snow—then the great thudding and shaking, her ears full of it, while they all stopped talking as if they were suddenly in a waiting-room, the light flickering, steadying, the echoes dying away . . . *it didn't happen* . . . Nothing could happen, with everyone so clean, and

Mrs. Lattimer knitting. But it was outside, just through that corrugated door, the war. You could smell it in the air, all the way up the muddy path where there were always feathers floating down from the chicken-run next door. In here it was safe, with collars and shoes clean; you could sit and turn the clean white pages, and be safe.

Major Bell was still in the shelters, with his clean shirt and shaved face, civilised: but the ground still shuddered and the smell was in the air. Just as they had known, secretly and without speaking of it, that the corrugated door might blow inwards at every next second and blot them out, he knew now that this elegant clock could tick away a death.

A sound disturbed her and she opened her eyes against the light to see a human face watching her; a flinch shook her. There were so many strangers—which was this? The man with a purpose . . . no. This was an old kind face with gentle eyes; to look at it was to see the light steadying and hear the echoes dying away.

"His Majesty would be pleased to speak to you."

CHAPTER VII

The girl was drooping against the mantelshelf, sick as a wilting lily. He would not go across to her. She would get over it, and might even learn to be content with her own petty affairs. One had to excuse her: she was English, one of the thirty million vicars' daughters, ageless, sexless, milk-veined. It was a misfortune, not a crime, to be born English. 'I'm not sure how English you are, under the stiff major's moustache,' she had said. A show of spirit—but no more spirit now, not even dignity. It must have been so awfully exciting, such gorgeous fun, to race after the big car in her taxi, sharing the same road with the royal darling of the debs; but the thrill seemed to have gone. There he was, the Rake of the Balkans, within flirting-distance of her eyelashes, but she wilted against the wall.

Because he might have to be shot? There were plenty more of that breed, thriving as thick as weeds from Drovnik to the Danube—in a week's hunting he'd deflower a barnful of peasant girls without a glance at their eyes. You wouldn't shoot the Dausmilian blood out of the country if you set up a machine-gun in the market-place and ran it till it seized.

Poor little English flower—but she didn't know when she was lucky. The Balkan buck was too busy with his broken-down throne at the moment, or he'd flex her across a couch.

His eyes caught movement and he saw Kosek approaching his master, whose eyes must have beckoned him, because Bell would have noticed a single finger move, anywhere in the room. Old Kosek went up to Nikolas in an attitude of surrender, as if his name had been called by the Almighty; there was nothing abject, he did not fawn; he considered his monarch so far above him that he could surrender his whole being and still keep pride. Bell had noted this measure of devotion, knowing that fanatics could be dangerous.

The ex-King was speaking to Kosek, who withdrew and now went down the length of the room to the girl. This might be amusing—did Nikolas intend five minutes diversion, to soothe his nerves? If so, the pale English flower would sleep tonight with a brand-new royal bastard in the womb. There weren't many Dausmilians in this island—perhaps he felt he'd been neglecting the place.

He jerked his head as the doors opened and Angelitri was escorted back. He was no bigger than Bell, but seemed more powerful: from flattened hips the body expanded upwards to great bunched shoulders with the disproportion of a ship's figurehead, and the neck was so short that the head was tilted permanently forward, so that his dark eyes must look upwards from the sockets, seeming to threaten, while the hunched body promised aggression, balanced like a bull's; but the portrait of brute force was altered by the eyes, whose light had such intelligence that one's instinctive defence was relaxed by them. Even here they were lit by humour.

"It is some few years," he said, "since I was led by the hand to the lavatory. I shall brush up my forgotten baby-talk." He stood poised on his small feet, the shape of his body suggesting that he was about to hurl himself upon the company.

"I'm sorry these restrictions are necessary, Baron, but you see we can't trust anyone."

The dark eyes looked upwards at Bell, dulled with gravity. "To leave it as clean as we found it?" He went across to the group of three men who were still engrossed in talk. He reminded Bell of the Executive, who had looked at him with dull grave eyes, saying:

"The report of his disappearance made as little difference as the report of his hunting accident. It was unfortunate that both statements were put out, due to lack of co-ordination in the department, because the plausibility of each was minimised. But the point is that the revolutionaries will not be satisfied until they see his dead body; and even then they may fight on, perhaps harder, because of their rage. Will you have one of these beastly things?" It was a packet of yellow Italian cigarettes.

Bell shook his head. "I'd like to know what you want me to do."

"First of all, you have to understand the situation, and the importance of the ex-King Nikolas at this moment." He sat back and surveyed Bell's face through thin blue smoke. "The shooting began only the day before yesterday, but there are already rumours over there that the Americans are coming in. It may be so, but the Americans are always jumpy about these things. Yesterday an official of the State Department said to the Press: 'If the Slavakians hold out for much longer, the incentive for America to take up arms may become very strong. Members of the National Security Council are already urging that tactical atomic weapons be brought into use to help the insurgents. The President would require the approval of Congress, and no Congressman will have a clear mind about the problem until after the elections this mid-week. But if the Slavakians are still fighting at the week-end, we shall be closer to a world war than we have been since August 1939.' I may have a word wrong, here and there; but that is the gist of the statement, and that is the substance of the rumours now rife in Drovnik. In addition, enthusiastic commentators of American radio stations in Europe, broadcasting in Slavakian, are using such phrases as 'Slavakians, we are with you in your great cause!'—and so on. A declaration of sympathy like that can undergo slight changes in the confusion of street-fighting. The rallying cry of 'Hold on —the Americans are coming!' has already been heard. It is untrue today, but it can be true tomorrow. It will depend a great deal upon what happens to Nikolas."

Bell was impatient. He did not want to understand situations. That was for others. He was an operative. This situation was perfectly clear already: anyone could read it in a newspaper. His voice exploded softly in the room:

"Are we to assassinate?"

The Executive gazed at him critically, his eyelids reddened by the raw cigarette-smoke. "It's like throwing you a live mouse, isn't it?"

Something moved in Bell's stomach, in his brain; a kind of life stirred in him, other than his. "I just want to know the job."

"Of course. But we have changed our minds from the original intention of murder. I'm so sorry—assassination. Nikolas will be unearthed, as soon as we can locate him, and held incommunicado. If it can be arranged, there will be an interview between him and President Imgrir Szados."

Bell moved in his chair, energised by amazement. "They'll kill each other."

"You think too much about death. They won't be left alone together, naturally. If Nikolas won't agree to our

77

terms, then your Mr. Peake will be asked to dispatch him——"

"What are the terms?"

"Secret. Don't look pained—I don't know them myself. It isn't in our province, you see." He leaned forward suddenly and fixed Bell's attention. "What you have to understand is the importance of this operation. Today the rebels are losing strength. The government, with the inconspicuous aid of Union forces and supplies from across the frontier, can restore order in Drovnik within the week. But if Nikolas decides to ask the Western democracies for help, and at the same time responds to the rebels' demand that he resumes kingship in Slavakia—*then* it will be different. Even if the West decides to keep a back seat, it will obviously display sympathy to the cause in strong terms; and Nikolas, if he is coming into the open at all, will have no choice but to offer his services on the throne. And then it will take a major offensive to put down the insurrection; and you cannot launch a major offensive inconspicuously. From the moment of its mounting, it will face the risk of challenge by N.A.T.O.: and if an ultimatum is ignored, we shall be nearer a world war—as it is already being said in Washington—than we have been since 1939. And this one would be atomic." He leaned back, and began coughing over his cigarette, his small bird's body jerking in spasms; but he kept his eyes on Bell. To a different kind of man he would perhaps have added: 'And so you will be working in the interests of world peace.' But Bell wouldn't find inspiration in that. His incentive was the knowledge that he was working against the country in which he had been born. It was enough for him, as a life ambition: to be a traitor.

"Where was he last seen?"

This man, thought the Executive, is the perfect operator. He is built like a beautiful gun: you can feel how hard and cold he is in your hand. You have no need to explain to him why this or that object has become a target. Tell him simply that it *is* the target, and you feel the long barrel swing.

"He was last seen at his villa in Basle. We think he is making for Geneva. Our political advisers believe it likely that he will try to reach London. That is why we have called you in. If he does in fact reach London, you will do whatever is necessary to hold him, under good cover, until the meeting with President Szados can be arranged. Bear in mind that he might not come alone. If others are with him, they will have to be held as securely. Bear in mind also that there are royalist elements in this country who will try to disturb your plans, if they suspect them. You will anticipate these complications, I know. We have supreme faith in you."

"I'll be on readiness."

"You will perhaps need patience."

But there had been no strain on his patience. Just before noon today the telephone call came through. The whole personality of the man had been in his dry pert voice: Bell could almost catch the reek of the yellow cigarette and see the dull, red-rimmed eyes—"It is definite that he will try to reach London by air. In company with him are Baron Petrik Angelitri, Sofi Mikayan, and a personal attendant named Kosek. The party will not be intercepted at Geneva, but will be allowed to reach London. You will then arrange matters. I have set about drafting in as many assistants as we can find at short notice. There will be upwards of thirty men at your disposal within the next few hours."

79

Bell said that he was satisfied, and asked only one question. "Where is the Roman Tart?"

"In a Swiss clinic."

"Then I may have to ask you to supply a woman, if we hold him for more than a day or two. Have one ready."

Perhaps there would be no need to trouble the Executive, after all. The sick lily was answering Kosek, looking embarrassed about having to talk to anyone when she was obviously about to bring up her nerves. Her lipstick shone as dark as a wound across the white face—and now she walked slowly beside old Kosek, staring across to the corner where Nikolas waited.

Angelitri had turned his head and was watching her.

Bell moved his eyes and saw that Peake was watching her, too, his thin beautiful face cutting a white wedge against the dark of the curtains.

There was another movement, and Bell saw that the Ambassador and his party had finished their discussion. As they came in a group towards the doors, he took a step forward to meet them.

"We have decided to leave, Major Bell." His eyes ruminated behind their glasses; his voice was sad.

"I'm sorry, Your Excellency. We could have advanced dinner, if you'd mentioned it——"

"You are very kind, but in these circumstances it might seem inconsiderate to ask His ex-Majesty to share our table. We have no wish to aggravate his humiliation."

The First Secretary was smiling faintly, looking at no one. The Counsellor was blowing his nose with a certain air of enjoyment, as a dog nibbles for fleas.

"There is one thing that disturbs us," the Ambassador went on sadly. "This particular house. . . . The police have only to knock at the door. I have it on good authority that there has been a general issue of search warrants, so that you would have no time . . ." Bell waited deliberately, letting him run on. "Our own presence here is of course an additional embarrassment. Officially, if we were to be discovered here, our reasons would be advanced and accepted; but their falsity would compromise your own position, as you may realise. . . ."

The man, thought Bell, talked like a correspondence course in Civil Service English, and his accent made it comic, like someone continuously raising his silk hat with his shirt-tail hanging out. I know you, thought Bell. Everything makes you sad. You don't approve of anything you're not running yourself—you don't approve of anything that goes on in the world at all: you feel very sad about the world and everyone in it; especially when someone makes a balls-up. I remember when Kisselmann made a balls-up at the March Tribunals, and tried to give you an explanation. You didn't let him sleep another night with his wife before you had him arrested and summarily shot. I remember how sad you looked when he was trying to tell you, that day when the flowers were opening in the public gardens below your window, when the first spring sun came out. Others are angry, or brutal, but you are only sad. I know you, Your Excellency.

". . . Had been consulted, I could have perhaps provided a more secure establishment for these exiles," said the Ambassador, his mild eyes plaintive, their wistfulness magnified by the glasses.

Not that I'm against shooting a man, thought Bell, it's the sadness that turns my stomach. He said: "There wasn't time, Your Excellency. We had only a few hours' warning, otherwise I would have been only too glad to consult you."

He stared past the Ambassador's head, keeping his watch on the room. The Baron wouldn't attempt anything violent: he was too wise. Sofi Mikayan and old Kosek had too much love for the peacock to risk his life— they all knew, they had all been told, that the first one to make a run for it would trigger off his death. The English girl hadn't the courage. But Nikolas himself would try it—work his rage up and then break out, berserk, to hell with the bullets: but he knew the risk, too. He wanted to feel the throne under him again and the saddle of his pet white stallion, and the jumping of the court strumpets in the afternoons. That life was a long way off, and he wouldn't journey far from here with a bullet in his spine.

". . . So that I am confident you will acquaint me of any untoward incident, Major, during the next few critical hours."

"I can assure Your Excellency."

In the brief pause the Counsellor and the First Secretary became suddenly active, like two lurchers who sense their master is making a move: the Counsellor stopped fiddling with his nose and tucked away the handkerchief, and the First Secretary smiled down at his shoes instead of at the middle distance.

"In the circumstances," the Ambassador said, "perhaps you will tender our good-byes to His ex-Majesty, on our behalf." His tone used the title as if it were obscene, something he was reading from a lavatory wall.

"A privilege, Your Excellency." He was invited to shake hands with them, in strict order of seniority, before he personally threw open the doors. "You'll forgive me, I know, if I don't accompany you to the hall." He stood sideways to them, keeping the ex-King in his field of vision. When they had gone, he stood framed in the arch of the doors and watched him more directly. It was essential to observe him with great diligence, and as essential to impress it upon Nikolas that nothing he did went unseen. Across the airy volume of the room their nerves were locked in the intimacy of a wrestler's hold. It must go on like this until President Szados came.

The girl was talking to him. Major Bell would have liked to know more about her. He had engineered the sudden meeting between the two of them, when she had come into this room, presenting her to him without any warning, watching her face. There had been instant recognition and then a medley of thoughts had filled her eyes, and he'd learned nothing. But she worked with Unic, and that building was a warren of internationals, some rabbit, some fox—people like Segrave, Messiter, Nadreanu, with their own internal sores or their political twists . . . but this girl? Whatever she was, she was safer here. If she were love-sick she could make her own moonshine, but the Executive had said: 'Bear in mind also that there are royalist elements in this country who will try . . .'

He must make a study of women, train himself in their psychology. First get rid of the hate that had soured these thirty years, since the acorns had lain brown among the leaves, their shine dulling and lighting again as the shadow passed over them, the shadow of his rugger boots, dangling from his hand as they had walked slowly, his father saying: 'I'm sorry . . . more sorry than you'll ever know. But these things happen.' First get the hate out, and then probe into their sharp glass minds, or one day they'd catch him again.

He could see the ex-King's face, but she had her back turned this way. She listened with her thin straight body.

83

Nikolas had acknowledged her presence only by a slight turn of the head, enabling him directly to face her. His body was rigid, legs apart, hands behind him: the stance of a statue.

"I thank you for coming to this house, but your gentle services are not required." And when the mouth closed he was a stone image again, the eyes dead, their sculpted stare directed towards her face, but not seeing it, so that she felt the onset of a slow, horrible sensation: that her own eyes were sightless and her body made of stone—that her name was on a plaque below her feet, forgotten by the living and already half unreadable under the creep of lichen. They would stand like this for ever, facing and silent.

But he had just said something. What had it meant? If she asked him what he had said, asked him to repeat it, the fantasy would be as horrible: of hearing a statue speak.

The old man had not withdrawn; she was aware of him, and remembered his kind face—and remembering, found heart.

"My . . . services, sir?"

"Are not required."

The old man made a movement beside her. She was to be escorted away. The interview was ended. To stay would be to cause embarrassment—but was there room for anything so trivial as mere embarrassment, in this place, on this night?

"I don't understand what they are. My services." Let me talk to you, don't make me go. I'm alone and scared to death.

"What are you doing here?"

"You asked me before, but I don't know. I was brought here."

The ex-King addressed a few words in Slavakian to old Kosek—but Louise answered the question in their own language:

"No, sir, I am not a prostitute."

They looked at her in silence. She no longer felt herself to be a cold stone figure: there is nothing so swift as an insult to warm a woman's blood. But the sense of unreality remained. Outside this house there were chalked placards along the London streets: a throng of people in Downing Street to see the ministers come and go: a babel of voices on the air from the international radio networks: the clacking battery of telediphones at Unic House as the reports flashed through Europe and the B.U.P. cables came in. *Where is Nikolas of Slavakia?*

He is here in this room with me, she thought, asking if I am a tart. She mustn't think about it, or she would begin to laugh. Her sense of humour was of that rare kind that picks on the ridiculous at the wrong moment: and when the laughter comes it is fed by the new absurdity—that one laughs alone, stared at by shocked faces while the dreadful noise goes on and the joy of the paroxysm quite overwhelms. . . . In the charged atmosphere of this room, where even an eyelid could speak, the sound of laughing would be unthinkable.

"I am sorry. I didn't know you spoke Slavakian." There was a reprimand in his tone, as if she had been eavesdropping. It was a wry thought: she had met this man only twice in her life, and each time had been humiliated. "Do you know my country well?"

"Very little. I was there for a short time, five years ago." She watched the shadows of those five years pass over his face. "I had the effrontery to present myself to you, without invitation. It's perhaps rather late to apologise."

In the full-dress uniform of a field-marshal with its braid and satin facings, gold epaulettes and sash, adorned with orders bestowed by half the monarchies of Europe, he had stung her adolescent eyes with tears as she had stood there among the group of gawky students—and she could remember each single detail, had kept them in her heart, a collection of exquisite miniatures . . . for the humiliation had come afterwards, to bring quick tears again, this time of chagrin and embarrassment.

Going down the great steps, their stones as shallow as piled leaves; the scarlet cloth of a sentry burning in the gloom where the sun was curtained by the palace roofs—'Louise . . . what a thing to *do!*' Their feet tumbling over the worn stone where other feet had climbed and descended on State occasions and the businesses of the court, on funeral and marriage days through the dark, lost centuries—the twittering hated voice beside her: 'Louise . . . I would never have *dared!*' The voice echoing sharp as a bouncing ball to the great sweep of the balustrade and the stones' shadows where the trumpeting of heralds had rung out and harness had chimed in the sunlight of the carriage drive . . . they clamoured about her, the young, cruel voices of her friends, leaping against the golden walls of her little daylight dream, the touching of the king's hand still on hers (I'll never wash it, ever again!), while their Leader hurried them down and hushed them to silence.

Every detail of the scene, and every thought: how dare an old woman with rabbity teeth and grey wool stockings and hiking-brogues presume to speak to *him* and talk about his 'treasure-houses' and his 'ancient kingdom' as if he himself were some kind of museum piece, a gaudy dodo! The Leader had been right beside her, and the smell of her iodine locket would last for ever—the pert matronly tongue delivering itself of clichés while the King of Slavakia had listened politely, not a muscle moving in that God-like face—and then the miracle: the Leader had finished and he was glancing over them all, the gaggle of wide-eyed foreign students, quietly greeting them since their Leader had explained their presence in his palace: and after the miracle (which was contained in the pip of time when his eyes had glanced upon her own), the sensation—the touch of the crimson rope against her skirt as she took the one step to the boundary dividing the dull educational world and the realm of true magic: the spark of surprise in his eyes and the movement of his hand as she held out hers to meet it: the sound of the light clear voice that must be her own—'I admire you, very much, Your Majesty.'

'Oh, Louise! What on earth came over you?'

Down the great steps and along the avenues, to the hostel, the quayside, the ship, with a madcap memory to relish on the journey and carry home: that ridiculous Louise making an exhibition of herself in front of all those people! No harm done, of course—but a wonderful story to tell the others at the college!

It shouldn't have mattered, at the time, because there was still the touching of his hand that she could feel whenever she thought of him in the next few weeks; and then it had stopped mattering—her friends forgot, and the nickname—the Student Princess—was dropped; and the magic faded too, its glow cooling over the months and then the years, the whole incident becoming a comic childhood memory. Yet the details were still sharp.

His face was smoother than this one that watched her now, a far less human face than this with its haunt of pain. The man had emerged from the trappings of majesty and stood facing a woman, Louise. It would be a sour pleasure to say: If my looks don't please you, there's no other choice. They say a cold bath helps, Your Majesty.

"Five years is a long time." It was said brutally.

"I know. And you wouldn't remember me."

He glanced to Kosek, who shuffled back a pace, his white head down like a horse under the rein.

"What is the news from outside?" the ex-King asked Louise.

"When I came away there was no real news——"

"Of the fighting."

"It goes on. Reports are confused, with only two rebel radio stations transmitting—and neither of them knows the true situation——"

"Which is?"

"We don't know either, sir."

"We?"

"I work for Unic Radio. That's why I speak Slavakian. The last message I heard going out was just to the effect that Your Majesty had arrived in London, and that it was confidently believed that you were here on behalf of your people and their cause——"

"On whose authority did that message go out?"

"Our programme chiefs are advised, in this case, by the Foreign Office."

He still had his hands locked behind him, but now

his shoulders were hunched forward and he spoke across his chest, staring downwards, speaking merely to shape his thoughts and vent their humours. "The Foreign Office. . . . There were to be representatives; there was a signal to the aircraft. We imagined there was some importance attached to the revolution of my people."

"It's the chief news, all over the world——"

"News? I am glad it serves a purpose. The world must have its news."

She was silent, studying his anger, hearing the petulance of his brooding tones and trying to measure his situation: that of a monarch forced from home, then to be given the hope of going back: and now this room for a prison, while the great events were at hazard across the barricades of the streets he knew and had lived in.

"They can't keep you here for long, sir. The police are making a house-to-house search in the district——"

"Your police?" His head jerked up and she was looking into the eyes of contempt. "This house was searched before you came here, while we were thrust into the back of a car in the dark with guns in our mouths—you overestimate the powers of your police. England's not practised in the pursuits of villainy—but you're right, we can't be kept here long. We'll make our own way out." He was gazing beyond her, and without turning round she knew he was looking at Major Bell across the breadth of the room, with a cat's dispassion. She wouldn't like to be looked at with these eyes.

"That man's sitting on a powder-barrel," he said softly, talking less to Louise than to the man at whom he stared. "If he'd wanted me dead he would have shot me by now." The words were so quiet that she was reminded of a cat's muted wickering in the throat as it stalks, watching the prey, enraged that a thing so small should demand patience and cunning from a brute so splendid. "I'm to be kept alive. I must have something he wants, and all the time I have it there's a chance for me. I wonder what it is. . . ."

He had forgotten she was here, but she didn't mind. It was fascinating to watch his complete and inviolable concentration. When she had been introduced to him this evening she had shivered under the penetrant stare that narrowed its focus to light her face and nothing else. Now it was turned on Bell, and she was invisible in the dark of his mind, thankful for the respite. At last she felt the warmth of the room—not the bright scorch of the logs that stung without warming—but the close soft air against her face and hands. The sickness had gone and wouldn't return: the shock was over: in those few minutes she had lived through long experience and was now by a few degrees immune. Undoing the belt of her coat, she was about to throw it back from her shoulders when she was aware of hands touching it. Someone was behind her. She swung her head, the black hair flying out.

Kosek gently took her coat, folding it across his arm as if it were spun glass. She felt foolish: her nerves were on show again. Her smile was wry. "*Gradtidji.*"

"*Pos nadridz, Duenaczina.*" The devoted eyes turned and made their excuses to the King, but he was not looking at Kosek. A calm had come to the room again as the two men exchanged the challenge. Louise began wanting to turn her head and face the distant yellow eyes—better to see them than feel them on her spine. Then the voice startled her by its nearness.

"Excuse my disturbing you, sir. The Ambassador asked me to say his good-night to you."

"That man wishes no one any good." He turned away, impatient with the Major's presence, with the stupid things he said, with his insistence upon formality in a situation that would better suit a jungle clearing than this house. There'd be an end to formality here, when his patience broke; an end to a lot of things.

Bell looked from the one to the other. Wasn't the Buck of the Balkans in the mood for love? She looked fetching enough in the wool sheath dress, her breasts pushing up and her skin pale under the soft black hair—he must have ridden coarser flesh than this. Perhaps after some wine. . . .

"We've a meal prepared, sir—I wouldn't call it dinner, with our makeshift facilities, but if you'd care——"

"I've no appetite."

Bell had expected it. The meal had been planned for the Ambassador and his party, with extra dishes in reserve. But Nikolas would be too angry, the girl too shocked, the others too anxious. "Some biscuits and wine, perhaps?"

"Wine, then."

"At once. Miss Cameron, I hope you'll eat something?"

"No, thank you."

"You're feeling better?"

"I feel very well."

He shrugged and turned to the ex-King. "If your man will lend a hand——"

In his own tongue Nikolas said: "Kosi, go with the Major, and check the wine carefully."

Passing Louise, the old servant said: "Your coat is on the chair, should you need it." Then he went with the Major to the end of the room where there stood a lacquer cabinet, its colours faded and the hinges dulled. He waited while

91

the Major opened it and selected a slim gold Hock. Knowing that Kosek spoke only a few words of English, he said in French:

"Unfortunately we've no ice here."

"His Majesty would, in any case, prefer a Beaune, sir. I notice a bottle there."

Bell found it for him and took the corkscrew, but Kosek begged permission to open it himself, and first inspected the seal and cork, his white head bent over the task. When he had drawn the cork he asked for a glass, and poured a little of the wine, sipping it slowly while the Major stood beside him, facing the length of the room, watching them all.

The Burgundy fondled the old man's tongue, smooth and innocent, and he was almost disappointed; at his age he asked for no greater privilege than to die in this way and so let his king live on. But there might be poison here, of a kind, for the man beside him. The English major seemed to forget that wine was the food of rage.

CHAPTER IX

There had been a room like this in the palace, Kosek thought, a long room with the hearth making a great stone arch in the wall. It had been the Audience Room. What was it now?

He was heavy with the need for news. They might still be fighting, or it might all be finished now. All might be calm, but for the dirge of funerals; or the true colours of the Slavakian flag might now be aflaunt above the palace roofs and the King's loved name the currency of voices through those rooms. But Nikolas would have his doubts. When the news had reached the villa in Basle that the people needed him he had been stunned, then bitter.

"They've waited a long time, Kosi. They weren't so free with their show of fealty when Szados marched into the palace."

Kosi had spread his hands, saying that those were different times; the storm had been a quiet one, but had come quickly, from nowhere. He used his gentle smile to excuse fifteen million people; but Nikolas remained immersed in his distrust. The one thought that started through him like a fire—and Kosek had seen it as clearly as if he watched the leap of actual flame—was that Szados might now be endangered, he and all his like who were lording it along the Danube. It was hate, thought Kosek, that had spurred him from his exile and brought him to England; not love of his people.

Yet Nikolas loved them. He had been formed by the

same alchemy as they, fed with the fruit of their same soil; his eyes knew the same patterns: the lift and trough of the mountain range that made the frieze of the sky to the west of Drovnik and the river cities; his ears knew the same tune of bells that carried across the wheat-lands from the dotted churches, when in the evening the sun went down across the thatch of crofts and the steam of oxen's breath rose grey as the night-coming mist. He knew the same red-sand roads, and the lope of dogs in the hunt; and certainly he knew the women of his land; no one could say that the King was mean with his seed.

But Kosek, better versed in his master's moods than his most astute advisers, did not waste his time in reminding Nikolas of his love for his people. Hate was the tune, for the moment. "President Szados will be up against it, if you give them the heart to fight on, Your Majesty." It was the first time he had dared use that title since Nikolas, with a litre of brandy in him, had shouted down the staircase of the villa, breaking the echoes against the walls—"*Majesty?* What majesty? I'm the king of a travelling-bag, didn't you know, damn you?"

That had been three years after Szados had forced his way past the guards and presented his ultimatum. The poison had a three-years' vintage, but was not mellowing as it aged. Now it was blacker; you could see his eyes bright with it; it curdled in his voice.

"Up against it?" The thought had lingered, chilling the very sunshine in the room. "Up against a wall, couldn't we have him, Kosi? Bullets in his belly as thick as flies. . . ."

Kosek thought, looking down the long room with the wine warm in his mouth: will the President have changed, as much as we have? He could hardly remember the man's face, but then it wasn't Szados's face that one remembered: it was a square negative face with blank eyes that said nothing—or it had been, five years ago. What was it now? Frightened? Nothing had ever frightened Szados. He was a kind of machine, without heat, or blood, or God, his boots jerking along the corridors, outstripping his escort, bringing the King's aide from the ante-room before he reached its door—"I demand immediate audience. Convey that message."

"You will please wait." Vralmar, the young captain, had barred his way, and from the music gallery Kosek, watching, had nearly choked himself wanting to cheer. Vralmar had been below the saluting-base a week before, when King Nikolas the Second had reviewed his troops on the parade-ground of the Kilvinjios Barracks, making a last show of defiance for the world to see through the eyes of its foreign envoys and the gentlemen of its press. Kosek had been there, but had seen no one but the King. He had himself arranged that brilliant uniform, draping the scarlet cloak across those strong, loved shoulders—the hem of it now spread over the rump of the white stallion that stood as if stone-carved while the Commander-in-chief of the Slavakian Army took the salute.

Five whole platoons had been marched past twice, to make a brave show of it, though few realised. The Slavakian Army was a whittled company, with its officers coerced, defecting, or filling the political prisons. But men like Captain Vralmar were left, to bar the door. "You will please wait."

A second aide-de-camp had appeared and stood beside the young captain, who told him: "The Minister requests an audience with His Majesty. I'll wait here." Seeing the attitude of Szados, he drew his revolver and stood with his back to the door while the aide went to convey the message.

Kosek had prayed that the arrogant robot would make a movement and give Vralmar his excuse. He gazed through the pillars of the music gallery, willing Szados to move, his ears longing for the shock of sound from the gun in Vralmar's hand. But only Szados's voice came, dry and regular like the rattle of a stone in a tin. "You aim at the heart of your country. You stand there protecting its archenemy. But you are young, and if you live, you'll learn." He swung round and paced with his back to the captain, so swiftly that the finger might have jerked on the trigger by nervous reflex; but Kosek, the pillars of the balustrade cold against his temples as he pressed his head against them, his eyes aching because he dared not blink, knew that it needed more than the reflex action of a finger to save Slavakia. Szados was not the only one; he was their chief.

At the end of ten minutes Kosek was sunk against the balustrade, sick with tension, listening to the clockwork click of Szados's boots as he paced the tiled floor, measuring off the seconds of this dreadful day. And when the door was opened and the aide emerged to hand the Minister a sheet of paper, Kosek knew that a dynasty had died.

Seventeen years before, a shot had been fired, and this was the echo: the opening of a door. The gap of time had closed and he remembered the face of the Crown Prince Nikolas as he had burst into the room where Kosek was busy at the wardrobes supervising the valets. The boy of eighteen had stopped short in the middle of the room, as if remembering that he could no longer throw himself and his infant miseries into Kosi's arms. But this face was a child's again, whitened by bewilderment, the eyes so filled with agony that they didn't see, couldn't look out from the chilled mind. "They've shot my father."

The stillness of the room was deafening: the ear had nothing to receive. They stared at each other and Kosek remembered that a pair of pin-stripe trousers had been in his hand, draped like a black flag from the hanger.

"Did you hear, Kosi?" In the car, driving through the riding-park. Two men, blocking the roadway. Then the shot. 'They'. Who were 'they'?

Kosi had heard. Not the shot, but the disbelief in the boy's voice, as if he had come here for Kosi to tell him: 'No, you're imagining things, Your Highness.' But all Kosi could say, after the stunned minutes had passed, was: "Then it's a black day, Your Majesty."

The day of the shot, 1937. Now the day of the sheet of paper, 1955, a day as black, but quieter. You could hear the birds outside in the palace gardens, and the far waterfall sound of the piano in the music-room where Elsina was practising, while the Minister read the sheet of paper, and Kosek from his high secret vantage watched and could do nothing.

Waiting by the pile of luggage, later, he heard Nikolas part from Szados with these words: "You'll bear in mind that the document is not an Act of Abdication, but a transference of authority. I don't regard my rights as abrogated, but withdrawn. They do not become yours. You will make your own rights and enforce them as you may. I have worked hard for seventeen years in the most exacting capacity that one man alone can assume, for the sake of my people and the Fatherland. I can only hope that you, once you realise the scale of your new responsibilities, will be able to——"

"Your train," said the President of the Slavakian People's Republic, "leaves in an hour."

Standing by the thirty-seven pieces of luggage, chief of domestic retinue, Kosek had seen the rage come to his master's face and had feared he would strike the President with his bare hand. But it did not happen.

"I shall require leave to visit my country as I choose, in the private capacity of citizen."

"Any application for a visa will be rejected," said the President. Kosek closed his eyes, and wished that he could close his ears. Would the President, being some kind of machine, tinkle like a tin alarm-clock when he was smashed? But Nikolas couldn't smash him. Szados was not alone. His guards were armed. From the shelter of his closed lids, Kosek heard the words that had then seemed so empty:

"Then I'll come without your leave, in the public capacity of king. I'll work for that day."

They were the words less of a crusader than a suicide. Szados knew that the ex-King could find strong support among the governments of Europe and America if he chose to look for it. Slavakia had given thousands of her sons to the Allied cause before the Panzers had rolled through the burning streets; and her underground forces had harried the occupying garrison until the Russian armies had marched in, in the name of liberation. Abroad, Nikolas the Second had established the reputation his father had sired: that of a strong ruler, practised in diplomacy, the loved monarch of a rich state, his reign interrupted by the onslaught of a martial enemy and through no defection of his own. Now he had fallen to the pressures of internal intrigue, sponsored by an enemy more subtle. There was no blame to him. If, in the free capitals, he could influence the twists of history, working for the country whose frontiers were closed to him. . . .

Szados had said nothing; but when the train had sped through the dark of the land that night, an explosion had wrecked the line, bursting like an orange flower in the mouth of the Danvislo tunnel that was still thick with the smoke of the train's passage. Whoever had mistimed the operation must surely have died against the wall of the Kilvinjios Barracks, paying the price of a fool.

Kosek remembered the sound of it. Though the explosion had burst a hundred yards behind the train, it had been like a charge in a rifle-chamber and had roared through the barrel of the tunnel—the guard had spoken later of flying fragments that had been blasted past the windows of his van.

The world had been shocked by the crack of the gun in the riding-park, when King Nikolas I had crouched suddenly forward in his car, his fingers already digging into the rent shirt, the oozing flesh, trying to pick out the bullet they had put there. Seven leaders of a fanatical group had been hanged. The Chief of Police had been dismissed. Special editions were run through the press in the major capitals. But when the Danvislo tunnel collapsed, the world had no time for more than a shrug. An ex-king had been lucky. Thirty seconds earlier and he would have been dead. But nothing else would have changed. Slavakia was a republic now, and there was another exile for the hotels of the Côte d'Azur. In these times, the museums were full of thrones.

Szados was the name. Imgrir Szados. He was the one to deal with. The click of his boots, the dry rattling voice, the face one never remembered. Had it changed in five years? It would never change, that face. It would look the same in its coffin: blank, negative, cold. It would never look as aged, as bitter as that loved face over there. That was a man's face, and even now a king's.

Kosek carried the tray down the room, ushering the wine into the presence.

"We thought," said Sofi Mikayan, "of starting a hunger strike." She studied Louise with bright date-brown eyes, her conversation an excuse for scrutiny. "But of course there has to be someone who will care if one wastes away. Here it would be a little ridiculous."

Louise had looked only once at Nikolas since she had left him to brood. He was still in the alcove, alone, balanced on lean parted legs, gazing down into his glass of wine. A few minutes ago his servant had taken the empty bottle away.

"In any case . . ."—the curious eyes drew her back— "it's impossible to ask the Baron his help in any project involving diminished rations."

Angelitri nodded thoughtfully. His massive shoulders gave the impression that he was about to force himself between the two women with a rugger ball, for all his stillness. "I have a reputation," he said in beautiful measured English, "of which I'm rightly jealous. I once out-ate a master chef during the Drovnik Exhibition of 1933. The feat occupied close on four hours." He looked neither at Louise nor Sofi Mikayan, but at the figure of the ex-King across the room, his mind divided between speech and contemplation. "There was a plan to send me aloft in an antique gas balloon and so commemorate the glorious death of its designer; and malignant rumour has it that since I'd no stomach for the voyage, I set out on the previous evening to prove that in point of fact my stomach was formidable—and far too ponderous an organ to burden a mere gas-bag the next morning."

Kosek was now with Nikolas. He had been summoned. The Baron watched from close beneath his eyelids. "Be that as it may, I remained on the ground, and waved my bottle of bismuth at the intrepid æronaut who volunteered in my place, to cheer him as he sailed overhead. He was picked up from the Adriatic some two hours later, soaked to the bone, and never spoke to me again. Since he was a noted vegetarian, I didn't grieve the loss of his thin companionship."

Nikolas had asked for another bottle, and Kosek was withdrawing, going across to speak to the Major. The King gazed into the bowl of his empty glass, as if seeking the future.

"So for the sake of my reputation, I shall shortly ask our warder-in-chief if the cold chicken he mentioned is still available. I have a flair for sensing when a balloon is about to go up." He turned his dark innocent eyes on Louise.

She asked hesitantly: "Have you any—particular plan in mind? I mean, to break out?" The Major was at the far end of the room with Kosek. The other two guards were not within earshot.

Baron Angelitri watched her sleepily for a moment. "Why should we dream of such a thing, Miss Cameron?"

Sofi Mikayan had folded her long white hands, giving them the shape of silence.

Louise realised that they didn't know who she was, what she was doing here. She was still alone. "I would help, you see."

"Of course," said Angelitri. "But whom would you help?"

They knew one another's names, watched one another's faces, had the choice of two languages for their communication; but they were strangers. Frontiers didn't end with barbed wire and swinging poles; they extended invisibly into the human heart, their presence intimated by the shape of folded hands and the surface innocence of eyes; and the password was changed every day so that you could never learn it.

"I'm afraid I've no credentials," she said.

"My question was too blunt——"

"This is the time for bluntness." On an impulse she turned and went quickly across the room to the doors and touched the handle before her wrist was gripped, and she was looking into the eyes of the drab little guard. Bell was half-way across the room——

"One moment, Miss Cameron." She waited for him. "You'll be given an escort."

"Thank you, but I've changed my mind."

She turned away from the doors. In the silence her feet were audible even over the carpet. Although she had been out of this room an hour ago on a mission to the lavatory, this was the first time she had been given physical proof of her prisoner status. Previously the business of getting her out of the room and back had been conducted formally, as in the case of Baron Angelitri. The escort had waited outside for her, and there was no means of fastening the door; but the operation had been 'civilised', according to the Major's code. Now there was the feel of the guard's fingers on her wrist and the memory of the warning in his eyes, the rawness of Bell's voice. She had lost the right of passing freely, without let or hindrance; she had no passport, and no credentials.

Panic stirred and the air suffocated: she was cut off from

a world so taken for granted, the world of near-by houses and street lamps, passing traffic. Its freedom was disallowed her, and she was on the far side of a wall whose existence she had never suspected. Would she die here? It would be among strangers.

She realised she was staring into the eyes of Sofi Mikayan and heard herself saying rather feebly: "You see, I'm here under duress, like you."

Angelitri said dryly: "Welcome to our happy band." But he didn't intimate that they would now trust her; and she didn't plead again.

Sofi looked at him, but Louise could not see her eyes; it was like being deaf and watching someone speak. "Are you sleepy, Petrik?"

"I lack air. I wonder if the good Major would let us take a short walk along the window-sills?"

"He's taken a pill, I saw him. Benzedrine, perhaps."

"When did you last sleep?" Louise asked them.

"The night before the journey." But Sofi's face was not tired; one could not imagine this face sleeping. "Except for a doze on the plane, which is always worse than staying awake." To the Baron she said: "Why don't you go and sleep? We shall have to take it in turns before long."

He was looking across at the King. "I might be needed."

"This could go on for days, Petrik."

"I don't think it will. Someone is expected here."

"How do you know?" Louise heard suspicion in the woman's tone.

"I have been watching Major Bell, and the others; and I have been listening. The King has been brought here for a purpose. An operation."

Sofi put a long pale hand on his arm and in the move-

103

ment there was the suggestion of sheathed claws. "Tell me about it."

"These are my beliefs, nothing more. There's nothing I can tell you, Sofi——"

"An 'operation'? How do you mean?"

"Brain-washing." He became less sleepy; his eyes were bright under their hoods. "Why else would they go to all this trouble? A bomb on the aircraft—a quiet massacre in the car—it would have been easier to kill us than let us live. They can't hold us here until a decision is fought out in Drovnik, because there's a risk of something going wrong, all the time—that is why the Major's nerves are starting out of his face. He has to wait, and keep us waiting."

Louise saw Bell at the end of the room, with Kosek, who was uncorking a bottle. Bell had left the room at regular intervals during the last three hours. "He goes out to listen to the radio," she said. "I've noted the times. The last time he went out I heard static when he changed the stations. He's keeping in touch with events."

Angelitri gazed at the Major, and turned his head a few slow degrees to watch the thin boy with the woman's face, the pale one who never fidgeted and never showed his hands. He was more watchful even than the Major; but the guard at the doors was a slack thing, bored with his duties. In here the numbers were three against five if you counted the women . . . if Sofi went to the doors and focused attention there, while he took the thin boy unawares, Nikolas could see to the Major. . . . But it was illusive, a plan like that. He had smelt cordite before and seen a pennyworth of blood ruin a priceless carpet (the Minister of Public Security, in the last year of the King's reign, tipping back in his chair with his legs kicking at the banquet-table and the ugly mouth unwiped, his eyes rolling; an unpleasant death for an unpleasant man). Planning, one must remember the trumps: the guns. They were out of sight, until suddenly . . .

They were not always in pockets. That one, with the bullet for the Minister, had been inside the white linen cloth, and no wine had flowed from the neck of the champagne bottle when the steward (hanged, now, for a good deed) had moved between the chairs to charge the Minister's glass. Beforehand they must have smashed the bottom from the empty bottle and slipped the revolver half-way in, the wine-cloth completing the disguise. And when the steward had moved softly between the gilded chairs the black neck had smoked as if with the spume of the wine as the sound had come, so like the pop of a cork that when the little fat louse had tipped back in his chair there were many who thought he was drunk instead of dying.

He had died like a monkey, all arms and legs and chattering teeth, looking up at Baron Angelitri with terrified animal eyes while the blood soaked across the starched linen and the elegant trousers, all formality gone, the high phrases forgotten, the decorations hanging crooked and the jewelled studs bursting apart as the monkey struggled on the ground, first Jekyll and now Hyde. No matter that he was the victim: he'd been a murderer all his life.

We change our places, Angelitri thought, and change our sides, all of us, killing across the frontiers, dying at Mons, pulling the bomb-doors open above Warsaw, Coventry, Berlin and Stalingrad, killing if we have a gun, dying if we've lost it. Man is as dignified as the stinking chemicals of his own making, a monkey in evening-dress.

The thin boy never showed his hands and there was

nothing under his clothes, unless it was a knife—he might be trained in knife-work; he was thin and pale and quiet, like a blade. The guard at the doors could have an arsenal under those bulging clothes; one could safely say a volley would come from that quarter. The Major would be armed: a man with as much fear in the eyes as that would surely keep a weapon to caress when the night thoughts came to scare him in the dark.

There could be no plan. The first to take the risk would kill the King; and the shot would echo in Drovnik, and kill all hope.

"Do you think," Sofi was saying, "they would let us listen to the news if we asked them? Whatever it is, we can do no harm."

The Baron watched old Kosek bring the wine to the King. The second bottle. "They'd let us listen if the news were bad. The thought gives me courage." Kosek withdrew, leaving the tray of wine on the shelf above the great hearth. The filled glass sat there like a big red plum. Perhaps he would approach in a moment and suggest that since life here was in the balance they should keep clear heads. They weren't at the villa in Basle, where one could drink until the morning with no harm done but for the frightening of the household staff. The issues of war and peace were pivoted here like a weather-vane becalmed.

"Let me ask the Major," said Louise; but Angelitri was not listening.

Sofi Mikayan thought for a moment and said: "If he refuses we'll know the news is good, as the Baron says. If we are allowed to listen, at least we shall know there's a world still going on outside. Ask him, my dear."

Bell was near the pair of doors talking to the guard, who

stood more erect. He told Louise: "There's no fresh news, Miss Cameron. The last report was a repeat: the city is calm, and the surviving insurgents are being rounded up. Amnesty decrees provide pardon for those surrendering arms before dawn tomorrow."

"You've no opinion of my intelligence, have you? And you daren't let me listen to your radio myself."

The yellow eyes registered nothing, even when they glanced across her face in fleeting interruption of their vigilance. "As you might know, the final news summary was broadcast more than ten minutes ago——"

"In English, yes. But there were two major freedom stations still transmitting at six-thirty this evening, as well as Europe Number Three and Vienna."

"The stations at Kresnik, Bandonitz and Vracz were re-captured by government forces before ten o'clock. Europe Number Three receives its reports wholly from propaganda departments in Washington, and the only news reaching Vienna will be from hysterical refugees crossing the Austrian frontier. I wouldn't waste your time."

"I don't think I have." She turned away and went back to Sofi and the Baron. "He won't let us listen," she told them triumphantly; but they did not hear. She followed their gaze. The King had emptied the wine-glass and stood with his head suddenly thrown back to stare across the room, as if he had reached some kind of decision. His eyes seemed illumined with emotion; his hand was clenched round the stem of the glass and now it snapped with a brittle sound. The bowl and base flashed white as he flung them into the hearth.

"Major Bell!" Energy from his body spilled into his voice. The nerves of its hearers shrank. "I'm in the mood for some exercise!" The shout had a kind of joy in it.

The thin pretty boy watched, his hands out of sight. The guard by the doors jerked a glance to Bell.

"What shall we do for exercise? *Answer, damn you!*"

The Major had to wait for the walls to stop ringing. From a tight throat he said: "I should warn you that if——"

"Warn the Crown, would you? But didn't you hear me? The Crown wants exercise!" The aura of his rage was such that if a bullet came his way one would expect to see it deflected before hitting him.

Angelitri was pale. "I beg Your Majesty——"

"Beg?" He stared into Angelitri. "Warn? Beg? What else, gentlemen?"

Beside Louise, Sofi Mikayan said nothing. She watched the King as a mother would watch her child in danger and out of reach, with a dreadful patience. The Baron did not move, but watched Nikolas with his head forward on the gathered shoulders. There would be no point in moving. The wine was in the King and the rage was out. Reason was suspended. He stood against them all, ally or enemy. The Baron had seen this rage before, in the years of exile when Nikolas had suffered the bitterness long enough and would tear it out like a cancer with his bare hands; as his father had tried to tear out the lodged bullet from his heart.

"Are you all deaf? Struck dumb?"

The only moving thing was old Kosek, hovering, a black suit with a white head, his eyes lifted to watch the enemies, his body between them and his master. It would be such a privilege . . .

"What shall we do for exercise?" The heat of the fire was against his back and he felt it and swung round so that poor Kosek had to dodge and edge like a goalkeeper as the King bent and lifted a half-burned log by its ends and stood with its flames in his arms—"Shall we toss the caber? Would it amuse us?"

Angelitri moved a step and Bell called a warning but the log went spinning across the room with its flames bannering out and then bursting against the wall where Bell was lurching clear. Sparks showered him. Kosek crouched, watching for the men's hands to move. Bell's voice: *"Don't kill him——"* and then the mad music of steel as the fire-irons were dragged from the hearth and sent whirling through the air to smash against the doors with a peal of broken bells, the small untidy man coming closer in a shambling run. The cough of his gun.

The King doubled, and his servant was kneeling against him fretting like a dog.

CHAPTER X

Throughout the night, messages cabled to Libertybeam London had so crowded on each other that they were cleared through special channels while the telediphones in Unic House kept up their clattering. Transmissions from European radio networks were monitored and edited for collation in London while Press representatives stood by for any hard facts that might bear printing before they were contradicted from another source: but when the first of the morning editions was on the street it was realised that no clear overall picture could be expected while Drovnik burned and the ether was jammed with the conflict of opposed ideologies.

"It is surely becoming evident," said an official spokesman of a legation in Paris, "that the news of King Nikolas's arrival in London has given the revolutionaries a great impetus in their struggle for independence, at a time when it seemed that their initiative had expended its force against the better-equipped Security Police and the People's Guard. But even if British advice were available to King Nikolas at this moment, it is doubtful whether he would be advised to return to his country while the strife continues. It would be dangerous to his person and his people's cause if he were to expose himself to a stray bullet even if he managed to escape the attentions of Union agents. If he is to return to his people, then his people have the task of winning peace in their cities before he can safely resume the duties of sovereign in Slavakia."

A comment from a German Press agency was briefer. "Since it appears that the ex-King has lost his freedom of movement and even decision, how can he influence the tide of events in his country except in name only? Would he, in fact, accept the throne again if the nationalists won the fight for independence? No one is sure of that: except those whose endeavours are so desperate that there can have been no time in which to doubt it."

A B.U.P. cable from Vienna carried more weight, having as its source the words of a half-dozen Slavakians recently engaged in the fighting. Now wounded, they had crossed the frontier as refugees. "The feeling in Drovnik and other embattled cities is that while Slavakia is fighting to over-throw five years of tyranny and re-establish her independence whatever form of self-government emerges, the hope of seeing Nikolas on the throne again as a constitutional monarch with a chosen parliament is driving the people to efforts that only a shared faith can achieve. While they live they find ammunition from nowhere, and when they die it is with an empty gun. The sad hordes of the refugees are made up of old men and old women, children too small to lift a rifle, and the wounded of all ages who know that their bodies would only litter the streets and hinder their friends if they refused this chance of leaving the country."

Individual stories were seized upon by correspondents at the frontiers, for these facts were from the horse's mouth. A man of over sixty—a farmer from Bandonitz—told reporters: "There didn't seem any hope, in the first two days, of any victory for us. Already the Security Police had started machine-gunning the scattered groups of students and factory-workers who had raided the barracks for arms. I told my family we would leave while there was time. Then we heard from our home radio station that the

King had gone to London and was trying to help us. My wife brought me the shot-gun we use for rabbits, and I went with my two sons into the town, where fighting had started near the radio building. We were there for two nights, helping to overturn trams and buses for the barricades. We used petrol-bottles and Molotov cocktails and sometimes grenades, and we put dishes in the roadway so that when the tanks pulled up, thinking they were mines, we could throw our 'bombs' at them. Then one of my sons was killed, and I brought the other away with me. He is tired, and I have lost my arm—it was a building that fell near us and there were big stones. I don't know where my wife is, or my daughters. I sent them to the frontier, so perhaps I will see them again." He looked up at them from the stretcher, and accepted a cigarette. "Tell the news of what we are doing. That is what we ask."

There were other stories, of tragedy, heroism, little victories won from the confusion; but this old man's testament of faith in the King pointed the argument in Europe that Nikolas was needed by his people. But no one knew where he was.

From several quarters the rumour spread that the British Government was holding the ex-King in concealment for his own sake, and listening to his proposals and pleas for aid while the revolution went on. But this speculation had a flaw: if Nikolas were free to speak, he would insist on sending a message to his people, saying that he was with them in his heart, and was working for them in London. Such news would have enormous effect in Slavakia, and could turn the tide overnight. But there was no message.

Pending a promised statement by the Foreign Secretary in the House, a statement was made by an official spokesman for the Foreign Office. It appeared in the noon editions. "It is not considered to be in the public interest, at this stage, to reveal more than that all possible investigations are now being made concerning the disappearance of the ex-King. No detailed account of their nature can be given without prejudicing the chances of their success."

"To be more brief," Messiter told his secretary at Unic House, "they're looking but not finding." He had arrived early this morning in response to the general appeal that all staff should work overtime to cope with the crisis. Putting most of his routine duties on one side, he had spent the morning between the monitor sections and the day-transmission studios, helping to assess the reports as they came in from Eastern Europe and to incorporate their information in the transmission programmes. The task of cross-checking the glut of information was exacting, and much was discounted as unreliable; but facts came to light on their own merit: at eight o'clock this morning the voices of announcers broadcasting from Kresnik Radio in southern Slavakia were heard against a background of shots, and twenty minutes later the station went off the air. There had been no mention of the attack that must have been launched against the building, for the announcers were desperate to send out the mass of reports they were receiving from the centres of the fighting, while time was left. A later report that Kresnik Radio was still holding out was discounted. The facts were self-evident: shots, and then silence.

Tony Messiter had taken a break for lunch, and in the canteen found strange faces, of people who normally worked here by night but who had come in with the day-shift. And there was a face he missed. He had asked his colleagues but they couldn't help; but Miss Thorne was in the canteen, with flakes of pastry falling over her pile of programme layouts as she sat with a bun in one hand and her pen in the other. "She has 'flu, Mr. Messiter."

"Are you sure?"

Miss Thorne's brown spinster's eyes surveyed the American's face. He was asking about Miss Cameron. If Studio Five was still booked for the afternoon Russian transmissions they would have to cut the English–Roumanian educational broadcast in Studio Four and switch to Slavakian News, unless Dr. Krosmitolf wanted to be awkward and insist on his programme space. The American had a kind face, a father's face. They said . . . but wasn't he rather old for a girl as young as Miss Cameron? A cold. No—'flu. There was a doctor's letter. That was unusual, as if the girl had expected to be disbelieved. This pastry would choke anyone. "Sure?"

"Are you sure she has the 'flu?" His patient voice came floating down from a din of plates and chairs moving.

"Yes. Oh, yes. She sent a certificate."

"A certificate of what?"

"Doctor's letter. It's in my office. Try there." Flakes of pastry fell like dead petals over the sub-heading: *Foreign Office Statement*.

"Why send in a doctor's letter?"

You would think Mr. Messiter had all the time in the world. But of course he was in love, they said. She thought for the fraction of a second about the word 'love', or rather glimpsed it drifting above her like a sugary flower, as meaningless as a coloured photograph of a place where she had never been.

"I really can't say." She brushed the crumbs off the script with her knuckly scrubbed hand. "Ask at my office. They'll be sure to know." Her office knew everything. There'd be ructions if it didn't.

This is PBX calling Miss Thorne. Miss Thorne in Box Two, please.

"Excuse me." A loose sheet dropped and he picked it up, the corner dripping with spilled tea. He tried to wipe it off. "Don't worry. The tea's very transparent in here." She hurried across to the telephones.

"Have you finished?"

He looked at the messy table. The girl balanced her tray on the edge. "Have I finished what?"

"With the table?"

"Oh, sure."

He went up to Miss Thorne's office.

The porter found him outside the door, with packages in his arms, and flowers. "She doesn't answer," he told the porter.

"You've rung, I suppose?"

Messiter was taken aback at the question. "Well, yes, I have."

Light from a high window shone on the man's pate, in the shell of which the thoughts must be circling, of bells and visitors and no answers. The scent of the flowers was rich in the silence.

"She's got the 'flu, you know."

"Yes. That's why I'm a little worried. There's nobody looking after her."

"You a friend of hers, then?"

"Yes, I am." It was nice to say.

"There's been such a lot of comin' an' goin', see, after she got herself into the papers. Try ringin' again."

Messiter balanced his packages of invalid cheer and pressed the bell. "Has a doctor been?"

"Oh, yes. That's how I know she's got the 'flu." The

old eyes gazed at the flowers, soft as butterflies. "Are they for her?"

"Yes."

"They're lovely, they are."

"Which doctor was it?"

"Eh?"

"Was it one of the regular doctors who call here?"

"Oh, I expect so. So many these days, you don't know one from t'other, do you? A nice feller. Not to disturb her, he told me."

"Do you have a key to this door?"

"I've got keys of 'em all." And all their secrets, his tone said.

"Then I think we should open it up, don't you? She may be needing something, and not able to move or call out."

"Best to let 'em lie and sweat it out of them, I always think." But after five minutes' patient discussion he went down the stairs and in another five minutes came back. He found Messiter squatting on the top stair. "We'd best keep quiet, see, in case of disturbin' her."

"Yes, we'll keep it quiet." He was inside the room just as soon as the door was opened, and put the packages down on the meal-trolly by the inner door. He tapped at it gently and then turned the handle, inching the door open. There was the sweet known smell of her in this room and he resented the man's hovering voice:

"Don't you go an' wake her up if she's——"

"Save it. She's not here." He held the door wide open. He had never seen this room, the bed, the pink lamp on the dressing-table, her things, the picture of Lombardy poplars askew on the wall. Underneath his alarm he was conscious of his resentment, having to share this moment that would probably never return. The porter's voice was awed by the impossible:

"She must be here! She's ill in bed, they told me!" His questing head jerked around and then upwards, as if she had floated to the ceiling and lodged there.

Messiter found the telephone in the main room and reported the facts to the police: Miss Cameron had shown no signs of incipient illness yesterday; a doctor's letter had been sent by hand to Unic House, explaining her absence; and this step was unusual; the doctor's name was Holden, and his note could be seen at Miss Thorne's office, Slavakian Section; someone purporting to be a doctor had warned the porter here not to let Miss Cameron be disturbed; the flat was perfectly tidy and there were no signs that she had left a sick-bed and gone out. He finished by repeating that this was the same Miss Louise Cameron who had been interviewed by reporters yesterday and whose picture had appeared in most newspapers, and that she might be of interest to those concerned with the disappearance of ex-King Nikolas of Slavakia.

He was asked to wait at the flat.

The porter had listened with his head on one side, fingering his bunch of keys. "Well, would you believe it?" he said.

"That can't be the police already?"

"Eh?"

"Didn't you hear a bell?"

"A bell?" He went out of the room unwillingly and when he had gone, Messiter stood alone among her things, his eyes like thieves in the silence stealing the shapes she had touched, seeing these new patterns that she had grown familiar with, and intimate. This much more he knew about her: the thin columns of the books along the shelf and the wilting cyclamen, the angle of the castor beneath the meal-trolly (the angle that she had made with the movement of her body when she had pushed the trolly against the wall there), the one green glove lying dead on the arm of the chair. Where was the other? Where was she?

It was absurd to feel this enormous loss for someone who had always been lost to him—more than that, even: never found. But he had never tried to find her, because of the years that would always be between them. He might have asked her out to a restaurant, long ago, and taken her for drives, spending a whole day by a stream, or in hills; and she would have asked him here, simply to return the hospitality—he could have been here before, nearer to her in this high small place that was her home than anywhere else on earth. Even, after days of confidences and an hour of wine shared in this room, she might have made love with him, out of kindness and loneliness, so that he would stand here now and remember how those books had looked when for a little while she had been altogether his, and how the cyclamen had been young and in firm bloom, then. But it was better to be here as a stranger and see it as it was, and as things were, wilting for the want of youth; because that would have been why it had happened: out of kindness. It was a kind of peace, to be here without regrets.

The green glove lay on the arm of the chair. He looked for the other, but couldn't find it. Was it important? Everything was important in this room: there must be a clue somewhere if he could see it. He went into the tiny kitchen, and then the bedroom, and came back. There were no signs anywhere that she hadn't simply gone out, and simply not returned. Three suitcases were in the bedroom and there were no drawers empty; on the draining-board in the kitchen were a few dirty things that she would have washed and put away if she had meant to leave the place for any time; there were vegetables in the pressure-cooker, prepared and ready for heating, and a pint of fresh milk on the table. She must have been here this morning, to have brought the milk in, unless the man who had called here had done that—the man who told the porter that she mustn't be disturbed. Was that the man who had written the doctor's letter?

The police were in no hurry. They moved slow, in this country, like the mills of God. He lit a cigarette and thought: she might have been taken away by the same people, or she might have gone off on her own to try finding out where the ex-King was being held. Either way, she's with him.

After five years, she was still in some kind of love, or would the adolescent fancy dissolve when it came face to face again? Of all meetings, this would be a strange one.

Voices rose from the hall, and footsteps. He went to the open door. The porter was plodding up the stairs with the enduring resolve of a mountain-climber, and two police-men followed patiently. Messiter said to them: "You may find a clue here but I can't. We should make better progress at Unic House, maybe. She was there yesterday afternoon and someone must have seen her leave—more than one person, probably. The commissionaires outside the doors might remember the time she left and the direction she took." He realised he was drawing hard on the cigarette, and the smoke stung his eyes. "There's a bottle of milk, though, in the kitchen here, that she might have taken in herself—or if she didn't, it was taken in by the man who called here and told the porter that she mustn't be disturbed, so that if you have finger-prints powdered we'll at least know whether she took the bottle in herself or someone else did it. In other words we'd have a clue to whether she was here this morning, or didn't come home last night."

One of the constables stood quietly in the doorway to the bedroom, his head turning slowly as he looked at details. The other allowed a pause after Messiter had finished speaking, and then said: "We'll start with your name and address, if you don't mind, sir." He waited with his book open.

Messiter dragged the cigarette out of his lips and threw it into the small stone hearth round the gas-fire. "I'm sorry. I'm a little worried."

"I can see that, sir."

Messiter gave his name and address, and they started at the beginning.

The porter, having remembered what one of the newspapermen had told him yesterday—that good money would be paid for any fresh stories, and that he could telephone to save time—had informed that journal while waiting for the police to come, using the phone-box in the hall; so that within the hour, the name of Louise Cameron was again on the front page, under the crabbed headline: Unic Girl Vanishes.

CHAPTER XI

The scene was confused. Bell stood over the shabby little man, furious.

"*You fool! You might have killed him!*"

"Only a wing——"

"That was luck! Get out!"

"I always hit what I shoot at, Major—you know that. He was running wild——"

"Send Antiquis here. Get some bandages and antiseptic."

Already he had been shocked into saying too much and his whole being was disturbed. There had been for an instant an eye to the keyhole of his mind, violating the privacy of years.

Someone was stamping out the embers before the carpet caught fire. The English girl was kneeling by the ex-King, with the old servant. Sofi Mikayan had given a bird's screech and was motionless, uttering unheard things that might have been a thanksgiving. Angelitri turned to the Major and might perhaps have attacked him with his great shoulders, but Bell had a gun in his hand. "For a retired officer of the British Army, Major Bell, you've picked a slack enough bunch of men——"

"He was perfectly right. He shot for the hand."

"But as you said, he might have killed His Majesty."

"It was unlikely." He watched the Baron lighting a cigarette. "And unimportant."

"You thought it was very important—but never mind.

121

Get hold of your wits again, and call that fellow with the bandages."

An odd little group stood near the hearth; Nikolas, between Kosek and Louise, who were holding his right arm aloft in a comic Hitler salute to stop the blood flowing. Louise was knotting a handkerchief at the wrist for a tourniquet. The King's anger was gone and he was sobered, gazing at Bell as if for the first time he recognised the enemy and judged his strength. Kosek was mumbling to him, perhaps apologies, while the smoke crept through the room to redden their eyes. One of the guards, emerging from behind some curtains when the noise had started, brought the fire-irons to the hearth and lowered them quietly. Louise said over her shoulder:

"Please fetch some hot water, someone."

"You will all appreciate," called Major Bell, "that even a show of impatience will provoke our use of arms, and that a bullet can go astray through no fault of the marksman."

In a strange voice Sofi was addressing oaths to him in her own language, but Bell turned to the doors and called an order to his men. In Slavakian, Louise asked Kosek if he would go and hurry the water and antiseptic.

"Through the bones—the bones?" the old man kept mumbling.

"We can't see until we can clean it. Please hurry." She held the King's arm upright as Kosek went away. "Are you in pain, sir?"

"No." His speech and eyes were clear and he was looking round him at their faces, so that she had the impression that the shock had in some way steadied him, and he was at last taking serious stock of the room, the people in it, and his situation.

Baron Angelitri came into her view, holding his hand out palm upwards. "It passed through," he said. He had found the bullet in the hearth with a chip of stone, its steel pinked.

"Then it might not have smashed a bone." She heard them bringing the first-aid things. "Would Miss Mikayan prefer to do this?"

"Unfortunately Miss Mikayan has fainted."

"Oh——"

"The sight of blood affects her."

Nikolas said: "Poor Sofi. Go and see to her."

Angelitri turned away and looked down at the woman on the settee. Limp and white of face, she roused soft amazement in him that someone so ruthless could become so vulnerable.

The Major was directing operations, having a small table moved near the hearth and the bowl placed on it, and the phial of iodine. Nikolas looked at Louise, quietly saying: "They all look the same—untidy men with nothing in their faces when they come darting up towards you. It was a man just like that who ran up to our car when we were driving in the park, my father and I . . ."

"I read about it——"

"You were too young."

"Not too young to read. Will you help me wash your hand? It's going to sting, with the iodine."

He said nothing more, but lowered himself into the chair they had pushed up for him, and rested his elbow across the table. A crimson trickle had crept across the tourniquet on to her fingers, and she remembered how once she had gone on feeling the touch of this hand long after she had come down the steps from the palace, chivvied by her friends; now there was his blood across her fingers. The floating image of a chandelier was shattered on the surface of the water as she tested its heat.

"Petrik!"

Angelitri loomed over the table. "Sir?"

"How is poor Sofi?"

"She is being fanned with vigour."

Louise poured some of the iodine into the water and watched it clouding and darkening.

"Petrik, that was insulting, wasn't it?"

"Even dangerous, sir."

"But my own fault, I suppose. Though I needed exercise."

"Next time," suggested the Baron, "perhaps a brisk game of chess?"

"That man smelt rotten. Of grease and garlic." He did not glance up at the Major, who had approached. "I tell you, my dear Baron, we've fallen among a rabble of thugs on this occasion. That little barbarian, stinking in his rags —and that tubercular pervert over there, watching me as if I were a woman—I'd be reminded of Alice's tea-party if it didn't smack of a snake-pit." He caught his breath as Louise began splashing his wound.

She turned her head to look at him, ready to stop if he wanted to signal her. The sight of his face communicated some of his pain and she looked away. He let out a breath. "Now I know where it went," he grunted.

"May I put your hand into the water?" The red of the blood mingled with the brown of the iodine in the bowl, and she had to steel herself against nausea.

"Yes. Put it in." He looked up at Bell. "Major, you must be most embarrassed by this mess of affairs. Where did you find that little assassin of yours? And where have you sent him? To bathe, I hope." Bell watched the red-brown water in the bowl. "He's an unlikely lieutentant for an ex-officer of the British Army. Is it the British Army, or the Foreign Legion? There's so little efficiency here, and not overmuch cleanliness. A certain display of tawdry pomp and circumstance, and drinkable Burgundy, but nothing else. A reliance upon firearms instead of wits and discipline—for instance you might have anticipated that sooner or later one of my party would show impatience and cause a disturbance for the lack of planned welfare. I can only take it that this is the first time you've been required by your superiors to abduct a personage higher in rank than a lance-corporal. Tell me if I'm wrong."

"If it calms Your Majesty, I'll apologise for the results of your own indiscretion." He said to Louise: "Take his hand out and show me the wound."

"The air is full of bacteria." She looked up into the yellow eyes.

"Have you had nursing experience?"

"Yes."

"Is it a serious wound?"

"It needs serious attention."

"By a doctor?"

"Of course."

"How much can you do, yourself?"

"Very little. I've no equipment and I'm not a surgeon. There are stitches needed."

"A doctor's been sent for. It will take him an hour to reach here. Do what you can in the meantime." He turned as the new guard, Antiquis, came up. "Well?"

"The telephone, Major." Antiquis was a broad neat man of middle years, quiet-voiced, an ex-seaman perhaps. He looked at no one but Bell.

"All right. I'll leave you in charge here." He left them quickly. Antiquis followed him to the doors and remained just inside them.

Nikolas looked up into the forlorn eyes of his major-domo. "Kosi, don't blame yourself. You couldn't have done more to qualify for your place in Heaven, and I thank you. Now go and attend Mademoiselle Mikayan." He watched the old man withdraw, nodding to please him. "Petrik, see what you can do with the windows, to clear this smoke away. Don't provoke the guards, but draw on your rich funds of diplomacy."

Angelitri contemplated a moment. "Your Majesty may find I'm unequal to the task. Nothing less than a bomb will open those windows, but——"

"Then ask the good Major for the use of one. I'm sure he carries them."

Still the Baron hesitated. "If—er—Your Majesty feels an urge to cause any further disturbance, perhaps you would give me a short warning, so that I can make my own contribution. On this occasion I was too surprised——"

"It wouldn't work, Petrik. That was an impulse, and not a good one. Do what you can to ventilate this place before we choke ourselves." When Angelitri had moved away, he asked Louise: "How is it, my hand?"

"Just as I told the Major, sir."

"I thought you might be deceiving him."

"You need a doctor."

"I need an army. What are those for?"

"To cover the wound on each side, before I bind it."

"Have you really had nursing experience?"

"A little."

"You've a gentle touch, like a woman's, not a nurse's."

She laid one of the cotton pads across the wound, lifting

126

his hand from the bowl and applying the other, while he helped her with his free hand.

"What is your first name?"

"Louise."

"I'll call you Louise, then."

She said nothing. When she had finished the bandage she moved the arm so that he could rest its elbow on the table. "Keep your hand upright for a while, please." She used the towel they had brought, wrapping it round his wrist and forearm. "That is all I can do, I'm afraid."

"You can talk to me."

"Very well."

"I'm told you've been trying to listen to the radio."

"It was no use, but I'm going to try again." She tilted his forearm more upright and he said:

"Bring a chair, Louise. You're tired."

While she was finding a chair the Major came back into the room. Sofi Mikayan, on the settee in the corner, was coughing. There was the low sound of Baron Angelitri's voice as he asked Bell what could be done about ventilating the room.

"We can't open any windows, Baron."

"Why not?"

"It would make sounds in this room more audible to people outside. I'm already worried about the gunshot, even though it had a silencer; and the fire-irons were even noisier. You have to co-operate, you see, in keeping the peace here; and of course you appreciate why." He stood squarely in front of the Baron; there was no lingering pique in his voice at Angelitri's manner just now, when he had told Bell to 'get hold of his wits again'.

"I'm not so sure," Angelitri said, "that you'd kill him, if the police broke in here."

Bell leaned a little closer, taking a few seconds to think before he spoke softly and quickly. "Baron, let me explain the position. Whether you care to pass this on to ex-King Nikolas or not is your affair, as obviously I shall divulge nothing that he mustn't know. My orders are to hold him and his party here until someone arrives. I am required to offer you all as much comfort as the situation permits— but to stamp out any attempt at disobedience, such as occurred just now." He paused, staring into the Baron's eyes. "Finally, my orders are that in the event of the ex-King's rescue becoming a likelihood I shall effect the immediate termination of his life."

Angelitri's shoulders were thrust forward, shaping his whole stance into an automatic challenge a foot away from Bell.

"Murder him, in short."

Bell said impatiently but without raising his voice: "The terminology of death doesn't concern me. In war, murder is valiant and mercy becomes cowardice. The death of this one man could save a thousand lives. It's not for me to judge or worry the point. But you've my word for this: I intend to carry out my orders to the best of my ability, to keep that man alive until the moment when his death becomes essential. That is to say, when it seems likely that he will be taken out of my hands. Such an event could be brought about by your own actions, and so I must restrict the opportunities. With a window open, someone might decide to shout an alarm in the hope of being heard from outside."

"But we all know the position."

"Yes. But it didn't stop the ex-King causing a serious disturbance."

Angelitri said: "His Majesty had drunk close on two litres of wine on an empty stomach."

"There are incitements to rashness even more potent than alcohol. Mere boredom will suffice."

The coughing of Sofi Mikayan caught at the nerves. Bell and Angelitri gazed at each other's red-rimmed eyes. The smoke was acrid in the air, yellowing the glare of the chandeliers and drifting in a faint blue haze across the room.

"Then we must open the doors," said the Baron.

"That can be done." He turned his head and called quietly over his shoulder. "Antiquis, open those doors wide."

Angelitri asked: "We are to be held until 'someone arrives'. Who?"

Bell signalled to the guard at the other door in the wall by the hearth, gesturing him to open it, saying to the Baron: "A high member of the Slavakian Government."

"Since we shall meet him, why can't we know his name in advance?"

"It would give you the opportunity of forming an attitude and deciding on policy before hearing his proposals——"

"Then he's well known to us."

"He is."

"When will he reach here?"

"Soon."

"Was it he who telephoned just now?"

"No. That was confirmation that a doctor's on his way here."

"I imagine," said Angelitri, "that your people weren't pleased to hear about the shooting."

"They realise that my job is difficult, and if they had a more efficient man, they'd use him."

"You take a good many risks, don't you, Major?"

Bell watched the Baron's face with overt attention, trying to judge its expression and catch a clue to his thoughts; but there was nothing, even in the eyes, except blandness; it was a diplomat's face. "Anyone," Bell said, "who is involved with international affairs at—shall we say—a private level must take risks. You will know that. We risk the sudden knocking down of all we are trying to set up. Death doesn't frighten us, but failure has to be lived with." They felt the cool air wafting past them from the open doors, and smoke swirled against their faces as if they stood in the littered wastes of a battlefield, a soldier from each side left behind and left alive to face each other with the fight gone out of them and the cause forgotten, while they looked out from their one face into this other's and questioned its identity, and also their own. "You regard me as a thug," said Major Bell, "but then you're a one for terms and pigeon-holes. You should have learned by now that the man who sits behind an elegant desk in his grandly-appointed study, signing his name to a warrant of execution with a gold-nibbed pen, is just as much a thug —or just as little—as the man who waits in the dark with a knife, and slips it into the victim; except that there's a certain honesty in the one who does the deed himself instead of leaving it to others. He is also responsible, usually, for fewer executions than the man who can sign away a dozen lives at one stroke of the pen. Nor does he salve his conscience with the plea that he does this for the sake of a nation. Each of them has precisely the same excuse: he is certain that the world would be a better place with these people removed from it. The difference between these two kinds of men is that the more ruthless has climbed higher and at a greater cost to others. If you want to talk about murderers, look for them behind the big polished desks, and notice how perfectly their trousers are creased."

Angelitri did not take his eyes from Bell until he had finished; but now he looked past his head, at the guard by the doors. "A thug is the man who enjoys the act. Men like these of yours."

"Don't suggest that a dictator—whether he calls himself a king or a president—doesn't think of the act when he signs his name to it, and doesn't enjoy the power he holds over people's lives. If any man with the power of decision over life and death had a moment's serious doubt of his own right to wield it, then he'd surrender it to someone with a smaller conscience. To a thug."

"And you?"

"I don't defend myself. But I don't defend the others, as you do. The men at the desks."

The Baron thought of the sad Ambassador, of Kisselmann and the March Tribunals, of Szados and the bomb in the Danvislo tunnel, of the Minister of Public Security with caviare on his mouth and the bullet in his vitals, of other men in other places, high places, just as the Major said. But there was a difference, still. Bell was like Colonel Stromjiik, and the little bandit of the Messini caves, and others whom the Baron had met and talked with and been sickened by. He found creation in destruction, and he would delight more in killing an animal than in ravishing a woman. He was a disciple of de Sade.

It would be impolite to charge a man with being the victim of his glands. There, but for the grace . . . "It seems a good reason, if a little devious, for leaving the windows shut."

Bell said with a strange slow smile: "I hoped we'd met on some kind of common ground, if only for a moment."

Angelitri turned away. "Small hopes die easiest in this world, Major." He went across to the settee where Sofi was now sitting upright on the cushions, to rub her long white hands for warmth, and soothe her fury that she had fainted and so denied the King her comfort.

"Major Bell!"

"Sir?"

Nikolas sat with his elbow on the small table, his forearm swathed in the towel. The girl had drawn up a chair and sat with him, keeping his injured hand upright to drain the blood away. The Major went over to them.

"I hesitate to criticise the service here, Major, but there's a bowl of blood and water on this table and I would like it removed. Kosek would give you assistance. And might we have those hideous chandeliers switched off? The glare is uncomfortable and our eyes are full of smoke."

Louise made a movement, but the ex-King stayed her.

"It might be difficult," said Bell, "to see clearly in here, without the lights." He beckoned Kosek, who arrived half running.

"What do you want to see? We've all been staring at one another long enough."

"There might be another disturbance, sir. We can't shoot so straight in the dark." He watched the ex-King's face for a sign of returning anger. If he tried to smash the place up again he would be taken to another room and restrained.

"There's firelight," said Nikolas, "and light from the doors." He studied Bell with his head tilted. "You can have a choice of promises. You can have my word that if those chandeliers go out I'll be peaceable. If not, I'll smash them out with a chair."

Old Kosek withdrew, taking away the bowl and medicaments.

The silence lengthened, and Louise put her hand over the King's where it lay on the table. In Slavakian she murmured: "Please take care. You need to rest your injury."

Bell looked down at her. A soft voice could work marvels here. If only she were on their side. . . .

"What's it to be, Major? It's a fair challenge, so why hesitate?"

"You're in no position to challenge, sir, but I've no doubt you'd stir up trouble again if you could. I'll accept your word that you'll be peaceable if we turn the main lights out. Naturally I have complete trust in your honour."

"Then we've struck our bargain." He watched Bell go over to the doors and speak inaudibly to the guard. Then the white glare of the chandeliers was cut off and the eye swam in a rush of colours and the dark until slowly the flames in the hearth grew brighter and the light from the doors shed a soft flush across the floor, shadowed by the Major's legs. No one moved and no one spoke. The room was transformed, and the mind took stock of the change, inspecting it with the tentative appraisement of a cat's whiskers. Light meant day-time and the dark meant night; for the first time in twenty-four hours, night had fallen in this room.

The amiable voice drifted across the shadows. "Thank you, Major." The white blur of Nikolas's face was turned in the light from the doors. "I see we have a radio in the other room there. Do you agree that a little music might beguile our ears?"

Bell watched the silhouette against the glow of the

hearth: the ex-King and the English girl with the small table between them and their hands resting on it, their faces turned this way, pale anonymous outlines.

In a moment he said quietly: "Antiquis. Go in there and tell Warren to find some music on the radio. He must be careful to avoid any snatches of news broadcasts while he's tuning-in, and he must be ready to switch off at once if they break into the programme with any announcement. See that he understands."

He waited in the doorway, listening while the man flicked through static and voices until an explosion of pop-music shivered the air, the vitality and monotony of its rhythm cancelling out.

"No, Warren."

From a new kaleidoscope of stations the man selected a concert orchestra, and Bell saw the ex-King nod.

Louise listened to the music, fascinated by the strangeness of its sound in this small place where so much enmity was in the air, as acrid as the drifting smoke with its smell of violence. This was the only common language among the higher animals. On these unspoken terms the music of Brahms had been played in Moscow, and the music of Tschaikovsky in Berlin, while blood darkened the snow in Stalingrad and the bomb-doors opened above Breslau.

"Does it please you, Louise?"

His face had lost its pallor in the fire's light; his eyes shone in the gloom.

"It's beautiful." Her eyelids stung with the smoke, and she was afraid her eyes would soon water and he might think she was crying for some reason.

"You are sleepy. There's no need for us to talk."

They were enclosed by the intimacy of the fire, related

by the table. A moment ago she had touched his free hand when she had entreated him to take care, and then moved it away again. Now he had felt for hers and their hands lay together, palm to palm. They sat together sharing the softness of the light and the easing rhythms of the music, with the romantic composure of the scene distorted by the smell of smoke and antiseptic, and the awkward shape of his right arm as she helped him to keep it upright.

"You were nearly killed," she said. The heat of this strong hand would be cold now, and these bright eyes dulled.

"Yes. That was a mistake, of course. I'm here for fattening. I still have a market value on the political Exchange."

"You mustn't provoke them again."

It would not matter what she said; nothing would be remembered when they left this house. The music and the light flowed through the open doors.

"You shall advise me, Louise. I've no one else."

"There's the Baron, and your secretary."

"They came with me out of loyalty, because I asked them. We were to do business with your government, if we could; but it would be my business, not theirs. Their earnest advice to me is——" He turned his head slowly, but no one had moved. The ruddied light was on the faces of Bell and Antiquis by the doors, Angelitri and Sofi Mikayan on the baroque couch in the corner of the room, the boy Peake and the two other guards near the curtained windows. "I would rather not talk about these things, Louise."

He turned his head back and studied her face; she seemed to feel the brush of his glance across her brow and hair, the touch of it on her mouth.

"In any case," she said, "you don't know who I am."

"This is all I need to know of you for now. An English face, small and cool, with pride in the mouth and a stillness that's a challenge to a man like me. I'm over-used to wanton promise in a woman's face."

His hand burned against hers; but it meant nothing; it had touched so many, cupping their breasts and burying in their hair, tormenting and delighting them and then forgetting them.

"I'm afraid," she said as gently as she could, "that I was a disappointment to you."

"In what way?"

"You thought I was a prostitute, fetched here for your diversion."

"I know these men, and the way their minds work. They are anxious to draw my sting, and it would have occurred to them as a reasonable method. There was no slight meant to you, but I apologise. The ways of our countries are different."

"The ways of men and women are the same." She must commit his face to memory, so that later, when the last chance of seeing it had gone for always, she could take the photograph off her desk at Unic House and drop it into the waste-paper-basket, and forget the younger face she had seen for the first time in the palace at Drovnik, and remember only this one with its lines of bitterness thrown into relief by the firelight.

"Have you a lover, Louise?"

"There's someone I love."

"Think about him."

"Why?"

"While I watch your eyes."

The heat of the fire lay against one side of her like something alive. It wouldn't matter what she thought or said; the minutes were dying away.

"All right," she said.

His hand moved against hers and he laid a finger along her palm; after a moment she encircled it.

CHAPTER XII

More than once Angelitri had thought of making an excuse to leave Sofi sitting alone on the couch, so that he would no longer have to suffer the humours emanating from her with the force of an electrical field; but it would be unkind to desert her, and so he stayed, pretending to doze.

"How long will they go on sitting there?" she asked, with a dreadful softness.

He had been watching the table and the two figures through his lashes, enabling himself to focus his thoughts on them and yet seem asleep if Sofi glanced at him.

"Until the doctor comes." He opened his eyes fully.

"It's dangerous, Petrik." Under the sound of the music they could talk as secretly as if they were alone in the room. The music isolated speech, so that nothing was heard of what Major Bell was saying to Antiquis the guard, or the ex-King to Louise, or Sofi Mikayan to the Baron. Even thought seemed confined by the music, so that Peake, solitary near the dark fall of the curtains, was closed in with these few minutes of his life, concealed in sound. He and the other guards in the room were as remote as if each were the sole inhabitant of a distant star.

"He has a strong constitution," said Angelitri.

"I don't mean his wound. It's dangerous to let her talk to him privately like that. We don't know who she is or what she was brought here for. Every word she says might be poison in his ears."

Angelitri wished that he had left her, and said: "If so, you can rinse them out for him in the morning. One word from you can purify a dozen from anyone else."

But the electrical field remained galvanic, and the Baron was resigned to subject his nerves to it, musing with irony that if Nikolas had been making love to the girl, Sofi would be content to watch and even approve the technique; nor did she really believe that he was in any danger of mental seduction, for the head of a state is well versed in the slang of intrigue, and this girl was too young to have learned it. Poor Sofi was jealous of the smell of iodine.

He remembered something the Baroness had confided to him, after the motor accident on the Swiss mountain road. Nikolas had been driving his Mercedes-Benz very fast and Angelitri had been with him, sitting silently and watching the road and the ex-King's temper unwind as the car was put at the bends with the tyres howling softly and the thin wheel trembling in the driver's hands until Angelitri knew that they were beyond the limit where safety was possible. The death-wish was in the King: he had seen it before. The rush of the wind had gone to his head and the lean whipping machine was carrying him to the edge of life and he didn't want to go back.

Perhaps it was Angelitri who prevented Nikolas from simply flinging the car at the mountain-side and exchanging bitterness for oblivion. As it was, they failed to pull out of a drift at a hundred and thirty-five k.p.h., and the beautiful Mercedes was sold for scrap a week later. They had been thrown clear and the Baron was out of the nursing-home within three days—it was said that he had brought down a barn with the impact of his shoulders, and he was pleased with the story. Nikolas broke an arm and regained consciousness in the cool grey room where people waited, watching the doctors and the white closed-eyes face of the King.

Later, Baroness Angelitri had said she was in the room when all the others had gone, and that Sofi Mikayan had come in and not seen her by the screens. "She watched him for some minutes, my dear, and then did a most surprising thing. You must not tell anyone."

Petrik had said: "Then nor must you. Not even me." But she had not let him escape.

"She leaned over the bed and kissed his brow. I was astounded!"

"It must have been difficult," said Petrik, "to keep so silent, being astounded. Only you could manage such a feat, with your superb aplomb."

"But are *you* not astounded to hear of it, Petrik?"

"The news you've been bringing me for fifteen years is becoming so sensational of late that even mild surprise is an effort."

"Sometimes I wonder if you really take things *in*. She *kissed* him!" Her hand, wilting under the weight of gems whose colours ran from amethyst to ruby, was laid conspiratorially on her husband's arm, making it look as if it were here that the rainbow ended. "Now tell me—did you know of this?"

"This?" The word might serve for anything, on the tongue of the Baroness. This enormity. This miracle. This scandal, comedy, tragedy—anything.

"Why, this situ*ation*!" His stupidity grieved her.

"My dear," he said, with a patience matured over fifteen years, "a kiss on the brow is hardly a situation."

"But she loves him! What could be plainer?"

"A lot of people love him, in their differing ways. You

140

do, and I do. His mistresses do, and so does Kosek, and the cat, and half the newspaper-reading teen-age population of the world. Some love him like brothers, some like whores——"

"Petrik!"

"Others like aunts or cannibals—there are so many kinds of love——"

"Your stupidity must be deliberate. She was kissing him, not eating him!"

"She would if she could, my dear; it's a mother's privilege to devour her young; and their appetites are enormous."

The jewelled hands had wreathed galaxies of frustration in the air. Sometimes it was impossible to believe that Petrik had ever left his cradle. "It was foolish of me to mention a word of it to you!"

"Not foolish. Unnecessary. I already knew of this—of this situation."

"How could you have? You were not there!"

"No, I was not."

"*She* wouldn't have told you of it!"

"Why, no."

"Then you couldn't have known at all." She watched him and waited for the admission that would complete her triumph in having been the sole witness to the kiss. He said nothing. "Only *I* knew!"

"And the King." The Baron had never made up his mind as to the benefit or otherwise of allowing her these triumphs, or denying them. He loved her dearly for qualities of which even she was sometimes unaware, and had no wish to take away these important little treasures that she coveted so much. "His eyes were closed, but he wasn't asleep." He stroked her rings, and thought how like a barnacled rock her hand felt, the gentlest hand in his life. "But don't tell poor Sofi."

She had never told Sofi. She had never told anyone. He was the exclusive recipient of all her news; and he knew that Sofi would be safe. It was sad enough to give a mother's kiss and receive no answering touch.

"Are we sure," asked Sofi beside him on the couch, "that a doctor will come?"

"No, but the idea is that his life should be preserved, for the time being, so they'll take steps to see that no complications arise, with his wound."

"You say it so easily, Petrik—'for the time being'. Are we completely powerless?"

"For the time being."

"But there must come a chance!"

"Yes, there must."

"Then what will we do?"

"All we can." He lowered his eyelids and the scene was shaded, so that the two figures might have been sitting there at a game of chess, or sharing wine, or divining the future in a crystal ball. They were silhouettes, almost black against the firelight, their identity burned away and whirling up the throat of the chimney with the smoke to join the nameless and the numberless.

Nikolas was a name for the man who sat over there, but the man in Angelitri's memory was different, composed of characteristics that had made a familiar pattern, so that the Baron could at most times prophesy that the King would or would not do this thing, that thing. But the pattern had changed. Just as the body of that man had slowly cast off its original matter and developed new cells year by year, just as its composition of atoms had altered and re-arranged themselves, the mind had moved through influences that had added and subtracted the essences that composed the man. And these influences had been stronger in the last five years, biasing him towards bitterness and away from fulfilment, until the events of the last five days had crowded upon him, exposing him to even greater change. Nikolas, the name for this fluid composition, had become unpredictable; and Petrik Angelitri's life had been devoted to prediction, so that he was first adviser to the Crown before Nikolas assumed it on his father's death. He was therefore miserable as he sat here watching the King through the slits of his eyelids, his one ambition to ease the predicament in which his sovereign found himself, before the march of minutes carried them both beyond return.

Whatever man that was over there, it wasn't the man who had striven to save Slavakia from the cataclysm in 1954, using all means short of brutality to purge the ranks of his ministers, bringing all the big guns of political warfare to bear on the enemy within, and campaigning among the world's governments for their support. During those last months he had lost sleep and ignored food, imprisoning himself in his study on the third floor of the Palace to summon his selected visitors and parley with them, friend and enemy, and assert his will over them.

As personal counsellor, mentor and friend, Angelitri had seen more of the King in those last days than anyone else had seen—even the Roman Tart, who had kept to her town house with her entourage of sycophants and flunkeys. For the first time since the Baron had sworn allegiance to the new king there had been no woman at the Palace for royal usage, not even a willing soubrette whisked by carriage from the stage door of the Colosijos Theatre for an hour in the private apartments. The pace the King had set himself had not slackened until the day came when he could see that his efforts had failed: the day when Szados walked in with his heels clicking like skeleton bones along the historic corridors.

There had been no moods, not a moment's rage to relieve his emotions of the strain. He had been dedicated, almost inspired by defeat, and had lost with his pride intact. Now he was a silhouette, passing the time with a stranger.

So many times Angelitri had waited, during this past day, to hear the old loved phrase come to his ear: 'Uncle Petrik, let's give our brains a rub and raise the genie!' There had been chances of speaking softly, of assessing their situation and forming a choice of decisions and a set of plans for action according to the turn of events whatever they might be. Even in Bell's hearing they could have discussed their position without revealing all they had in mind—could even have talked in a makeshift code, formulated by shared experiences: 'We could pursue the well-known Elsina policy'—for Bell could not have known Elsina, the child princess who had often held the entire Palace in subjection when she chose to exert her immeasurable charm for her mischievous purposes, paying out the silken threads as subtly as a spider until the whole of the household staff and the Crown itself were quivering on the web. They could have talked in front of Bell, weaving round the subject of their situation until he was provoked into letting fall a word of his own plans for their future, so that by a few degrees they might learn what best to do against the enemy.

Nikolas had done nothing to these ends. Perhaps it was simply because the man who will fight to the death for what he holds is not the man who will fight for what he has lost; or because the bitterness of exile had corroded him beyond repair; or because the warrior who will rout the foe in the open field however he may be outnumbered is the captive whose heart will suffocate in the claustrophobic cell.

The Baron listened to the music that filled the air. If only it were the music of words—of news from Drovnik!

He realised he was standing up.

"Where are you going, Petrik?"

"Going?" He looked down at Sofi. She could be as still as a tall, pale lily in the gloom of night, living out the hours alone, thriving on silence; but his mind craved movement, and drove his body to it. "I'm going for a walk, my dear. I shall walk from here to the Chinese cabinet over there, and make a smart turn, setting course for the console table and circumnavigating the chaise-longue to complete the round trip before retiring from public life to write my book entitled *Round the Room in Eighty Seconds.*"

She looked up at him from his own huge shadow that was cast by the fire, her red hair and bright brown eyes catching its reflected glow; then he left her. Even the slight exercise of pacing over the carpet stimulated his mind, and it ran again through the possibilities and methods of escape for the King; but there was always the lock and bar of Bell's warning: whoever tried to escape would take the King's life in his hands.

He passed through the flood of light that came from the open doors and, seeing Antiquis, stopped, and stood a foot distant from the man, staring solemnly into his face, aware of Bell's yellow eyes questioning. Antiquis looked him back without any expression, standing as erect as a paraded trooper under inspection. Angelitri wondered, who is this man? What writhing convolutions of the heart's motives had brought him all the way from the cradle to stand here at this moment and in this room?

Saying nothing, he turned away and continued his itinerary past the Chinese cabinet, and deviated towards the youth with the white wedge for a face and cold glass for eyes, and stood in front of him to look at him. He was so different from the other one, Antiquis! Whatever had brought Antiquis here at this stage of his life, it had nothing in parallel with the way this boy had taken.

Petrik Angelitri was looking into the eye of a bird, into the lens of a brain so unanswering that he might have peered into a bead of bright water and expected it to cloud with thoughts. Yet Peake must be thinking about him, busily, perhaps wondering if he were to be attacked by this man, whose shoulders were like a battering-ram in the moment's pause before it is run against the enemy gate. He must be thinking deeply about Angelitri, yet his hands did not move, nor did his eyes tell anything. They stared at stone.

The music floated between them and neither heard it.

"What is your speciality, my child? The stiletto?"

The eyes flickered as if the human voice had called a wax-work to life.

"He's dumb," said Bell, and Angelitri swung his head and looked into the yellow eyes.

"I thought he was dead." He felt the accelerated beat of his heart within him. Bell had come up so silently. To defend the boy if he were attacked? Could Peake work only on the offensive? Or had he come up to save an accident—a misinterpreted movement of Angelitri's hand, a flash of panic and the steel slipping in with a spark's quickness? A snake struck like that.

Why had Bell come here? To ask the same question of him, perhaps.

"Can we help you, Baron?"

"I doubt it. Our ambitions differ." He turned away and continued his pacing with a policeman's boredom, hands behind him, thinking of the boy. Dumb from what? Birth? Shock? Was he a part of this pattern because his affliction had set up a trauma and deflected his mind from the norm, or had the trauma come first, of some other and earlier cause, striking him dumb and deflecting him? One mustn't pity the people who would murder one in the dark, from envy that one's life was light. This was the scheme of things. One womb had once held this man, another that; beneath their uncertain feet the world had spun counter for each. The conscience had to be lived with, and the right to survive defended. The laws of the animal kingdom remained uncomplicated despite the angle of the bowler hat and the shine of the watch-chain, the diplomatic documents and the non-aggression pacts. The human was not humane.

He returned to Sofi, who said without looking at him: "She is now doing all the talking. She began by listening, and now she is talking. You'll have to stop them."

When a child is hurt, thought Baron Angelitri, its mother's place is at its side. Sofi was suffering the neglect of a natural law. "It is a long time," he said, "since you had any sleep. It will work wonders for you."

"I'll sleep when he is safe."

"He may never be safe again."

"Then I'll never sleep again."

Women of Sofi's kind had a penchant for the dramatic; but he did not pretend to himself that she wasn't serious.

147

He could feel her seriousness; he sat in its aura. The Chinese cabinet would have made a more peaceful companion, and he had been foolish to come back.

His eyes half closed against the irritation of the smoke that still hung in the air. He watched the King for a while, and the girl, Sofi's wicked enchantress who had been summoned here to turn Nikolas into the marble effigy of an unknown political prisoner . . . the girl who not long ago had been sick with fright at finding herself here at all. She was probably telling him her life story, and Nikolas would be listening with his thoughts carried along on her voice to haunts of his own choosing. 'The golden rule, Uncle Petrik, in listening to a woman is simply this: if she is plain, leave her; if she is pretty, imagine her to be saying all that you would wish her to be saying in that soft voice of hers. Bearing in mind, of course, that you've got yourself into a dangerous position to start with, if you are actually having to listen to her at all.'

But Nikolas had been the first to find out how powerful was the influence of women over the most important men. One had come close to killing him, and her name had never been mentioned in the Palace after the night when the sabre had rung on the stones of the forecourt and the shouts had wakened the staff.

He had drunk nothing that night, yet Starita the white mare had been dragged from the stables in the dark and he had leapt to her bare back and charged the steps with the sabre whirling and his eyes mad. The grooms had been terrified and one of the guards, roused from a doze, had loosed off a bullet that made the air whine past the head of the rider, and was reloading when someone called for him to hold his fire—it was the King.

Lights had come on when the alarm was sounded and

doors banged everywhere, and people were shaken in their beds—"It's the King, sir!"

"*What* is the King, man? What's happening?"

"Not himself, sir——"

"Fetch my boots then."

On the great sweep of steps, figures running and halting, voices calling. Shadows, questions, a light bobbing as a man hurried with a torch. The white shape of the horse as she was ridden to frenzy, her hooves ringing on the paving—the glint of the blade as the sabre swung about. And the dreadful shout—"*My queen's gone!*" As if he addressed the Palace itself, the listening stones that housed the ghosts of the dynasty whose dead faces were ranged along the galleries to look down upon the living and watch them in their tournament with the odds of life. "*She's gone—my queen's gone!*"

And never known where. Tales came later: she had been taken ill on a secret journey and had died; had become mad and was locked away; had fled upon an assignation, prey to a Rasputin; had taken herself to a convent in the north.

The fact remained. The man with half his heart cut out was berserk on the Palace steps, and the white mare foamed in the gloom as she was driven at the doors and down again with her tail flying and her eyes mad as her master's, until she lost footing and pitched him across her mane among the throng of grooms, herself falling as she broke her leg. Within the hour, Nikolas was in his bed, and heard the shot from below.

"What's that, Petrik?"

The Baron had gone to the windows. "Starita," he said.

"No. Helena."

Before dawn he had woken from his bruised sleep. "Who's here in the room?"

Angelitri had answered from the chair, chilled in his dressing-gown and with no thoughts that could warm him.

Nikolas said to the dark: "I knew this was coming. For quite a long time." And after that, he had never mentioned his queen again.

Angelitri had drawn his own conclusions, but had told nobody. The only woman whom the King had loved was gone, and life went on. Solace must come from wantons and peasant girls along the path of the chase, their faces never seen by the royal lecher whose heart seemed coldest when his blood burned.

Was it always her face he pictured beneath his closed eyes, and was it hate for her that crushed them under him, not love for them? Angelitri did not know; and now the King was unpredictable: he was looking at a girl in the firelight, while her voice reached him through music. A girl, thought Angelitri, not very unlike Queen Helena, with her pale skin and the dark curves of hair, the luminous eyes. Perhaps the memory had its reasons.

"Petrik, I want you to listen to me." He turned to Sofi, knowing what she would say, for the words had circled the air for minutes now, as angry as bees. "We must find out who that woman is and what she is here for. We have a duty to Nikolas, and must protect him. You must go to the Major and ask him about her, and find out what you can." But before Angelitri had time to answer, the music stopped and the voice of a French announcer replaced it.

Bell took quick strides. "Warren!"

Silence came.

Angelitri was watching the King and saw that he did

not turn his head, but went on looking into the face of the girl.

Sofi Mikayan stood up.

"Don't disturb him," Angelitri said; but she left him and crossed the room. He saw Bell come back from the doors, and got up, looking at them all in turn, to make certain there was no mistake; then he went over to Bell. "The news must be good, Major."

"One can never tell; it's always so distorted."

"But a man like you would always tell the truth. What has happened to Kosek?"

"He's not here."

"Quite so. He has not been here for some time. Nearly an hour."

Bell watched Sofi Mikayan speaking to the ex-King. "He is sleeping, in another room."

A casual enough lie, because if old Kosi were no longer able to keep to his feet he would curl up here like a dog, where his master was.

"He is a servant," said Angelitri, "and knows nothing of affairs. You'll find it useless to question him." But Bell had turned away. Men were moving through the ante-room and in a moment they came through the doors. Two guards and a stranger whose eyes blinked nervously as the main lights were switched on again.

"The doctor," said Bell.

Angelitri looked at the man from the outside world.

CHAPTER XIII

Miss Thorne was not in her office at Unic House when the two men called there with Messiter. A secretary sat with a stack of reports as high as her typewriter. New sheets were going into the machine from the left, and her cigarette-butts were going into the ash-tray on her right. She looked as if the movements of her hands would go on weaving this work-pattern until someone came in here with a strait-jacket and took her away.

"Do you know where Miss Thorne is?"

The fingers clamoured at the keys, and from the nicotine-fed robot the word came: "No."

"We have to find her. These gentlemen are from the Yard."

They waited until the pale face looked up at them and its blue eyes focused. "Yard?"

"Where would we find Miss Thorne?" asked Messiter. It was like this all through Unic House, the pressure.

"Studio D, I think."

"Will you please phone down, then?"

"Could you take that one?" Her hands flew at the keys again with the frenzy of a hopped-up pianist.

Messiter picked up the telephone, and in a moment was put on to Miss Thorne. He said: "I'm in your office. Can I see the letter we had from the doctor who attended Miss Cameron?"

He had to wait because she turned away from the telephone to call something to someone down there. When she was with him again she said: "What?" and he went through it all again, and finally had permission to search her desk; but he was sure, as he put the receiver down, that she still had no idea what he was talking about.

They found the letter, signed by Dr. Holden. The men took it away with them. Could they contact him here if they needed to?

"If you start from here, you'll catch up with me somewhere."

When they had gone he tried to talk to the secretary about Miss Cameron, but it was like trying to talk to a machine that someone had forgotten to switch off when they went home. He gave it up and went down to the Monitor Section.

Miss Thorne met him in the passage by chance. "Did you find it?"

"Yes. I gave it to the police."

"Oh, good." She passed on, and turned back, for the word had filtered through the nimbus of her preoccupation. "Why?"

He explained about Miss Cameron.

"How odd," she said. But he didn't know whether the thought at the back of the stare was about Louise, the police, or the afternoon programme schedule; and so he left her staring. People were difficult to communicate with, of late.

The air inside the Monitor Section was stifling and the place crowded. The swing-doors were fanning open and shut all the time, blowing out the stale air of the room and blowing in the stale air of the corridor. He picked up a pair of extension head-phones and sat with them in the corner, shut in with the voices of a different world.

The transmitter at Kresnik was the strongest, and was

still holding out despite the fact that the government forces must realise that it was the most dangerous to them. Messiter had been listening only five or six minutes when he heard:

"Kresnik Radio is now changing to seven and a half megacycles on the fourteen-metre band. Please continue to listen to our broadcasts and acknowledge them."

He waited, while a hand reached out to the master switchboard and moved the dials. In a moment he was receiving again.

"New freedom stations are now operating in Losvricz, Viln, and Duna-Teranik, and we will repeat their signals at intervals of one hour. Reports from Drovnik say that the first regiment of an organised resistance army has been formed by Colonel Bojransi at the Kilvinjios Barracks. It is composed of civilians from the age of sixteen upwards, and the remnant of the loyal soldiers who were trapped in Mosincz Square and massacred by a Union contingent of machine-guns late last evening. Colonel Bojransi declares that he has a plan of campaign, a regiment of men prepared to die for the King, and sufficient arms, food and medical supplies to last them for a week."

Messiter watched the faces of the others listening along the desk. No one looked up. They were probably used to hearing it, but this was the first time he had been down here for three hours. Not to die for Slavakia, or freedom— but for the King.

"Supplies of food, arms and ammunition are still coming in from the outlying areas, running through cordons and ambush to reach Colonel Bojransi's forces. In the Duna-Teranik district, a people's council has ousted the central authority and has set up its committees, so far unchallenged."

Messiter switched to the new station at Losvricz, ten miles from the Austrian border.

"All this morning there has been heavy gunfire on the hills along the south fringe of the Losvricz Plain, and ambulances are blocking the roads to the frontier, their progress hampered by refugees on foot. We have no accurate reports from the battle area as yet, but we have seen a squadron of bombers flying in from the north and it seems likely they are heading for Drovnik. A message from the offices of Szina Diurna reached us at middle-day. It read: 'Enemy forces are encroaching on this part of the town and we are preparing to defend our building until it is blasted from beneath our feet. We have very few weapons—three light machine-guns and some grenades, apart from a dozen rifles of obsolete design. At the end of the street below our windows we can see people dealing with the first tank as yet to have appeared in the fighting area. They are throwing grenades into the driver's window. It is a minute later and the tank has just exploded, sending up a fountain of flame. We cheer. We can see people running from it to the safety of doorways. But it is one tank out of many to come, and even if our reinforcements arrive in time we shall be lucky to hold out for longer than one more day here.' There has been no further message from Szina Diurna. Here near the frontier, the scene is confused. The roads are black with people and vehicles as refugees make the final stage of their journey to freedom —and exile. Many of them have come to our building for water and for news, and they ask: When are the Americans and British coming in? They tell us they are with us, but they are not here. What is the United Nations doing? But we have no answer for them. We would like to know ourselves. Since yesterday, Western journalists and members of the International Red Cross have been crowding at the frontier posts along the three main roads from Austria, but so far they have not been allowed to pass. These doors must be opened—not by our own efforts, which are directed at the saving of our cities and our capital, but by the United Nations. We are prepared to die here where we stand, but what is the West prepared to do, while the blood of Slavakia is running out?"

This morning there had been a message from New York quoting Senator Linkerdall, and Messiter had found a Telex copy on his desk. "An hour ago we were told of the situation as it is now in Slavakia. Drovnik is surrounded by a ring of tanks, and bomber squadrons have been over to assist in reducing the city to ashes. If ever there was a chance of saving a nation of people from death, that time has now come. Action by the United Nations could stop this slaughter of a people whose only fall from innocence is in that they wish their land to be free. There is more to it even than this. To those who feel that because they are not Slavakians they have no concern in the life and death of Slavakia, I would say: let them be concerned, then, with their own lives, because their own lives and families are threatened by what is going on out there. The peace of our whole world is in grave jeopardy, and the shell that leaves the gun in a Drovnik street can land in Times Square, any day now."

"What do you think?" someone had asked Messiter, and he had said:

"I think we'll go in."

"With atomic weapons?"

"Not with spears."

"Then there'd be world war again."

"It's coming some time—why not now?"

"I think you'd just like the excitement."

"Sure, I'd just love the excitement. I'm just crazy about watching the fall-out in the sunset while my eyes burn out of my head."

He listened to the voice in the ear-phones: ". . . But while the journalists are waiting at the frontier to come in, the refugees are going out, and they will tell their story, and perhaps convince the West that in a few days their chance of helping us will have gone. We are fighting here against the evils that soon might threaten them also; we are fighting for them as well as for ourselves. If we are too small to save, their world will be the smaller for our going, because the territories of the enemy will be larger by these few square miles of rubble and littered bones once called Slavakia."

He listened for two hours and then went up to his office, dictating his survey and passing it on to Editorial. When he left, he found an early evening paper on the table under the notice board, and read: Mystery of Unic Girl: No Trace.

There were two columns, and a picture of Louise.

"Mr. Messiter?"

"Himself."

"Miss Thorne would like to see you in Studio B if you have a moment."

He went down to the claustrophobic cells from which the news went out to the world.

"You seemed," said Miss Thorne, "to know something about Louise. I wanted to ask you before, but there wasn't time."

"All I know is that she's missing."

"But——" She could hardly say: But you're in love with her, aren't you? And would that mean he knew anything

157

about her disappearance? "But wasn't it you who informed the police?"

"It was."

She gestured vaguely. "I hoped you might know something." A copy of the newspaper was on the desk. "This is quite disgusting, of course. We shall protest to the editor."

He looked at the paper; it was a different one, he realised now. "Disgusting?"

"Haven't you seen it?"

She passed it to him. 'What is the mysterious link between Louise Cameron and the ex-King? Why did she follow his car from London Airport last night to Richmond? Why was she waiting at the airport when his plane landed? We are reliably informed that this is not the first time that their names have been linked; and the answers to these questions might well enable the police to locate the ex-King and his party.'

Miss Thorne was impatient. "It's ridiculous."

"Oh, sure."

He read on. The search was now concentrated in the Reigate district, following the clue discovered early this morning when a suitcase clearly belonging to the ex-King Nikolas and full of his effects had been found in a ditch along the road between Richmond and Reigate. It suggested that Richmond was not the limousine's destination, two nights ago. From the Redhill and Reigate area there were reports of such a car having been seen there, shortly before midnight.

"It's a reflection on us," said Miss Thorne.

"I'm sorry?"

"A reflection on Unic, this *Sunday Scandal* approach. We shall lodge an immediate protest."

"You do that." He put the paper down and glanced at the big clock. He was off duty until the emergency shift at midnight and would need the sleep, but he would stay here, and maybe borrow one of the P.O.'s beds. He could be located more easily, if the police or anyone else wanted him (or if she phoned . . . but why should she phone him?).

"Don't *you* think it's romantic nonsense, Mr. Messiter?"

He looked at the waiting face with its righteousness begging support. "They have to print something," he said. "People get tired of being told that there's a new world war on the doorstep. It's cosy that warnings of radiation effects and Civil Defence instructions and the opinions of scientists and generals should be leavened by the mention of a human heart."

Her indignation backed to the wall. "I call it frivolous to drag in this kind of thing when the whole world is in the balance."

"They say it's what makes it go round."

He left her to smoulder, and went up to the Telediphone Room to pace along the rows of glass panels, and for a long time the only words that seemed to be jerking over the long white sheets were *Where is she? Where is she?* until he told himself that there was nothing he could do, except phone the police at intervals in case they forgot to keep him informed.

The black words pattered down like raindrops in orderly lines. ". . . And soon after the street was cleared, people began gathering again outside the British Embassy, as quietly as a crowd collects in Downing Street—but the scene here is different, with the pavements strewn with the rubbish of battle, and some of the people looking like hospital cases with bandages round their heads and their arms in slings. Occasionally a single voice is raised in Slavakian, and one man called repeatedly in good English: Will you help us? Do you mean it when you say that you are with us? What are they thinking, in London and Washington and Paris? And an hour ago the British Ambassador appeared in the main doorway, just to wave a hand to them and smile. They asked him to make a statement, but of course he could not do that."

In the next machine an International News Agency report was being fed on to the sheet with yesterday's date-lines:

". . . Whenever a small victory is gained, a flag goes up—the flag of the monarchy that has been hidden away for five years in this unhappy city. In some of the windows the shattered glass has been replaced with a portrait of King Nikolas, taken from an attic or a cellar, or newly painted or chalked on a board or a piece of cardboard; and everywhere his name is to be seen on walls and doors along the broken streets. It seems impossible that this loved name has had to be kept secret for the last five years, a crime to utter in public and even in the privacy of a house.

"The curfews and amnesty decrees are still being promulgated in the city. No one is obeying the curfew, and only one man responded to the amnesty decree providing that the surrender of arms would ensure the bearer's pardon. This man left a group of his friends and limped to the doorway of the Parliament Building, handing over his rifle to the Government guards. The barrel was twisted almost into a knot, and half the butt was missing. As laughter rose from his watching friends he turned away from the doors and was half-way across to rejoin them when a guard drew his revolver and shot him down. Heroes like this man are born every minute in Drovnik, and die the next."

In the glass of the panel Messiter's face was reflected, so that the black words crowded visibly in the outline of his head and became his thoughts; and he saw the man's knees double and the dust rise where he fell, and heard the laughter grow silent.

"Oh, Mr. Messiter . . ."

He looked into the face of a pert girl.

"There's someone on the phone for you, in your office."

"Phone?" He knew what it was like, now, to look vacantly at someone, as all the others did.

"In your office."

He nodded. "Thank you." He walked out of the noise into the quiet of the corridor. The man with the gun had died because he was poor. If the gun had worked, he would have been a rich man with a valuable possession, and he could have shot the guard. With a machine-gun, a millionaire, with a rifle, rich. But that man died a pauper. The values of the animal world held good for men, and the killer was king.

He found Mac in his office, clipping layouts for the studios.

"It's Continental, Mr. Messiter."

"What?"

"From the Continent."

Messiter picked up the receiver and had to wait until the operator re-established contact with the caller. It was Willi, his opposite number in Zurich. They asked about each other and about Willi's wife and Messiter's family and then Willi said:

"We have a flash here, and I thought you should know about it. Szados is on a plane for London. He took off at——"

"What? What was that, Willi?"

"Szados took off for London half an hour ago——"

"Imgrir Szados, President?"

"The same. We got the news a bit late because——"

"Oh, sure. Anything else?"

"Nothing sensational, but we'll keep you informed if there's any——"

"Do that. Till then." He put down the receiver and checked his watch. "Mac, fill me in a form. For Top Directive. I'm going on special leave." Zurich–London was two hours, now ninety minutes for this flight. Aldersgrove to London Airport was eighty minutes, leaving ten for prayers and traffic-jams.

"Leave, sir? As from when?"

"From now."

CHAPTER XIV

The sun had gone down behind the buildings and the Square was soft with twilight, and very quiet. The leaves of the plane trees made a pale green canopy above the iron railings and the parked cars and the sand-bin on the pavement, not far from where Messiter stood watching.

The air was so still that the flag over the portico of the house across the road hung unmoving. The only disturbance in the last hour had been made by a murmuration of starlings, a great cloud of them drifting down from the parapets of the tabernacle and dissolving among the trees. Sometimes a car had come up to the Embassy and people had gone into the building. Other people had come down the steps and walked their way home round the Square, and once a party of three men had hurried out to a waiting taxi and been driven away—but Messiter had been there within a few yards of them, and the face of the President was not among them.

Men sat in some of the parked cars, smoking cigarettes, talking, getting out and strolling along the pavement and through the evening's peace; but they never went far from the building, and their heads would turn at the slightest sound from its direction. One of them was known to Messiter: Peter Vaquier of Atlantic Press Associates, whom he had met several times in New York.

"You think it's him?" Vaquier had asked.

"It depends who you mean." He gave him a cigarette

and they lit up, standing idly together, watching the doorway over the road where the policeman was stationed.

"The big Slavakian cheese."

"There are so many, aren't there?"

"Still the oyster-mouth, Tony? Don't ever change. But let's just suppose it's him. What would he be doing in London?"

"There's Madame Tussaud's, and the Tate."

One of the Press boys a little way down the pavement was even using field-glasses, snapping them up to his eyes whenever there was a movement across the road. Wasn't there some antedeluvian English law, Messiter wondered, against a man using those things in the public street? Or could he plead bird-watching?

"They say," Vaquier opened up again, "that the ex-Crown Prince is on his way from Brazil."

"Is that what they say?"

"Would you think it made sense, though, if he was?"

With Pete Vaquier it was always like this. He would go on taking no for an answer until you suddenly realised you'd said yes, and he'd be off in a cloud of dust with your exclusive story. But he was a nice enough guy, for a shyster.

"I wouldn't think so," said Messiter.

"But suppose he has ideas, about helping his old man to get back on the throne, and then cashing-in on the proceeds?"

"They don't sound like his ideas. They sound more like yours."

But the thought stayed for a moment in Messiter's head. Prince Carl was the only survivor among the three sons. The other two had been in an aircraft when the Russian armour was going in and the German armour was going out, and the sky was a starfield of shells. But Carl had no interest in the throne. Vaquier was just feeding him ground-bait.

A man came out of the Embassy and tucked a paper beneath his arm. A bowler hat, a regimental tie: this one could pass.

"Did you pick up the scent from the airport?" asked Vaquier.

"Scent?"

"We had the tip from Vienna, ourselves."

Messiter watched the Englishman go round the corner towards Buckingham Palace Road. He knew that Vaquier hadn't been at the airport: how then had he been sure that Szados would come straight here to the Embassy? Or hadn't he been sure? Mere surmise? But you didn't ask questions of Pete Vaquier; the answers would accord with policy, not truth. The thing was: why had Szados come to London at all? He was certain he knew. He must go wherever Szados went. Not through those doors where the London bobby stood: that was Slavakia, inside. But when Szados came out he'd be in England again.

There was a back entrance to the building, a gate in the mews behind the Square. But Szados wouldn't use it; he was a front-door man. He was the man who had walked down the front steps of the Police Headquarters in Drovnik two years ago in morning sunlight, knowing that his name was number one on the execution list and that Polsti's men were in the building opposite with their orders and their fingers crooked. Why was there no fusillade? Perhaps because there was something about Szados that made you feel that even if you shot him down in this world he'd get you in the next. He had met Szados, once; he was about the size of Napoleon and about as evil—though not evil, quite.

There was no evil in a snake; but it was not human. A conversation with Szados had the eerie tone of a discourse with a man who was blind and deaf, because he didn't look and he didn't listen. "Your activities during the last twelve hours amount to espionage, Mr. Messiter."

"Then my Chief of Mission should be informed."

"You have been twice discovered in a prohibited zone."

"I lost my way."

"You will leave this country on the four o'clock plane to Vienna this afternoon."

"If you want to expel me, you'll have to use the proper machinery and hear my official appeal against any charges you may level against me."

"Notice of your departure has been circularised, and you will be escorted to Bandonitz Airport in good time. We regret the necessity of withdrawing our hospitality, and thank you for your services in the cause of understanding between the United States of America and the People's Republic of Slavakia."

The door had opened. He felt exactly like an index card being flicked neatly out of a file.

At his Embassy he had lost his temper with the Counsellor, Major Jim Phelan. "They can't do this! The constitution doesn't sanction this kind of treatment! If that short-arsed puppet slings me out of this country today, I'm going to take the dome off the White House the minute I hit Washington!"

"Look, Tony. We have a policy, and it comes from under that very dome. For a little while and within limits, President Szados is to be given rope——"

"Let me have it and I'll deliver it in person, express!"

"President Szados," said Phelan soothingly, "is nearing the end of his term of office, for reasons that are top secret

166

in any language. But the U.S. Embassy will remain; and if you want to, you can come back——"

"To this comic opera? What does Uncle Sam use for guts these days?"

"Wits."

The plane had taken off at four o'clock on schedule, and he was on board, his nostrils still queasy with the smell of the hair pomade that the feminine-waisted guards used. That was over three years back, and Phelan had been wrong. Szados was still at the top.

When Szados came out of that building, it would be down the front steps.

"New glass going in," Vaquier said.

"Yes."

A workman was lifting a sash, on the second floor, and plying putty along the frame. Vaquier watched from beneath the brim of his hat. "I was here when they bust it."

"You were?"

"We got pictures. My chief wanted to use the caption: Rioting in London, but even for this place you couldn't call it a riot. There were around fifty people, a lot of women among them, and two or three banners—'Free Your People and Free Yourselves'— things like that. They were here over an hour, with one guy going up to the steps and making a speech—talked quite a lot of sense, with half a dozen police boys standing around just watching. I couldn't see who threw the brick or whatever it was—but you should've seen those boys move in! The people themselves seemed pretty mad at the one who broke the window. Then a van arrived and took him away, and the crowd got its orders to quit. Ten minutes after, you wouldn't know a fly'd been there."

"It was different in Drovnik."

"You can say that again!"

Messiter had been in the Monitor Section when the first broadcasts had come on the air. He and the other people in the room—a lot of them Slavakian-born—had listened frozen while an unidentified underground free transmitter began crossing the Drovnik beam. For a second or two the signal had faded, to come in more strongly as the reader made his report: ". . . Although the crowd was now large, it was not hostile. I myself was among it. We were gathered outside the Parliament Building to ask President Szados to consider our ten-point declaration, as his Committee had already promised to do. There were about ten or twelve thousand of us, half-filling the Square. On the steps of the Parliament Building stood a band of Security Police guards with their revolvers drawn, and others were at the windows with automatic rifles pointing down at us. One man in the crowd went up to the steps and shouted to a guard: 'You are a Slavakian, and so am I! Why do you aim that thing at me?' And he knocked the revolver from his hand; but some of the guards grabbed him and hustled him inside the building—and the crowd became angry and there was shouting, and someone threw a stone, and then others, until a tear-gas bomb burst among us, and a woman screamed, thinking it was a grenade.

"The students on the fringe of the crowd began surging closer to the building, and more stones were thrown, breaking several windows. An ambulance was trying to get through the crowd and we fell back to let it pass, thinking someone was wounded; and then when the ambulance stopped and the doors were opened we saw Security Guards pouring out of it. I can remember the people pressing round me and shaking their fists at the guards as they ran to join the others who were facing us along the building.

Someone cried out: 'Why are you afraid of us? We are your brothers!' Then a stone smashed a window on the first floor, and in a moment we saw Radicz, the Chief of the Security Police, coming on to the balcony. I don't know whether he meant to speak to us, or whether the next stone hit him by accident, but he made a signal to the guards and there was a rattle of guns. They were firing into the crowd—not over our heads to warn us, but into us, into our bodies as we stood there with our empty hands.

"The world should know how it all began. I have just left the Parliament Building and my friends of the underground are still coming in, some wounded and all enraged. They say there are a thousand dead in the Square already, and that a tank has come up from the barracks. I don't believe that there are a thousand dead, but I know there are many, because I have seen them myself; and there were women among them. So this is our first communiqué from the front line, which is our cellar door. We don't know how it will all end, but this was how it began."

The man pressed the putty along the window frame, whistling, his face catching the last of the sunlight; the sound of his whistling carried across the calm air, and the policeman looked up at him for a moment as if at a lark.

It wasn't a good wish to have in your mind, this itch of the hand for the unfamiliar feel of a cold butt, so that when the foreigner (who had nothing, really, to do with you) came down the steps of that English house, you could squeeze your finger, and do the job that Polsti's men were scared of. It would be a clean mathematical operation, a question of range and direction, an invisible line drawn from your hand to the moving shape of the biped as it came down the steps—nothing personal about it (except a lingering humiliation that still begged atonement? You will leave the country on the four o'clock plane. . . . But you don't kill a man who has simply irritated you). It wasn't a good thing to want to do, even if you knew it might save a thousand lives.

Messiter watched the house, and the steps, and made himself picture the scene as it would be, with the figure halting, toppling, his companions frozen for an instant into a tableau—the policeman moving suddenly this way (because that was the crazy way policemen behaved over here, running towards trouble on the fixed assumption that an Englishman won't shoot a policeman and that a foreigner is always a bad shot). That would be the scene, if he had a gun here with him, and if he used it. But would he? Forget the tag about human life being sacred: sacred to whom and to what? God? Then let God reach down His hand between the bullet and the man, just as Polsti's men had expected the Devil to do. Sacred to man himself? There was nothing sacred to man but his own need to survive his own brother, if necessary with the help of a gas-chamber or the cobalt bomb. Forget that one. Would he shoot, then, to save the lives of others? Even a thousand—even fifteen million? Where did it become worth it, to him, to give his own life? At a thousand, two thousand—where, what figure? He wouldn't do it for one, even for ten. When did the scales tip?

Messiter, you had a gun in your hand and you knew that if you shot Szados you would save many lives. Why didn't you shoot him? Because I felt I was doing more good in my job, trying to persuade them that our way of life is better than theirs and that war doesn't pay. *Is* your way of life better than theirs? We like your nerve, Mr. Messiter. The wars you've fought have paid you very well.

Leaving aside your generous desire to force on other people the ideologies you've been taught to believe are perfect, and the natural regret you feel that your wars have left you so embarrassingly rich, we'll put it this way: would you have shot that man if you'd been quite certain that your own life would be spared? We'll put it so clearly that you can't misunderstand: if you knew that after shooting that man you could have tossed your gun among the trees over there and walked off unmolested, pardoned even in the very act by the righteousness of it, would you have shot him?

Probably.

That's no answer.

I need time to think.

Take your time.

No. I wouldn't have shot him. Because that would have reduced me to his level. We've got to stop thinking in terms of shot for shot, or it's no good, is it? We can shoot the Szadoses, and they can shoot us, but it doesn't prove anything and it doesn't get us anywhere. We've been too long at that game already, and it's only because the beast in man enjoys it—that's to say it relieves the hate in him for himself, and the guilt in him that he has to get rid of, and the fear in him that if he doesn't kill first he'll die— it's only because we've all come out of a sheltering womb into the blinding light and the noise and the knowledge that we're not, after all, the only one in the world, and that everyone else thinks we're the smallest and least important—it's only because we have in us the brute biological tendency to kill that we can wrap it up in righteous phrases: war to end wars, war for our children's sake, war for our freedom, war to defend our way of life. To make a war you need three things: a belief, pride and a military band. The belief doesn't have to be a right one, so long as it's the particular lie you were taught by your all-wise fathers who made this world so beautiful; the pride can stink, because there's no kind of pride that doesn't; and the military band can play off-key—but you'll keep in step, because if you don't you'll be called a pacifist, and be afraid that your wife will be raped by enemy troops (instead of blown apart in the shelters) and leave unsatisfied the little shaggy beast that still lies curled up in the subliminal mind, its feet naked of your smart shoes, its acids odoriferous despite your careful hygiene, its mouth empty of your subtle languages, its brain untutored in the shifts of civilised philosophies.

Without the little primeval beast the world would turn mad. It keeps us sane. Without it we would lose our reason at the thought of designing a machine with which to lay waste a city of people who, like us, bear children and live in houses, and brush their hair and grow flowers, and send Christmas cards to their friends here in our own cities and listen to our music as we listen to theirs. The beast is our reason, so that our reason allows us to think that it is wrong to lay waste those cities. But it doesn't stop us doing it.

The whistler thinned the evening air, festooning the thread of his tune across the leaves.

"Pete."

"Yeah?"

"If Szados came down those steps, and you had a gun, would you shoot him, if it was legal?"

"Why?"

"I'm just asking."

"I mean why would I shoot him?"

"Can't you think of even one reason?"

"Well," said Vaquier in a minute, "he's a bastard."

"Would you shoot bastards?"

"No, I didn't mean I'd shoot him. I just said he was one."

"You gave it as a reason for shooting him."

"Well," said Vaquier, "I didn't mean he was that big a bastard——"

"How big a bastard would you shoot?" He'd never asked Vaquier so many questions in so few minutes.

"I wouldn't shoot them at all. What the hell are you talking about, anyway?"

"So you wouldn't shoot him. Szados."

"What for? He's done nothing to me."

"He's done an awful lot of things to other people."

"Sure he has, but they can do the shooting themselves, can't they?"

"If they get the chance, yes, they probably will." He said no more, but watched the policeman at the frontier, the stone flight of steps dividing one half of the planet from the other half, East and West. In a little while the workman stopped whistling, and because of Messiter's thoughts it was like a flying bomb cutting out.

Then Vaquier said: "You mean because he's a bastard to the Slavakians?"

"Let's not go all over that again."

"Well, you started it. I mean, are they so innocent?"

"Of what?"

"I dunno. Inhumanity. Would you have liked to be a Jew, in that country, when it was free? Hell, they taught Hitler what to do with Jews! Now it's their turn, isn't it?"

"Do we all have to take it in turns to hate one another?"

"It seems it's the way it goes."

"Yes, it's the way it goes."

"But I mean, why the hell should I shoot Szados? I think you're nuts."

"Yes, I expect I am. Cigarette?"

"Sure. Is that just your hand in your pocket?"

They lit their cigarettes and Messiter smiled. "Yes. I wouldn't shoot him either." He watched a dog that went trickling past them; it doubled on its tracks, caught by the scent of a bitch and chasing it in a kind of drunken hurry along the railings until the papery scuff of its paws faded from sound.

He looked up at the windows of the Embassy again. A minute went by, and Vaquier asked: "You seen something?"

"What like?"

"Anything." He eyed Messiter obliquely. The guy had seen something, all right. He'd gone as stiff as a shot cat.

Messiter tried to relax, but felt the blood beating at his temples. His thoughts flew and circled round this new situation, working out what it meant. But it was difficult to control this sudden rush of thought, standing within an inch of a man like Vaquier.

He began strolling, and Vaquier said: "You going somewhere?"

"No. I've just got cramp."

"Sure. In the mouth."

He idled his feet along until he came to the man who had the field-glasses, and said: "Would you mind if I took a look through those things?"

CHAPTER XV

The man, thought Mr. Turocz, did not look like a police-man, with his neat grey suit and pocket handkerchief and calm English eyes. At home they always wore uniform, even Radicz, the biggest, his hat a black halo.

The other man, also in peaceful clothes, sat at the desk and made notes; it was his colleague who talked, leaning his haunches against the edge of the desk and looking obliquely down at Mr. Turocz. Andrey had said:

"Now don't be afraid, Bjelik. They will only want to ask some questions, and there's nothing you have to hide."

"They are police." He had been trembling, and ashamed of it; but his father had whistled a tune in the street, as a person will in the spring when he forgets for a moment that only a bird has the right; and the truck had been coming along and had bundled him in, hands tearing at the tailboard as he protested and then struggled, knowing that friends were on the pavement and that Bjelik was already running down from the house—but the truck drove on and they pulled him in by the arms, and all Bjelik had seen of the man whose seed he had once been was a scarecrow figure of arms and a head, a face staring in bewilderment and becoming smaller, soon to be lost in the street's perspective. Bjelik had run after the truck as far as the corner, calling that he was coming, until one of his friends shot out a foot and tripped him, and picked him up, saying: "Don't be a fool. It's too late. Do you want to be taken, too?"

He had hit his friend across the face and gone back to the house where half a big bed was now to be empty, so that his mother's body would no more be aware, even without touching, of the warmth beside it that had been there for nearly fifty years. It hadn't been much of a whistle, because his teeth were not his own, but it had been in tune, notes recalled from nearly forgotten music, and it had sounded thinly across the spring flowers of the park and become part of their charm; but the pipe and tobacco-bowl would be taken away from the window-sill inside the house where in a moment the woman would be sobbing, her heart robbed of half a century's love.

"They are police," Bjelik had told his brother, obstinate with fear.

"Listen, Bjelik. In England the police are servants of the public. You are a guest of the public while you are here, and so the police are in your service too——"

"You are crazy. Even in our country, before the war——"

"It is different here. The point is that you have nothing to hide. Therefore you have nothing to fear. Answer their questions, and help them. I will be waiting for you outside."

Andrey had come with him, and was outside now. It was a brave thing to do, even for a brother.

Although the man spoke in English, he looked all the time at Bjelik, who watched the interpreter. It was very strange to hear one man's thoughts coming from another man's mouth. However long he was in this room, he would never speak to the security officers themselves; yet their minds would have been engaged.

"You had no knowledge at all that the ex-King was arriving in London that evening?"

"None at all. It was a great surprise to me."

"It was a surprise to you. When?"

"I am sorry, I——"

The interpreter waited, then translated the unfinished answer.

"When did you first hear that ex-King Nikolas was in London?"

"The next morning—yesterday. There was a broadcast from Unic Radio. I was there, in the building——"

"With your brother?"

"Yes. I came to see him—that is why I am——"

"Wait, please."

The interpreter was a Slavakian, but he had been here so long that he spoke with an English accent. It made him a kind of no-man's-land, a mouthful of languages with legs.

"You didn't hear the ex-King was in London until yesterday morning. But you stayed some hours in Miss Cameron's flat the previous evening."

"Yes, she left a message for me at——"

"Wait, please. Miss Cameron knew the ex-King had arrived in London—she had seen him at the Airport and had followed his car. Didn't she tell you about it?"

"No. She said nothing of it."

"Nothing at all?"

"No. Nothing." Why did the man pause so long? The one at the desk watched him, and so did the other. The interpreter watched the man standing up, and Mr. Turocz looked at them all in turn. The room was full of the silence, and no one moved, even a finger: but inside these round, hard heads with the flesh drawn down to make a mask . . . so much was happening. Then Mr. Turocz remembered. It was frightening to think that they suspected

177

he was leaving something out, when he had truly forgotten it!

"Another of your people," she had said, "arrived tonight in London. Did you know?"

"What is his name?"

"He used some other name, I expect."

"I am not to be trusted. I understand."

Trust was a dead word with a cold shine, like chivalry.

Would it be worse to say yes, he had just remembered, or to go on staring them out? They couldn't have seen into his very brain, into his memory itself, to know this thing that he had himself forgotten! And his face could have shown them nothing, being innocent. But now it was no longer innocent; he could feel the duplicity awakening in his eyes, and the tightening of his jaw muscles, the prick of sweat across his scalp.

It would be worse the longer he waited. Yet it was not important. It would *seem* important, when he blurted out that he had forgotten! They would think—what did these people always think? That you were lying, whatever you said. They were police.

"I was forgetting," he said suddenly and desperately to the interpreter. "Tell them I was forgetting." The man nodded and Mr. Turocz heard his true words turn to the gibberish of another language. Then they were waiting for him to go on. He had begun trembling; the room gathered cold. "The lady—Miss Cameron—told me that another of my people had come to London that evening. I asked her his name, but she wouldn't tell me. She didn't trust me. But she must have meant the King. I have only just remembered. But that is all I knew of him, I swear to you."

It had seemed as if the three men had closed in on him,

that the room was contracting, slowly crushing him with its silence. Andrey had deceived him! These were police.

"Why didn't she trust you?"

His hands hung down from his knees and he looked at the floor. "Because nobody does."

"Why is that?"

"I am foreign. Who will trust me?" His face jerked up at them. "I know that I might be an enemy and that you can't vouch for me to your superiors—you have no proof— my papers are not proof—but it is dreadful to *know*"—his hands pressed against his chest, enfolding sincerity—"to *know* that I mean no harm to England, and not to be able to tell people without seeing their faces doubting me the moment I speak!"

The passion in the words cooled on the voice of the interpreter; they became a monotone, with all the sincerity gone, so that he looked ridiculous with his hands pressed to his chest like an actor who holds his position while the curtain slowly lowers.

"As long as you know yourself, Mr. Turocz, your conscience is clear. That will help. You realise we have to be careful, with refugees already entering the country. Have you met any of them yourself?"

The voice was friendly, and when he looked away from the interpreter to the man who had spoken he saw a smile. One could tell, even when the words were strange, when their tone was friendly; and even a foreign face can fly the international smile. But these were police. Their smile meant nothing.

"I have met some of them, yes, at Unic House. They came in today by aeroplane. They are glad to be here, where it is free. They are happy to be in England."

"We're glad to have them." It was said dutifully,

slipped in politely for the interpreter to toss like a biscuit. "Do they talk about the ex-King?"

"But of course. They know the King is in London."

"Do they want him back on the throne?"

"Everyone wants him back. They are fighting for him."

"Have you been to Reigate?"

"I am sorry?"

The man at the desk made a note. What was he writing? What did they think he had said that was important enough to write down?

"It doesn't matter, Mr. Turocz. Have you been to Downing Street?"

This name, too, was untranslatable. The man at the desk wrote it down and gave Mr. Turocz the slip of paper.

"Ah, yes! My brother has been showing me round London—the Palace and the Horse Manœuvres, and Saint Jane Parks—and he took me to this street, where people were gathered. He gave me a shock, for a joke—he told me a revolution had started. Then we saw ministers coming out, and people cheered them——"

"And the Embassy?"

"Embassy?"

"Yours. The Slavakian Embassy."

Mr. Turocz looked at them all in turn, but could tell nothing from their faces. "I do not wish to visit the Slavakian Embassy." Suddenly he was on his feet, talking into the face of the Englishman who must wait for the interpreter to cool all the passion away as the words flew from mouth to mouth—"They are not my country-men. They are foreigners. I have no secrets for them—they have their own spies here in your capital. I have not come here to throw bombs at your Queen or shoot at your ministers in Downigen Street—my name is Bjelik Turocz

180

and my family has been in Slavakia for many hundreds of years! I and my father and brothers fought against Germany with you not long ago, and there was a picture of Mr. Churchill in all our homes, and King Gregor Six in his uniform! My King"—his hands held his own king jealously against his chest—"*my* King is a great-grandson of Queen Victorina of England, and he went to school here and can speak like an Englishman—as well as you can speak! I am not an enemy! Police are always enemies! *I* do not trust *you*! Do what you wish to me! Have me shot! Imprison me! I care nothing!"

His words echoed against the interpreter and became unrecognisable. Even a little of their passion was left, because he had been shouting, and the interpreter had been forced to shout too in order to be heard. Now the silence was down like darkness. He was no longer trembling, but sweat ran down under his clothes and he breathed as if he had been running. Now it was all over, but he did not care. He was tired of being questioned and of all the different faces that peered into his own, demanding him to tear his mask away, when there was no mask. He was himself! It did not matter what his name was—he would even give up his name and his country and throw away his papers to the wind—they were nothing to do with him, with this man that he was, alive in the world, a part of it.

He said into the man's face: "When I stand in the sun I make a shadow! Have you ever had to do that? To look down and make sure there's a shadow on the ground—to reassure yourself that you *exist*? Have you? Because when so many people question who you are and what you are doing and where you come from and where you are going, you begin to wonder what you are yourself—and you begin to wonder if you are anything at all! It is more than being a *kind* of thing—it is being a *thing* that becomes an ambition with people like us! We do not want to be happy any more, or rich, or loved even. We want to exist! So shoot me! And if the bullet is stopped by this *thing* before it hits the wall, then I shall know that something existed!"

His coat hanging open, he stooped against the man like a bird with its wings in tension to attack. "I want you to shoot me, Radicz, against your wall where all the others have been shot! *I want you to shoot me, do you hear?*"

The Englishman noted the web of pink veins across Mr. Turocz's eyes; they had become as wild as the eyes of a horse that is too frightened to do anything but lash out with its hooves. Mr. Turocz had lost orientation.

The door opened and a face looked in.

"You all right, sir?"

"Yes. Why?"

"I thought I heard some shouting."

"We were having a shouting-match to stir the echoes of this ruin. You might fix some tea."

"Right, sir."

"For four."

The door closed. He looked again at Mr. Turocz. The fever was dying; he just looked tired.

"I know how you feel, Mr. Turocz." The commandant at Oflag IV had been a man like Radicz and the questions had gone on for eighteen months.

"You cannot know."

"Anyway, there's some tea coming. Perhaps you'll join us before you go?"

"The man has a nerve!" said Crowther heatedly, so that Stross smiled behind his public face, knowing that

Crowther's heat could be switched off in an instant by the right word. Crowther was an ambulating gamut of emotions, and when he was angry, fear was in the queue. The only thing that could level him out for a few hours at a stretch was his Placidex; this evening he seemed to have run out.

"Certainly he has a nerve," said Stross, and watched the starlings go swooping across the avenue of leaves towards the lake. It was time to go home, but Margaret would want him to take her to the Vaseys, and half an hour in the company of General Vasey was enough to turn a chap into a conchie on principle. Besides, Margaret would ogle him, oblivious of her lined powdered skin that was so white and clear in her magic mirror on the wall, and of the twittering platitudes she poured forth as conversation. Better to watch the starlings from the window here and listen to Crowther's indignation.

"Even if his visit isn't official, he can't just slip through the airport and vanish into his Embassy!"

"He has."

"I'm surprised we had no instructions to meet him."

"But he didn't request to be met. We'd have looked rather silly standing there waiting for him, merely to be given the brush-off."

"I do wish you'd spare me your Americanisms."

"I think they're rather effective. They get to the point; and the point, Charles, is that if President Szados wishes to visit this country at short notice and without pomp, there is nothing to stop him."

"I really think you admire him."

That was Crowther for you. Half what he said was nonsense and the other half misinformed; yet here and there a truth was struck and sparked like a stone; moreover, it was seldom the sort of truth that you could admit to. Admire a man like Szados? In a way. A bulldozer was an ugly-looking machine, too, but there were always people to pause and watch its relentless disposal of all in its path.

"I don't think I'd put brute force very high as a human quality. The man merely has his rights and reasons."

"What *are* his reasons, then?"

"For coming to London? To talk to ex-King Nikolas, I'd say——"

"But no one knows where he is!"

"Szados does."

"That's just guesswork," said Crowther, who always challenged a good guess when it was made by someone else.

"I'd rather rely on my intuition than half a dozen reports from well-informed sources. Work it out for yourself: Nikolas heads for London immediately he hears that the throne of Slavakia would be vacant for him if his people overthrow the present régime. He needs British diplomatic support for his proposal to accept that opportunity, as an assurance that he has the blessings of the West. On arrival he is abducted with such efficiency that our personal faces were turned a horrid shade of red. Only a powerful organisation could have brought off that coup, and we know now that if that plan had failed there were plenty of alternatives ready for springing. Two days later the President of Slavakia is also in London, and vanishes as quickly——"

"We know where he is—at the Embassy."

"Becomes as quickly incommunicado, then."

"But what can he possibly have to say to the ex-King? The time for talking's over, and the shooting's begun."

Turning to look at Crowther's pale bright face, Stross

thought: He's glad it's begun—it excites him; just as I can admire a man like Szados, in a way, he can enjoy the peace of London better for the distant sound of shooting; he is an arm-chair revolutionary, if one can imagine a man with a watch-chain and paper collars and a rose-bud in his button-hole even hearing the word 'revolution' without a shudder.

"Well?"

"Well," Stross said, turning away from him, "my view is that Szados will have a proposal for Nikolas. They daren't kill him, because he'd become a martyr, and the blood would really be up. At the moment the Slavakians are a determined people fighting hard for their freedom. With their king dead they'd turn into tigers."

"They daren't keep him alive either. Every house in Richmond's had a police search, and now they're combing Reigate. Any minute now we're going to hear that Nikolas is free—and the effect on his people will be the same: they'll fight like tigers to win his throne for him. I can tell you, they're in a cleft stick."

"That's why they've sent Szados to talk——"

"But to what purpose?"

"If I were Szados I'd force the ex-King to broadcast to his people. To tell them he doesn't feel justified in disturbing the constitution of the country by reinstating the monarchy when the present government appears to be guiding affairs with ability. Something like that. Imagine the effect."

"My dear Edmond, they'd simply go on fighting!"

"According to military attachés in Drovnik, there are now two hundred thousand troops in Slavakia with twelve thousand tanks to soften up the revolutionaries. They are fighting against these odds, and with no overall leader, and with no real faith that we or the Americans or anyone else in the world will join them in the struggle. A message from their idol, Nikolas, saying that neither he nor the Western Democracies feel that this revolution can or indeed should succeed, would strike to their very heart and they wouldn't recover. If I were Szados, that would be the line I'd take; but don't forget that Szados has a brain as well as a pair of jack-boots, and my policy in his place might be childish compared with his own."

"I must say it seems rather childish to me."

Stross gazed down at the cars parked in a line along the avenue. One or two were drawing out: people going home, too warm in their dark suits and bowlers; but the sunshine roof would open and the rush of air would be cool, and there was the lawn, at home, and ice in the fridge. Other cars were crawling along the line, looking for a space: a man in a dinner-jacket, a girl in a soft blue dress moving like a hyacinth blowing in a breeze. But over there were the barricades and the rubble, with masonry flaking and falling, and people on the ground, crawling with a gun, a swarm of beetles on the march with single antennæ thrust forward through the dust. A life could end here with the watch-face smashed at twenty to seven and the mouth sucking at the stony breast of a cobble, or there at a minute past with a friend's face stooping and calling too late, the eyes glazing on the last image of a boot or a falling lock of hair, the smell of cordite slowly filling the head as thought seeps away and silence descends, and the long night comes.

Her dress soft blue; her laugh sounding under the leaves; the sky giddy with starlings above her head. Which was the dream—this street or the other? They could not exist in the same world.

"... And standing like a lot of sheep in Downing Street, and round Eros."

Stross looked at the faint reflection of Crowther in the window. "What?"

"Panicking. I ask you, how *can* there be nuclear war, now or at any time? Who's going to start it?"

"Our side started the last one."

"Started it? You mean ended it."

"It ended because the other side didn't have any bombs."

"They have now."

"Yes. So they'll start it this time, or America will. There's no one else who can."

Crowther came up to the window to see who this moron was. The same old Stross. "What *is* the use of starting a war that'll bring life on this planet to an end?"

"I don't think anyone claims the idea to have any *use*. But if this revolution isn't put down, the rest of the Danubian states will join in, and Communism will have its death-blow in Europe. In Poland the people are already in ferment, and Hungary looks like having another try. Once they're all in——"

"But for God's sake, even the death of Communism is preferable to the death of life itself, for a Communist!"

Stross turned and looked down at Crowther. What was it like to be Crowther? "Yes. But they don't think we'd start it. The only way to prove an intention beyond any doubt is to act on it. Threats aren't enough any more. We're all driving ourselves into a position from which there's no way back."

Crowther frowned out of the window. "We'll outlaw the thing, rather than commit suicide. That's my view."

"Ban the bomb, and stick to the good old-fashioned

block-busters? You really think that humans are capable of burning each other's cities down and at the same time keep an agreement with the other side not to make another bomb in secret and drop it? And if they are, why stop at the block-buster? In a few years we could perfect those toys and produce one that would sink this island overnight. Why not limit ourselves to grenades and machine-guns—or pistols and daggers? Where do we draw the line? Why not a cock-fight to settle it all?"

"You're being so absurd, Edmond."

"Yes. What nonsense to think of staging a cock-fight when we can destroy the world so easily."

"Your arguments don't honestly hold water. If I may say so, they never do. They're impractical."

Stross pulled the window down, locking the catch. Big Ben sounded three-quarters. What was it like to be Crowther, with his model trains and a pretty wife with a Birmingham accent and no brain? Or Szados, a human bulldozer with no heart? Or ex-King Nikolas of Slavakia, with no throne? The women would be a comfort, of course. He didn't have to stand listening to a girl waffling about Whistler and drinking Pernod, just for a glimpse of the cleft in her breasts while the itch and the fear chased each other round and round inside the head: those breasts, lying against his arm, moving against him while her legs strained and enclosed his—but if Margaret found out, and if the Office found it. . . . What was it like to be Nikolas the Second, walking through a world of open thighs? Boring, perhaps. You can have too much of anything, even that.

"You're not prepared to be honest with yourself," said Crowther.

No, it could never really become boring.

"Would you fancy a drink, Charles?"

"Aren't you going to the Vaseys?"

"No. I got Beatrice to ring up home."

"I suppose," said Crowther as he trotted down the stairs beside Stross, "that the moment they unearth him, we'll be dragged out of our beds."

"Nikolas?"

"Of course."

"I don't see there's much we can do now. The thing is to dissuade him from returning to the throne, if it becomes vacant; and that sticky wicket can be left to the P.M."

Crowther stopped, and stared down at Stross from a little higher up the staircase. "*Dissuade* him? I thought the idea was to support him!"

"Did you? But that would be fatal."

CHAPTER XVI

The King's hand throbbed. A few minutes ago she had made him move the fingers, but pain had knifed down his wrist. Now he kept them still, and felt only the steady throb.

"When I go back," he said, "will you visit me?"

"I'd be quite lost among all your splendid concubines."

"I've no love for them."

"You've none for me. It's just that I'm young, strange to you, and the only woman within reach with those two qualifications——"

"You remind me of someone I once loved more than anyone else."

"Then I'll make do with providing a reflection. It's not really a reason for visiting your country. When we leave this house, if we leave it alive, all these things we've been saying will become untrue; but I'll remember them. You said them beautifully, and it didn't seem as if you'd said them so many times before——"

"Never those same words, Louise. Your fair little face belongs only to you, and as I look at it, new thoughts come, and turn into words."

She pressed his free hand. "In our idiom we call it ringing the changes. But you've never been in this situation before, and nor have I. It makes my happiness exclusive, and that's why I shall want to remember these few hours with you. I didn't realise a woman could experience such delight, with only the touch of a hand, which is all we have. I envy the others, Nikolas."

"I envy him."

"The man I love?"

"Yes."

"He's not very happy."

"He must be happier for having you."

"It won't be for long."

"Will you leave him? Why?"

"We shall leave each other."

"But why?"

"It's in our stars."

And there would be no one to torture her; outside this house there were no steps down which she must run the gauntlet of her friends' tormenting, before she could be alone with the memory and the last of the touch of this man's hand. Yet oddly, it would be welcome this time. 'My dear, the things you let him *say* to you . . . why didn't you stop him?' Because I loved to hear them. 'But weren't you *ashamed*?' No one was listening, except me.

Where were they now, the shocked voices of the innocent? Had they been only in her mind? They were gone now and so was innocence; her hand had played with his in the firelight, and nothing had been left unimagined between them, and they knew it. Perhaps after all she had out-whored the splendid concubines and been the first to make love to him like this. It would serve as her consolation later.

She was talking to him again without thinking, in the way she had learned so quickly in this last hour, perhaps because she knew that their time wasn't long and that if he remembered, it wouldn't matter, and that if she did, it would.

"The next time, when you're with someone, think of my face, just for a minute."

"I'd rather it were you, Louise."

"I would too, but it won't be."

"I've never wanted anyone so much."

"I expect that's true, but only because it's impossible. With no one else in the room you'd have taken me by now, and it would be over, and you wouldn't even feel like talking to me. I'm very glad it's got to be like this, because you'll remember me for longer, and so for a few minutes in a year I'll be inside the King's head, a powerful influence at Court. You see, I'm really getting the best of this affaire."

"You talk so much with your head."

"My heart's in my hand." But there's only your body in yours, these warm, strong fingers merely an extension of your Majesty's genitals. I don't mind. It's a heady privilege. Will you really think of me, sometimes, when you are reminded of me by someone's face, or the way her fingers move among yours? Or when you smell iodine. . . . 'The smell of that stuff recaptures a most romantic scene for me, Doctor.' 'Yes, Your Majesty? How odd.' How awful.

"Why are you smiling, Louise?"

"As an antidote to sadness. My medical training was very thorough." Gently she drew away her hand. "When you are home again, send me an invitation."

"But you won't accept it."

"No, but I want it for my mantelpiece. His Gracious Majesty King Nikolas of Slavakia takes pleasure in commanding the presence of Miss Louise Cameron for an hour's diversion in the Royal Apartments. I'll veil it with my most purple silk scarf when friends visit me. When you smile, you look like a boy again."

He made to touch her hand again, but she prevented

him. "It's over, Nikolas. It was glorious, and I feel sated, as if it had really happened. Poor you: it's less easy, I know."

The music stopped, and they heard the voice of a French announcer. Major Bell called to one of the guards, and Sofi Mikayan stood up. But she seemed to be coming across the room to them, so Louise touched his hand again on the hard, bright surface of the table.

"Your Majesty has been most gracious."

Standing over them, Sofi Mikayan had the tall mien of an admonitor; the fire's light burned in her eyes and made more vivid the red hair. Louise looked up at her and knew she had become an enemy.

"I beg leave to inquire after your Majesty's injury."

There was movement in the ante-room behind her.

"Dear Sofi, I am well."

Louise could feel the ray of the woman's eyes on her hand, joined with the King's.

They heard voices and then suddenly the chandeliers blazed above their heads and bleached the shadows.

"I must disturb you, sir. Dr. Holden has arrived." Bell stood beside Sofi, and as the stranger approached, Louise left her chair and smiled briefly to Nikolas as she moved away. She found Sofi beside her.

"I do hope you haven't tired the King, Miss Cameron. His injury has left him weakened."

Lightly, she said: "I've never been in the presence of a stronger man; but if I'd realised you were anxious, I would have reassured you——"

"I am certain you would. But you see, I've known the King for so long, and can recognise his characteristic signs of fatigue."

They stood outside the group of men who were gathered round Nikolas: Bell, Angelitri, the doctor. Sofi watched their backs, and no movement of Doctor Holden's escaped her as he set out his things.

"It must be a responsibility for you," Louise said, though she had no particular desire to cross swords with this woman.

"But of course. He is the head of a sovereign house with dynastic obligations to fifteen million subjects. The Baron and I share the duty of protecting him in every way. You'll forgive me, but we know nothing about you, and it worried us to see how strong your influence has become since you arrived in this house. The King seldom grants nearly a whole hour to a stranger's wish for conversation."

'Nearly'. Had she been watching the French clock over the hearth? Her malice chilled the air, its coldness emanating from her.

"His Majesty seemed pleased," said Louise, "and we found so much in common——"

"The conversation was general, I assume?"

"Very particular."

"It may seem unusual to you, Miss Cameron, but my obligations to the Sovereign require my asking you what subject was discussed, since it was particular."

"More, really, than particular. Private."

"Never mind. We shall ensure that there are no further opportunities for private discussions with the King. You force me to put it bluntly." She turned on Louise the sad smile of the victorious who in the moment of their triumph suffer a little with the vanquished.

"The King doesn't seem a man to tolerate interference even from loyal friends, Miss Mikayan; and in England the commoners claim the sovereign right of talking to whom they please." But with each word she could see the red-brown eyes hardening, and knew that she was in the presence of the implacable. How true was it, that this woman was devoted to the protection of the King? In a woman like this, what did the word protection comprise? Among other things, possession certainly.

"I will ask the Baron to explain to you that wherever there is a king there is a court, and that obligations are required automatically of all those present within the circle of its influence. You may be persuaded to more discreet behaviour, as you seem addicted to the company of older men, and will respect what the Baron has to advise."

As Sofi Mikayan moved away, Louise wondered why it was that so much jealousy could parade itself, conjured up by a mere conversation between the King and a stranger, in sight of all these people. How much did the woman suffer when Nikolas passed days away in the company of the Contessa di Medici, his most intimate confidant? Her very soul must be corroding with the acids of jealousy!

'The company of older men' . . . it had been said before. Nikolas was Tony Messiter's age, the age her father had been when the staircase had collapsed and she was a child in the open doorway, suddenly alone in the ruin that had been home. Sofi might be right; but there was no purpose in trying to trace the convolutions of the human heart; it must beat to its own free rhythms. She had become one of those who loved the King, seeing in him something that she in her particular need wished to possess; it didn't matter what it was; it had his face and voice and it was enough.

The doctor was shutting his cases, looking at no one.

"He will require to rest," he said in an odd embarrassed voice, addressing Bell.

"In bed, Doctor?"

"Upright, in a chair."

It was as if the King were a horse with ulcers, to be discussed but ignored. Louise moved back to the table and he smiled to her. His right hand was raised in a sling and held against the other shoulder. The doctor spoke again. "Who applied the original dressing?"

"This lady here."

She received a critical glance, a mere lift and fall of the man's eyes.

"Was it satisfactory?" she asked.

"Yes, if there's no allergy to iodine."

"We had nothing else here. May I have instructions for nursing, Doctor?"

He gathered his things. "I'm leaving the syringe and capsule. In two hours, inject a second dose of penicillin. You can use a syringe cleanly?"

"Yes."

"That's all, then. See that he rests."

Nikolas spoke to him. "We'd like to hear the news from abroad. What is happening in the Balkans?"

The doctor looked at him, but there was nothing in his eyes except the formal recognition of one human for another.

"The Danube still runs from its source to the sea, and they say the blossom is out."

"You have a poetic imagination." Nikolas stared up at him from the chair. "But the blossom was out a month ago and it's mostly over, now. It's the blood that's out, redder than any blossom, and if you told us it's no longer flowing and that the revolution has been put down, we shouldn't believe you; so you may keep your news to yourself. And please spare yourself any professional anxiety about my being allergic to iodine: it was applied with the blessing of kind hands. We thank you for your services."

"Major Bell, perhaps you'll see me out. And there's the other matter."

Antiquis shut the doors when they had gone into the ante-room.

"What does that mean, Petrik? 'Other matter'?"

"I don't know, sir."

"Where is Kosek?"

"Sleeping, sir, in another room."

"Poor Kosi."

There'd be such rage if he told him Kosi was missing. He would demand to see him and assure himself that Kosi had met no harm; and they would disallow him; and there would be further blood let. The inevitable required acceptance; it was one of the laws of diplomacy.

The doors opened and Bell stood there.

"Mademoiselle Mikayan, may I have your assistance for a moment?"

She glanced at the King, who got to his feet. "No!"

"It is necessary," said Bell.

The Baron moved to the doors. "I'll accompany her."

"That isn't possible, Baron."

Louise was beside Sofi and asked the King: "Let me go with her, Nikolas."

"Why do you need the assistance of Mademoiselle Mikayan?"

"It is a delicate matter——"

"I don't trust you——"

"You've no option, sir. Miss Cameron can accompany her, if she wishes."

"Don't be anxious," Sofi told the King, "but rest your wound. That is Your Majesty's duty to us all." She joined

Bell at the doors. "I would prefer to go alone."

"Louise will go with you, Sofi. I command it."

Bell stood aside for them as they went into the ante-room. As the doors were closed Sofi murmured: "There was no need for you to come, Miss Cameron. I prefer you to go back."

"She can remain here," said Bell. "Warren, see that she doesn't follow."

Hands slipped down her arms and took her wrists, pulling them behind her; the man's breath was against her neck. The Major followed Sofi and when she had passed out to the hall, turned and looked back at the guard. "Keep her in this room for ten minutes and then take her back. Your behaviour will be correct and I shall ask Miss Cameron whether that order was obeyed."

He left them.

"He knows me," the breath came from behind her. "He knows what I'm like." There was pride in the bestial mutter.

"If you let my hands go, I won't try to get out of the room."

"But they feel so nice." Slowly he was pulling her hands against his body, and when they were forced to touch him she brought down the pointed heel of her shoe on his foot and heard pain hiss on his breath. For a moment his grip was relaxed and she wrenched her hands free, spinning herself away from him. When she turned to face him he was crouched in the middle of the room, waiting to spring at her.

She said: "You look like an ape. Can't you stand upright like a man?"

Slowly he straightened his legs. "I should've knocked you out."

"Why didn't you?"

He was a dark quick-eyed man with a pallor that deepened the black eyes and hair; he looked as though all his life he was coming up against people who tamed him for their purposes.

"You try running, and you won't know what happened to you."

"I'm content to stay here. Why are you doing this? I mean, working for the Major?"

"I hate people's guts."

"Yes? Why?"

"I like it."

She let the air move against her wrists, keeping them away from her body. She would have liked to wash them. "Why do they need Miss Mikayan's help?"

"She's in the way. Like the old boy. There's too many people about."

"What's happening to them?"

"I can't say, can I? You'll soon know. That's why you appeal to me so much. I'd like it while there's time. I don't fancy them when they're cold and can't move any more."

CHAPTER XVII

The fire was burning low.

"Petrik, are we completely powerless?"

"Yes. Completely."

"Without their guns. . . ."

"But they have them."

"It's all they have——"

"But it's enough. With men or nations, the guns are the ultimate authority. We know that."

Nikolas stared at the guard, Antiquis. Did he understand Slavakian? Even more softly he murmured: "Kosi can't be sleeping. He wouldn't sleep anywhere but in here."

"I think," said Angelitri, "the Major is worried. He's decided to separate us."

"You don't really think that. You're afraid that I'll do something rash——"

"We can only wait, and hope for an opportunity——"

"They won't kill me, Petrik. They need me alive."

"I know. But they'll shoot for the other hand, and you'll lose even that advantage."

The king failed to draw the eyes of the guard, Antiquis. He stood against the doors, looking idly down at his big hands, never lifting his head.

"I shall want an assurance that Kosi and Sofi are unharmed, Petrik."

"How will you know if they lie?"

"I shall know." He brought the flat of his left hand down across the table and saw the guard's head jerk up and the gun jump from his pocket. In English Nikolas called: "Where did you train?"

"The Major's unit."

Nikolas looked back at Angelitri and spoke softly again in their own language. "That one has no silencer. How can they risk the noise?"

"They know that we can't rely on that. Please have patience. It's the only way. If there's a chance, you know I shall take immediate advantage of it."

"You are my strength, Petrik, even if you are against my being King again."

"For your own sake, sir."

"I know. But I think it's the only mistake you'll have ever made in my sake's cause."

"When we are free again, I'll try to convince you——"

"If I am free again I shan't want to live, unless it's in my palace where I always lived. There's your place there if you want it. Otherwise you can remain an exile with your bags and boredom—you may have the patience for it, but I've not."

The doors opened and they saw Louise come past the guard, slipping in lightly, just as Helena had moved in the privacy of their chambers, quick as a girl, free of her public poise.

"She is so like——"

"I know, Your Majesty."

He would always call him that, in front of others, though Nikolas preferred their relationship to be less formal when alone. But the King had never abdicated; to Angelitri he would always be King. If only he could persuade him not to attempt that climb again to the throne! When his people had expected nothing of him he had worked hard for them and made Slavakia a name among nations; if he went back, they would expect everything of him, and the Union would use all its strategy to undermine his efforts until the time came when it could ask the country: Is this what you fought for: this shadow of a monarch whose powers have been bled away in the years of his exile? For Nikolas would not be the same. He was not the same now. Nor was Slavakia the same. Before the war, Nikolas the Second had perpetuated the reign of his dynasty with the authority he was born with and the powers to which he succeeded; his rights were unquestioned, his position unchallengeable. If he were to go back, it would be by the permit of his people who had shed their blood to regain him; he would be their leader on probation and they would watch his policies, ready to criticise. He would become a mere referee in the political arena, a figurehead without substance, and a go-between. Nikolas could never be King again even if he took his meals on the throne and slept on it until his fine body was hunched to its shape. That day was over when his name on a document was law without question.

"The temper of the people has been changed, sir," he had told him in Switzerland. "The whole world has been changed by the war and the new sciences."

"The world's made of people and the temper of a people is in its history, Petrik. My country is used to kings and it doesn't want anything else. Even a bad king's better than foreign dictatorship, and by God I was a good one!"

They had talked for days, for years. For Your Majesty's sake, Petrik had always said, and had not dared to say, for the sake of Slavakia, too. If Nikolas returned to his beloved throne it would be the final step to the grave; he had survived expulsion by an enemy, but when his own people turned him out, the Swiss or the Spanish or the English would find him along one of their roads with his broken toy.

But Angelitri was the servant of his loyalties. If the King lived through this, he would go home with him to the Palace, and be with him until the end came. At least he would be there to leaven that day's agonies.

The guard shut the doors and stood as he had stood before, watching his hands.

"Louise . . . where have they taken her?"

"I don't know. I was held in the ante-room." She touched his free hand. "She'll come back. There's no reason why anything . . ."

"And Kosek? You didn't see him?"

"No."

"Are you afraid, Louise?"

"Why do you ask?" She could see her face in the gilt mirror on the wall, but it was not like her face at all, so white, the eyes so large; yet she wasn't afraid. Old Kosek had gone, and now Sofi, and for ten minutes she had been alone in a small room with a man whose lust for her was in his eyes and voice and hands; but he dared not attack, so he had slaked his heat with sadism, watching her face as he built upon her fear, sly as a lawyer, until she was prepared to think that his was one of the last faces she would see, and that death would not be easy. Closeted with such a man, her nerves alert for the danger of his losing control and coming for her, she was cut off from mental perspective and was stifled, as happens to the imprisoned and to those awake in the hour before the dawn when there are no friends to bring comfort by their mere presence: she had believed in horror.

Outside the law, time receded a hundred thousand years, even here in a house on the edge of a great city. The power of these men was absolute and there was nothing they could not do; they had only to wish, to act. To knock insensible and then to rape, to torture or murder, to disfigure or to mutilate, to drive mad, to lay waste the whole person, body and mind—to possess until replete and then discard, this was their right, because a hundred thousand years of civilisation had invented the means of killing from a distance, whereby a grain of base metal could be impelled through the air by explosion to penetrate flesh and disturb the pattern of the animal body. Here lay the supreme authority of the twentieth century after the birth of Christ. The gun.

"No," she said, "I'm not afraid. Only a bit sickened."

Nikolas spoke softly in Slavakian. "Petrik says we must have patience, and he's always been right. He says we are being separated, in case of trouble arising. Now there are three of us left. We will stay together."

"Yes."

But the elegant French clock showed the first hour of this new day. When the long hand had gone another circle, where would they be? Flight 6 from Geneva had arrived at London Airport just twenty-six hours ago with these two strangers on board, and already the King was wounded and the air was tainted with the smoke of the log that had blazed across the room; his secretary and his servant were missing; and the doors of this prison house were as strong as ever.

"The instructions are," said Angelitri, "that Your Majesty should rest. I have arranged cushions in the armchair."

Nikolas was resting when Bell came in, some fifteen minutes later. "Mademoiselle Mikayan asks me to assure you that she is in no way uncomfortable, sir."

"For all we know, you might have murdered her."

"Your injury isn't troubling you, I hope?"

"No man likes the loss of his right hand, but it'll mend. It has a lot to do, Major."

"I would advise you to sleep, sir, if you can. Fatigue won't assist in healing." There seemed a new attitude in him, a returned confidence. "I should like to remind everyone that although facilities here are improvised, they are nevertheless available—a modest menu, comfortable beds. . . ."

"And built-in skeletons in all the cupboards," nodded the Baron. "You run an estimable *ménage*." He stared without expression into the yellow bland eyes, but could learn nothing from them. The brain behind these eyes knew where Sofi was, and Kosek; the knowledge was locked in the dark of the skull and nothing could bring it forth except the threat of something the man feared. What did he fear? Nothing that they possessed. "Where have you taken Mademoiselle Mikayan, Major?"

"She is quite safe."

"I didn't ask whether she were safe. Where has she been taken?"

"To a place of my choosing——"

"And the servant? Where is he?"

"At our disposal——"

"In the same place? With Mademoiselle Mikayan, or separated from her?"

"You'll forgive me if I excuse myself from answering your questions, Baron——"

"It interests me, you see, that you can't answer them. Why not? Because of what we might do? What might we do? What *can* we do? There must be something we can do against you, or you wouldn't withhold information from us. I'm becoming fond of the idea that your position is not unassailable——"

"My position isn't that of an enemy. You make it sound as if I were an enemy."

"I've known better friends."

"I work under orders. The people who order me acknowledge a way of life that happens to be my element: that is why I work for them, to support them in their ideals and help them further their aims. Your way of life is different, and you work for different ideals. Therefore we are opposed in what we do, but not in what we are. In different circumstances—that's to say if our aims in life were in harmony—I would take pleasure in entertaining you as a host, showing you round the garden, offering to drive you to the airport in time to catch your plane. But if I did that, you'd be back in the services of an ideal which I feel to be wrong. So I am obliged, being diligent, to restrain you. But it doesn't make me think of you as an enemy. I wish you could see that."

"I'm afraid the argument cancels itself out. A man is the instrument of his aims and you can't split them into two entities."

"You can alter both the man and his aims, given time——"

"Not with a gun, which is all you have——"

"No. The gun is to restrain the man, while he is subjected to mental influences."

"Our brains are too agile to be washed. Like cats, they don't take kindly to water."

The Major smiled, and for a moment his new assurance had almost the light of benevolence. "I don't mean brainwashing. I'd call it a persuasion to right thinking."

"That's what they called it in Korea——"

"That is what the East called it. But you called it brain-washing. Actually it's not a bad name, because brains gather dirt so easily, and hygiene is a valuable step in progress. Even in the name you give our process, you unconsciously seem aware that your own brains are unclean."

"So we're to regard you—I mean you personally, Major Bell—not as an enemy but as the chief of a sanitary squad?"

"I'd like you to regard me as your host, while in this house. As such, I feel concern for your welfare, physical and moral."

Baron Angelitri studied this man for some seconds in silence. Was this an act, or was he simply childish, still a schoolboy with paranoic delusions? It was difficult to tell; but there was much of the schoolboy about Bell that revealed itself in brief instances.

"Forgive me," Angelitri said, "but your arguments don't convince me that you have the special mental qualifications essential to a brain-washer. I would go as far as to say that you could expound your theories until the trumpet blows for doomsday without so much as rinsing out our ears."

With a sudden flash of bitterness Bell said: "If I had the power of influencing men with my mind, you wouldn't find me here as a common jailer." He seemed about to say more, and the Baron waited, for nothing.

"This other man," he said in a moment, "this 'high member of the Slavakian Government', I think you called him—that will be his task, will it? To lead us gently into right thinking?"

"Yes, Baron."

"Suppose for a moment—ridiculous though it may seem —that he fails?"

"It's unlikely. But in that event, arrangements will be made for the early discovery of the body of the ex-King, who will be found to have taken his own life." The yellow eyes were deflected downwards to the arm-chair. "I hope your ex-Majesty will pardon my mentioning this in your presence."

For half an hour the Baron had been eating in the ante-room. Someone had been frying eggs and bacon, and the smell had crept through the house to this room. "I won't offend anyone," he said, "I'll have it put on a tray in there."

One of the doors had been left wide open: Major Bell was agreeable. His nerves had found stamina, and although he watched their faces and hands and every one of their movements as keenly as before, the vigil seemed to strain him less. Angelitri wondered what kind of drug he was using.

At about half-past two, the Baron stood in the doorway and said: "The coffee is very good. Might I bring a cup?"

Louise, talking to Nikolas on the couch, was uncertain what to do; coffee would wake her up, when it might be best to drowse off and fortify her nerves; but if there was to be no time for sleep, she'd be glad of the caffeine. Nikolas shook his head, so she declined too. The Baron went back to finish his early breakfast. It was not yet light in the windows; dawn was still hours away.

For a few minutes Bell sat with him, and relaxed sufficiently to smoke a cigarette, watching Angelitri and exchanging a word when invited.

"When were you last in Slavakia, Major?"

"Three years ago."

208

"On a mission of duty, I take it?"

"It wasn't a holiday. I spend my holidays in Cornwall when I can. I like remote places."

"And were you in Slavakia before the change of government?"

"Oh yes. I was military attaché in 1947."

"That's how you came to know the language."

"And the people."

"You must have friends there now, in the fighting." He would have taken a third piece of toast to go with the marmalade left on his plate, but the smell of the Major's cigarette was alien, and he poured some more coffee instead.

"Yes, I've friends there. Fewer than you have, of course."

As if Bell had called their names on a roster Angelitri remembered Johanin Beurt the Lord Great Chamberlain with his one short leg and brilliant mind—Grosji the Minister of National Economy, immured among his budgets and ledgers, self-imprisoned in his chosen paradise of figures and finance, withdrawn from the frivolities of social pleasure and leaving his wife to savour it for both of them until she could no longer conceal her pregnancy and he shot her for a whore, knowing that the seed could not have been his, for he was sterile—and the Count of Vralinzi, still in prison for his royalist declarations in the Press: or was he released now? They were breaking into the political prisons already—it was the last news before the King and his party were brought here to a prison of their own. Vralinzi . . . he'd die for Nikolas, beg for the chance; with as little imagination as poor old Kosi. And Stefan the Major-Domo, with his squint and circumstance and shoes like black glass——

"Perhaps you'll see them again, Baron . . ."

"See whom?"

"Your friends. There's a world outside Slavakia, for people to meet in. And later, when there's peace again——"

"Peace where? In this world?" But he was thinking of Stefan again, reminiscing. He had slept very little; the coffee should wake him soon.

"I expect you realise," said Bell, "that the people would have welcomed you as President, any time during your exile?"

"They would have welcomed a drooling peasant providing his blood was pure Slavakian instead of a mixture of Vodka and Muscovy sauce——"

"I mean of course under friendly guidance."

What would Vralinzi have said? His favourite phrase, perhaps: 'I'll have your cancerous giblets on a sabre-point, by giddy God!' "I don't really fancy myself," he said without much passion, "as the puppet of a foreign power dancing on my own King's tomb." No, Vralinzi could say these things better. He had bellowed his oath from the window-bars when they had taken him to the Barracks, and even Szados had——

"I'll leave you to finish your meal in peace, Baron, if you'll excuse me. It's time Miss Cameron carried out the doctor's instructions."

"Time?" Angelitri looked at his wrist-watch, but it had stopped long ago. What was time? He looked up, but Major Bell had gone.

Louise was taking the hypodermic needle from its case when he came into the room. He told her quietly: "If you can persuade the ex-King to sleep a little, after the injection, it would do him good."

"I'll try." She prepared a wad of cotton-wool; the sweetness of ether came into the air. "Will you help me with the sleeve?"

The clock chimed three-quarters. She snapped the pip of the capsule and drew in the solution, watching it rise along the calibrations. He had said, 'it was applied with the blessing of kind hands.' This too; but a hypodermic was a strange instrument of love.

She smiled down at him.

In Slavakian he said ruefully: " 'Then let the gilded dart of love fly in . . .' "

" 'And wake thy heart.' " She turned his face gently away. Bell was not close enough for his breath to carry. The needle went in and she watched the fluid-line recede slowly over the seconds.

Her hand trembled for the first time as she took the syringe away. Bell took the swab and threw it into the hearth, where now there was no more than a glow of embers; then he came back and stood with his hands behind him, looking down at the King. Antiquis was watching them from the doorway, and once glanced across at Peake.

The King tried to say something before his head lolled sideways. When Louise turned round she saw Bell standing over the King, lifting one of his eyelids. He straightened up and called to the guard by the doors. "Tell Warren we're ready."

Louise was by the chair, taking the King's wrist, feeling the pulse. "Major Bell—what happened?" She looked up into the face of stone.

Warren came in. She gripped Bell's arm. "What was in the syringe?"

The Major said to Warren: "You and Antiquis. Mind his arm."

Louise ran to the doors. "Baron——"

He was sitting at the table, his head slumped across the white cloth. The coffee-pot had been knocked over, making a wet brown stain.

CHAPTER XVIII

The ambulance drove fast and sometimes rang its bell across road junctions, though inside the sound was muted, a distant telephone. Street-lights went floating past the smoked windows, unreal and far away. Inside, two low green lamps burned, so that every face was a goblin's, and hands looked dead.

Major Bell stood against the panel, his shoulder near the small window that opened into the driving-compartment. He would like to sleep. When they got there, he could perhaps sleep, at last. The floor swayed under his feet as the soft springs flexed; the motion was soporific, and he blinked his eyes often, and every now and then straightened his back.

A straight bat and a straight back, his father had told him as they had walked round the pavilion together, for the first time without her there. "I don't honestly see why she couldn't have turned up," he had told his father, "if you say she's not ill or anything."

"You'll be home in a few days, old boy. You can see her then." And it had been the last time, on those holidays. It was autumn again before he knew. The acorns had winked among the tufty grass, burst from their cups, some of them crushed white by passing feet. "I'm sorry . . . more sorry than you'll ever know. But these things happen." It sounded almost reassuring: this was nature in its course; in autumn the acorns fell, and while you sat doing prep, or scrummed-down in Low Field, your father was with someone else, and your mother was drinking tea at the solicitor's; and next autumn they were different acorns falling, and the golf-bag wasn't in the hall at home any more —these things happened, and you weren't to mind, even when the ambulance came and then weeks later, back at school, you were sent for by the Head.

"Bell, I've some bad news for you, but we know your character, here. You'll take it well." The thin domed head, the eyes frightened by having to do this; the arm round his shoulders. For Christ's sake, he'd wanted to say to the Head, get it over—I know what's happened. She's dead.

A straight bat and a straight back . . . and a new woman, not there with him at the hospital, though—the weather was wonderful on the Côte d'Azur, too hot to move, really, and such a bore.

"You're not old enough, Pip, to understand. When you are, I want you to know all about——"

"I'd rather you didn't call me that again."

"Now we've got to keep friends, old boy, because——"

He had walked away. The father, the son, and distance lengthening between them, other objects—trees, a building—taking shape between their two figures. Looking back, just a small upright object that might have been a tree-stump in the distance. These things happened.

"You've reached here," the Colonel said, "by a pretty roundabout route. You missed Borstal by an inch, and I call it lucky."

"Yes, sir. I've been very lucky."

"You'll have to remember that you're no longer a kid. You're nineteen, and if you play the game with us there's a rattling fine future for you. But there's one thing you'll have to grasp. A rabble is a group of men. Add discipline, and you have an army. Add comradeship, and there's a

miracle. And that's what the British Army is—a bloody
miracle, when it has men like you in it. You've been given
a rough ride, until now. Forget it. Because if you don't,
it's going to go on being rough. You're not bad material.
The only thing wrong with this report-sheet is that it's a
record of revolt. 'Lacks discipline.' 'Resents authority.'
'Won't co-operate.' 'Mistrusts friendly advice.' Take
Sergeant-Major Hobson—a damned fine soldier and a man
with a head and a heart. He's more patient with you than
a mother could be with a child, but you won't give him a
chance. He's tried cussing you up hill and down dale, and
he's tried talking to you for hours on end, father to son—
I know—he's talked about you to me, and so have others.
But that's his report, here: 'Mistrusts friendly advice.'
Why? Do you know why? Have you thought about it?
Talked about it to him, to anyone? Talk to me about it—
the door's shut and we can say what the devil we like."

Hobson, a good man, yes. Dead now, Arnhem. "Keep
your head up, kid, and keep in step." The way he said it
was wonderful, grunting it out, the strength of his only
philosophy pushing up out of his hard body like an oak
thrusting its life out of the earth. Head up, and a straight
back: it was the same thing and you couldn't trust it. It
was the same bloody lie.

But the war was good. A young man could get his fill
of gun-smoke, breathe it into his blood—and the prison
camps did you good; you could break down their authority,
treat it as a full-time job, because there was nothing else
to do. A cosh was nothing, when you'd made them see
that you weren't going to accept their bloody authority.
It was almost a let-down when the Russians came out of
the east and broke the camps open, except that here at
last was hope for you: a race of men who could stand on

215

their own feet without being cradled in some infants' monastery with its own proud tie and traditions, without having to use a fatherly arm like a crutch, only to be crippled when it let you down. The Reds had a goal, a big one, the world; and they were going to win it. If you got in the way you'd go down, whether you were keeping your bat straight and head up or not. Climb on board or get run over, take your choice.

"It is unusual," said Comrade Molshilov, "for an Englishman to renounce the implicit claims of his country. You have spoken about yourself, and from the account of your life we can see the cause of the philosophical attitudes you have adopted. But a man does not accept an ideology the precise opposite of his earlier teachings simply because of a disruption of his home life. You see why we cannot trust you until you have proved yourself."

"Then give me a test, Comrade." It was a good word, and he still liked to use it to them. Not boss or beggar, but comrade, another man joined with you against that rotten bastard, life.

The test had been too easy. The man's name was Smith, a good old English name; he was the representative of a firm trading in vegetable oil produced from sunflower seeds, and lived for part of the year in England, in the village where he was born, and part in Moscow, in a flat above his firm's agency. It was discovered that much of his spare time was spent in the company of the wives of Party officials and that certain oddly-phrased cables were going to London, signed by a different name. His *pied-à-terre* was searched and afterwards tidied carefully; and Bell was sent for. There was to be no awkwardness. Two men, an Englishman and a Canadian, were at that time under arrest in Moscow awaiting trial for espionage, and the exchange of political overtures between the Soviet and the West were already subject to disharmony.

In the late autumn of that year the body of Mr. Smith was found under a tree on the edge of his village green, a few yards from the cricket pavilion. Medical evidence of the time of his death was supported by the fact that the night had been windy, and that acorns had fallen on to the body.

Philip Bell had overthrown the final authority, conscience.

The ambulance dipped and swung, and he braced his shoulder against the panel behind him, looking down the small shadowed vault of the interior. Their faces were all green in the low radiance; they all looked dead. They might be the ghosts of the Revolution, the after-lying cadavers lit with the phosphorous glow of shells, reminders that if you fight with your own species, busy as a jackal for scraps of power, this is the way you finish up, win or lose.

His eyes jerked open again, their red lids scouring across the conjunctiva; the green light washed into his skull.

Baron Angelitri sat hunched on the attendant's tip-up seat, hanging his big hands down. Louise spoke to him, but he didn't answer; yet he was fully conscious. She moved along the aisle between the bunks, looking again at the King's face. He was still inert. She decided it must have been Pentothal in the hypodermic, by his immediate reaction and subsequent coma. The Baron had drunk coffee with a drug in it, a mild dose, possibly even one of the drugs one could buy at a pharmacy as a means of dodging life; it had dulled him, no more, and reduced his nuisance-value. They hadn't expected him to break into a rage like Nikolas might have done, here with only a thin panel concealing them from the outside world.

She had asked the Major: "Where are we being taken?" But he had said only:

"It's not a long journey." It might mean anything.

Sofi was still in a coma, but Kosek was conscious, his eyes moving slowly as he tried to re-orientate. She had told him that the King was safe and it had satisfied him.

Bell had said: "You are the only one left fully alert. We have decided to rely on you to look after the others. You'll understand how foolish it would be to attempt to raise any kind of alarm during the journey: you would be silenced and the others would be left helpless. Obey me, and no harm will be done."

His voice had buzzed in her ears and she had held on to the rail to steady herself as the ambulance moved off. Twice during the journey she had dozed off for a few seconds; their faces had swum against hers and the green bulbs had gone floating away, and suddenly Bell's hand had gripped her arm. "You can sleep when we get there."

"I hardly needed drugging, did I? You know exactly what you're doing." She talked to stay awake. "It must have been like this in the ambulances during the war. Has there ever been a peace-time for you?"

He had not answered. Behind her she knew there was Peake, standing against the doors. Warren was in the driving-cab, and Antiquis was driving. They sounded the bell again and went swinging through a curve. From outside it must look natural.

The rail struck her across the brow and a sunburst flared against her eyes. The Major was holding her. "You mustn't go to sleep. Take these." He was opening a capsule and she tried to focus her eyes on it. "Swallow.

them whole," he said. She took the two pills and dropped them on to the floor.

"They might be anything." The hollow metal rail trembled to the vibration of their movement.

"You mustn't go to sleep."

"No. I daren't."

She was driven through the night and the nightmare, but refused to let her eyes close again, keeping herself awake by movement, putting one hand higher up the rail, then bringing it lower, shifting her feet, stroking Nikolas's hair back from his brow—and as the vehicle swayed through a corner she was thrown against the edge of the bunk and his face was near hers, and so she kissed his mouth and for a moment was lost in the strangeness as denied thoughts came flying in and made time and place quite meaningless, while her mouth rested on his, this once.

Through the ventilator in the roof she heard the soft rush of leaves. London lamps, antique, elegant, smudged their light across the smoked windows and then the ambulance stopped.

Bell came past her and spoke to Peake in an undertone. The only words she caught were: "any . . . danger . . ."

The ambulance was reversing, and now stopped again. A door clicked shut and there were footsteps outside.

Louise prepared herself for the unknown. So little was known in the nightmare of the last twenty-four hours; identity had been dissolved; it had been a day of strangers. The idea that eventually she would be returned to life and to known things had almost no meaning now. The gas-fire in her flat and the picture of Lombardy poplars on the wall—the photograph of Nikolas II of Slavakia on her desk at Unic House—the kind, calm face of Tony Messiter—they were becoming no more than objects in her memory, losing their associative significance. A few hours ago, slipping her coat on because the logs in the room were burning out and the air was cooling, she had found, in the pocket of the coat, a green glove; and there had been a moment of panic at the idea that had sprung at her: this one glove was only the reflection of another in the lost life; there had never been two of them; she was on the other side of the looking-glass and there was no way back.

She needed to sleep. Tomorrow, in the daylight, things would seem normal. Tomorrow? That idea, too, had lost its identity and was only a word. It had been dark when she was taken to the house, and yesterday's light was gone; it had been night ever since, without end. It was night now.

"Wait at the far end," said Bell, and made her move between the bunks until she was pressed against the panel with the small window in it. His nerves were audible in his voice; suddenly he was keyed-up again, a yellow-eyed animal in the gloom. The doors opened at the rear of the ambulance and he was silhouetted for a moment, turning away from her, a shaggy thing now faceless.

The cool air came washing in. The doors were fixed open at right angles and a man said softly: "Back a bit more." The ambulance jerked and then crawled in reverse for a few inches until the doors were almost touching the gate-posts behind them. Bell opened the gate. There was a garden path and the vastness of a house, grey as a prison in the starlight.

"Careful with his arm."

Two of them took the stretcher out and the King's face

lost its look of death as it was touched by the pale light from the sky.

She tried to follow, but Warren was inside now, forcing her back.

"Angelitri," said Bell.

The huge shoulders blocked the doorway. "Where is this place?"

"Antiquis, help him down. Hurry."

Kosek was off his bunk, holding on to the rail, and Louise steadied him. "It's all right," she said in Slavakian, "you've been asleep——"

"I am worthless to him. Worthless."

"There's nothing you can do for him. We are all safe."

They took Sofi Mikayan out on the stretcher and then the green lamps were switched off and the whole world went grey. Hands reached up and she saw Kosek taken down the step to the ground, an old man thinking himself worthless. A glove was nothing: what was it like to have lost the past?

A breath was on her neck and she touched cloth as her hand moved—a sleeve. Peake was behind her, a luminous white face in the gloom a few inches from her own. He had come past her when she was talking to Kosek: he must have; he wasn't a spirit.

"Speak no evil," she said, to get her nerve back.

Men moved round the ambulance. Bell called quietly: "The girl now."

She saw that the doors of the ambulance were close against the gate-posts, so that no one could squeeze through. Bell was waiting for her. The air was heady.

"Warren, lock the gate."

The engine of the ambulance was started. Bell walked up the narrow pathway beside Louise; his voice was no longer nervously pitched. "As soon as various other factors have been brought into line, Miss Cameron, we are going to ask the ex-King to accept certain proposals. I don't imagine you'll refuse to help us persuade him."

"Why should I help?" Her shoe brushed against flowers and her head buzzed with the need of sleep; she tried to walk more steadily. Was the Major stupid? She was an enemy.

"Because he might be ready to forfeit his life, rather than agree. You have influence over him, however temporary. His life will be in your hands perhaps more than in any other's. I might mention that the ambulance wasn't originally intended for this journey; if there had been a serious incident at the house it would have been used for the discreet disposal of the dead."

They reached some steps, leading upwards to the grey unknown place. He touched her arm. "Don't let the next kiss be a farewell on a cold mouth."

CHAPTER XIX

Lights burned in some of the windows of the Embassy, and the beat-man noted the fact, and mentioned it in his next routine report to Operations. But towards dawn they began going out one by one, until only a small high window glowed saffron against the ink-blue sky.

Some of the Embassy staff had remained out of their beds—a butler, three footmen, some chamber-maids and a chauffeur—to assist in the reception of the party of late guests; but none of them had seen the face of the notability who was said to be among them. Before the staff was dismissed from duty, the Counsellor spoke to them personally.

"We have important guests with us. You have all been chosen for employment here by virtue of your excellent records and your long-established reputation for discretion. You will appreciate that the arrival and the identity of our guests are very secret and must remain so." He fiddled with his nose and stood inspecting his handkerchief with interest, a habit that had become familiar to the Embassy staff. A footman had once suggested the reason for this nasal preoccupation: 'He's making sure he hasn't blown his lights out.' The Counsellor folded his handkerchief and put it away. "You will be receiving orders from Major Bell throughout tomorrow, and they will be obeyed without question. If, however, you feel that any particular order seems contradictory to others received from members of our Mission, you may consult me or the First Secretary."

The small high window whose light still burned was the bedroom of a chamber-maid who had vowed to write a letter each day to her young man. She was not to know that before it left the Embassy it would be censored, for this was a rare occurrence.

When the party of guests had arrived, the Ambassador had been in his dressing-gown and had talked with Major Bell for a few minutes.

"I may say that I am distinctly relieved, Major, by your late decision to act upon my advice. His ex-Majesty and his entourage will find themselves more comfortable here, and we shall enjoy better sleep." His sad, grey, massaged face was a study in composure, impervious to the invisible sparks of hate from the other man's yellow eyes; he knew how Bell hated him, but his spirit thrived on it; love was suspect under the pressure of human affairs, but hate was always to be trusted.

"I'm always ready to take Your Excellency's good advice, but in this case I delayed on account of prudence. There's a big staff here, and they're not all known personally to me. In the event of an incident, the news will leak out that the ex-King is here, and the house will be surrounded by noisy crowds."

"The house can be surrounded by the entire British Army without disturbing us, Major." His light-rimmed glasses were directed on Bell's tired face as searchingly as a surgeon's head-lamp. "In your obvious condition of fatigue you may be allowing the fact to escape you that this is Slavakian territory. And incidentally"—he looked down sadly at his hands—"the people in this house, including yourself, are, of course, subject to Slavakian law, of which I am the prime custodian within its walls. I suggest that you go to bed, and enjoy the sleep you have earned. We shall look forward to a longer discussion in the morning, when you are refreshed."

The dressing-gown was of plain black silk, flowing like a shroud from the grey face. He looked like a penitent, Bell thought, a saint dying of sadness for the world. Appearances were deceptive, when a snake could look like a saint.

On his way upstairs to the Residence, Bell saw the girl going into her room. "If you'd like a bath, Miss Cameron, just let a chamber-maid know. This place is better appointed."

"I'm too tired." She leaned in the doorway and for an instant he felt something approaching pity, but did not recognise it. "What will happen if I sleep?"

"You'll be the better for it."

"I don't want to turn my back . . ."

He said: "This is London."

"That doesn't mean anything to people like you. What part of London?"

"The Slavakian Embassy."

Her eyes opened wide, staring, drugged-looking. "That's why . . ."—she moved a limp hand—"everything's so elegant."

"I'll wish you good night, Miss Cameron."

"Will I have a guard all the time?"

"Yes. He won't annoy you."

The man was inside the room when she closed the door, a stranger she hadn't seen before, a slight body in neat clothes, a young negative face. He spoke to her in Slavakian and asked if he might help her in any way.

"I'd like to be left alone."

He was sorry, it would be contrary to orders. But the young lady should forget his presence and save herself embarrassment. He stood near the door, dissembling, while she looked at the room, which was small, beautifully decorated, a woman's room.

"What's through there?"

"The bathroom, Ma'm'selle."

The thought of hot water and clean rough towels swam like a mirage in her mind; but she would fall asleep in the bath and drown, unless the man pulled her out, and would he stop at that? It almost didn't matter. Sleep came up against her face and she ached to fall forward into its soft deepening colours. She dragged her shoes off. A breeze moved the filmy curtain at the window; the sigh of leaves washed in against the ceiling. She unzipped the sheath dress and looked across at the man.

"If you do anything, I'll tear your eyes out."

He looked politely at the wall. "I can assure Ma'm'selle."

Was he like Peake? He didn't look like Warren, something out of a cave. She laid the dress over a chair and climbed between the sheets and lay in their coolness, unbelieving of their benison. Colours swam across her eyes and she closed them, but they reeled through her brain in rainbows. She asked if the curtains could be drawn against the light, and the question was repeated until she became aware of her own mouth forming it. He said from miles away: "Does Ma'm'selle wish the light out?"

"Yes, the light."

Its glare burst inside her head, then slowly all the colours drained away.

Glass smashed and she dragged the weight of her body on to one shoulder. Light flickered against her eyes.

"We can't let them," she said in almost a shout.

Someone called out in Slavakian, from another part of the house. She was alone and the room had shrunk, the hearth had vanished; the air was clean of smoke. She felt deeply afraid, remembering the drugs. "Can't let them." A man swam into focus and she leaned up on one arm, ready to tear his eyes out, because she remembered saying she would. "Go away." She could smell the overnight scent of her own body and looked down. She had never slept in her underclothes before, except when she and Joanna had been made drunk at the Thompsons' flat, and Clive had been there, and his hands. She pulled the blankets up. Was she drunk? Drugged? "What was that?" she asked.

"Someone has broken a window."

His voice was chillingly clear and polite. She remembered his face. He was like Peake, or she would have been hurt by now. The animal thoughts asked questions. Men thought of violence, women violation. A man could blow up a bridge (Mark had said, at the Thompsons' flat, earnestly talking through the drink, partitioning the world for her in what he called psycho-sexual dualities), but a woman could only be raped. She said: "Window?"

"An accident."

Voices shouted a long way off, and seemingly below. Her scalp crept suddenly—"Where is he?"

"Ma'm'selle?"

"Where is the King?" She was out of bed, looking for her dressing-gown and slippers, but there were no wind-bowed poplars on the wall; this was an unknown house. She had left him in a room, a small beautiful room, a kind of prince's tomb, lying alone in the narrow bed with his dark eyes closed and all the anguish at peace; old Kosek was on the upright disciplining chair nearby, suffering the pains of the devoted, looking at no one, merely inwards to his dreadful failure, still perhaps murmuring in his mind, I am worthless to him, worthless.

They were going to ask the ex-King to accept certain proposals, Major Bell had told her; so he wouldn't be murdered tonight. There'd be a new day for them all, because Nikolas was wanted alive.

"He is not to be disturbed, Ma'm'selle."

"What's the time?"

"Not quite twelve o'clock——"

"Twelve what? Midday?"

"Of course."

"When did we arrive here?"

"During the night, Ma'm'selle."

"It's tomorrow, then?" But it was never tomorrow. Her mouth was parched. Going into the bathroom and pushing the door closed she was confronted suddenly with his face in the gap; the door shivered; he had put his shoe against it. "Go away," she said, furious with sudden dawn intolerance of interference when the light is pale and new, and people must talk too early.

"If Ma'm'selle wishes to bathe, the door must be left open. I am sorry, but——"

"Ma'm'selle," she said, "likes privacy when she has a bath——" but his shoe was still in the way, and when she drew open the door and struck at him with her nails hooked he caught her wrist, and they faced each other in absurd embarrassment for seconds on end.

"I have my orders," he said.

Voices still shouted from below. "You must not go near the window," he said while her wrist burned in his grip. "I should get myself into great trouble."

"Please let me go."

"You make it difficult for me, Ma'm'selle. I have my——"

"Let me have a bath. I won't go near the window, or do anything wrong. I just want to wash."

When he freed her, she thought: I'm acting like an animal, as they do; it's infectious. This is London. "You can leave the door open," she said. "What's your name?"

"Franz." The Christian name of the trained servant.

"German?"

"Austrian, Ma'm'selle." He seemed relieved that they had shed their anonymity. His face was young and sensitive, but the hand on her wrist had been iron. He respected orders, and feared punishment. "If I remain here, Ma'm'selle, I can see all of the window. It is enough."

She turned the taps and took off her underclothes. The water stung and she felt like a lobster, and the ache crept down into her feet and burned there. The light from the frosted window glared; her eyes felt reddened; the steam smelt of mushrooms. "Franz."

"Ma'm'selle?"

"Is the King asleep, still?"

"We are not enabled to say."

"Is this the Slavakian Embassy?"

"Yes."

"Who were the people shouting?" The heat of the water was delaying her awakening; she turned on the cold tap and felt the coolness lapping at her feet. She was in a strange house, a foreign house, inside the walls of a frontier yet in the middle of London, with strangers shouting—you could never tell what language a crowd shouted in; it was a herd cry; outside Buckingham Palace at the end of the war they might have been calling in any language to the King of England, loud in their fever of victory and demanding the sight of high persons to focus the moment upon—here they were shouting again, through a smashed

229

window, calling without a language except that of the human herd. This, too, was London. She began shivering.

"I don't know, Ma'm'selle. An accident."

The whole world was an accident, a lunatic with its poor brain turned in upon itself, a gun in its hand, turned on its own heart. German? No, Austrian. And I am English, but we speak Slavakian. Our flags have different colours and we are proud to have been born in our different lands. I am English, and proud of it; you are Austrian, and proud of it; other people are proud of being Chinese and American and Russian and Brazilian and Afghanistani and Kuria Murian—we are all proud of being whatever we are; we are all a proud people, each ready to kill all the others because their flags and languages are different. It doesn't matter if the mountains of India and the mountains of South America are the same indistinguishable mole-hills from the cabin of a stratocruiser, or that the buildings of the governments look smaller than mud-huts, or that you can't see whether one of those teeming lice has a gun in its hand or not, is powerful or not, because from that height, even from that small height, the lice can't be seen at all. Who would guess, Franz, that we are the representatives of the dignity of man? But we are. You can tell how important we are, because although I am a naked female wallowing in water and you are a male with seed in you that biologically would cross well with mine according to the laws of Nature, this is onyx I am lying in, and the taps are nickel, and the soap scented and expensive; and round your neck you wear a ring of fibres harvested from the earth's plants and then woven and bleached, cut and shaped and made flat with a heated iron, and treated with a carbohydrate to keep it stiff and polished-looking— over the centuries, this is what man has decided to carry round his neck; in other parts of the planet the people wear rings through their nose, but here it is round the neck; and we have rules about its shape, and its height; a speck of dirt, a pin's-head of black, on the shining white ring would cause comment, and it would have to be changed or the people would say, Franz has a dirty collar.

We observe the proprieties. Is your eye to the crack of the door? It would be unthinkable. We are the civilised. The window is frosted so that strangers shouldn't look in—but the other window, what about that? Disorder has risen, and someone has broken a window. Down there, on the spinning globe of rock and water with its forests of lichen, one of two thousand five hundred million lice has smashed a fragment of glass; and the globe spins on.

I wallow in my water-hole. When I can get it, I prefer Lanvin soap; the scent is different from this by a subtle shade. And you prefer Robin starch, Franz, for your collar? Life can be so full of difficult choices.

The shouting began again outside the house. She emptied the bath and splashed herself from the cold tap, fully awake. It was no good looking through the wrong end of the telescope to see the truth. It was no truer that way. You had to fit in and conform, accept the conditions and the *status quo*. For those who didn't, there were the asylums.

Standing on the wet floor, drying herself, she realised that it was no accident that she worked with Unic, in the Slavakian Section, with his photograph on her desk. It had been the only place, after the walk down the long flight of steps, the touch of his hand still felt. One imagined that chance governed behaviour, but it didn't. There had been a dozen jobs open to her, and this one had interested her because it would be worth while, a challenge to her laziness in learning languages, and she would be working among foreigners, so that some of her cramping insularity would be broken down: those had been her reasons; and then, by chance, at the airport . . . but it hadn't been chance at all. From the moment she had walked into the doors of Unic House to begin work there, years ago, she had been following a direction which had led her to the terrace where the cool wind blew and the thin rain swirled past the lamps where the bowsers refuelled the aircraft. And both of them five years older.

The shouts died away. "Franz, would you please pass me my dress?"

Standing in the doorway with the towel, she watched him back cautiously, keeping her in sight. "I've no bombs, or anything, Franz. They're all in my other pockets."

"I have worked hard to reach this position, Ma'm'selle. I wouldn't like to lose it by failing in my duties."

She put on the dress and washed her nylon briefs in the hand-basin, leaving them on the towel-rail to dry. All the fatigue had gone. There were questions to be asked: about the smashed window, the shouting. When she had brushed her hair she used a lipstick and said: "Franz, take me down to see King Nikolas."

"I am afraid——"

"Franz, if you don't take me downstairs I'll make quite certain you'll lose your job here. Will you please understand that?"

"I have my orders, Ma'm'selle." His eyes were like his hand now, cold iron.

"I shall make it evident that you attacked me. There'll be a lot of noise and excitement about it." There was a certain relief in using a tart's trick in these elegant surroundings, when the proprieties were held in temporary respect. "Take a few seconds to think; then I'll begin."

She went to the door and he passed her quickly, standing with his back against it. There was conflict in his eyes. This wasn't a difficult man to manage; the pick of the thugs would be guarding the more important guests.

"If you wish," he said, "I will take you downstairs, but it won't be for me to decide whether you can see the ex-King."

"Then open the door."

"Ma'm'selle will behave?"

"As impeccably as you have."

The Ambassador came down from his office and found Bell waiting for him.

"There's no cause for alarm," Bell said.

"I am not alarmed."

Police were moving the last of the small crowd in the roadway below and there were no more shouts. The Ambassador said sadly: "It improves the soul to relieve the heart. Even the sheep of monarchies know that. I wished to talk to you for a moment, Major, before we call our other advisers in. I am obliged to you for presenting yourself so promptly."

Take the poison out of you, thought Major Bell, and you'd make a maiden aunt for someone. He suffered another minute or so of diplomatic platitudes—the word 'circumstances' was used four times—then the Ambassador said: "I have had a word with Dr. Holden, who, as you know, has called here to examine the ex-King's hand. A phrase he employed has set me thinking. At the moment the ex-King is physically well, but of course emotionally disturbed by these events. We have given thought to the matter of calming him with narcotics as a preparation for the discussion with the President this evening; but it might prove dangerous. We do not wish him to accept our proposals under any form of narcosis, however mild, and then revoke later at a time when it might be that our plans would suffer irreparably."

Bell waited. There seemed no particular response to be expected. His own views on the advisability or otherwise of drugging Nikolas weren't likely to interest the Ambassador, if only on the principle that they weren't those of His Almighty Excellency's.

"But the position is this, Major Bell. Either he accepts our proposal or forfeits his life. While we are not concerned with his life, since kings and politicians curtail their longevity in any case by the nature of their vocation, we are very closely concerned in his future if he chooses to live, on our terms."

The Major said, because of something in him that he was hardly aware of: "The alternatives are absolute, are they, Your Excellency? He accepts our terms, or is assassinated?"

"No. He accepts our terms or is found to have committed suicide, Major. That is important. The effect is the same: he will still decompose, for all the royal crimson of his blood, but there is world focus on his person at this time, and his death will be public property. As I understand that you will play a major and gallant part in the proceedings, I thought I might remind you that suicide is to be the outcome of his refusal, whether or not there are a few of us who will realise the truth. To answer your question: yes, he accepts our terms or renounces life. The alternatives, as you put it so briefly, are absolute. There is no chance of compromise. Why did you ask?"

"To make sure what I'm required to do, Your Excellency, in the event of his refusal. I have my orders already, but I wanted Your Excellency's confirmation."

"You have it. Now with regard to the preparation of the ex-King for his conference with President Szados, I feel we have an opportunity of calming the man beforehand, with one of Nature's oldest sedatives. There are no two greater enemies in this world, possibly, than President Szados and the ex-King Nikolas; and the latter is known for his rages when challenged by stronger forces. If we can confine the conference to mental considerations, unconfused by dictates of emotion, we shall be granting our cause greater service."

You're so proud of your English, Your-bloody-Excellency, that it's a job to know what you're talking about. But do go on. You'll have to pipe down fast enough when Szados comes.

"I doubt if the ex-King can be persuaded to enjoy a good luncheon; nor in his case is wine a tranquilliser. But this young woman we have with us: you say there is some form of adolescent infatuation manifested, and of course Nikolas will content himself with anything female, especially after a few days of abstinence. She appears to be attractive enough to satisfy the somewhat undemanding requirements of brute lust."

He waited for a comment, but Bell was bored with circumlocution. He assumed an expectant expression and let the silence go on.

"So I suggest," the Ambassador intoned sadly, "that you arrange matters during this afternoon so as to enable the ex-King to seduce her. Your guards can safely withdraw for the occasion, as he is most unlikely to think about anything else while preoccupied with the copulation."

CHAPTER XX

Old Kosek came into the room where the ex-King and
Baron Angelitri sat together in the middle, on two chairs
as if in a waiting-room. This was as far as they could be
private, for Peake was by the windows and Antiquis at
the door.

"Well, Kosi?"

"It is a small demonstration, Your Majesty, in the
square outside the house. Someone threw a stone and
smashed a window. The police are dispersing them——"

"What are they demonstrating? Do they know we're
here?"

"No, Your Majesty. There are strong feelings against
the present government of Your Majesty's country."

"A stone. That's a small enough start."

The morning light was pale in the windows and a
watery sun was clearing the roofs behind the house. For
a long time the ex-King was silent. Angelitri brooded,
sometimes glancing at his face. It wasn't easy to judge
his mood this morning. The effects of the drug had passed
and he seemed no worse for it. The doctor had called an
hour ago, and had been allowed to dress the wound, but
not one word had passed between them; it had been,
Angelitri had thought, like a mechanic adjusting an
engine, in the silence of accepted incommunicability.
There had been no attempt to make an injection, of penicillin or anything else. Any such attempt would have
failed, or led to such a scene of violence that the whole

situation would have run out of control. Nikolas was not prepared to risk a further surrender of his mind. Likewise Angelitri had refused food and drink until Kosek had been allowed into the kitchens to supervise the catering. The Embassy staff accepted the old man as a superior, and confined their intercourse to sly questions: he was retainer to a royal house and must have a fund of pre-war palace scandal, and they yearned to hear it.

He supervised the preparation of coffee, and offered no titbits in exchange for the privilege. He took the trays personally to the sitting-room and hall and watched the cups until they were raised. Despite this, Baron Angelitri had drunk no coffee this morning; he contented himself with water from the tap.

"Uncle Petrik, let's give our brains a rub and raise the genie . . ."

It was the old call to arms and the Baron responded, his head jutting from the huge shoulders, his eyes resting on the King's. Perhaps there was something to be saved from this diminished spirit.

"With all my heart, sir."

"We haven't much to go on. Someone's coming to see us—a 'high member of the Slavakian Government'. According to Bell, our minds are to be worked on, though I don't believe he knows for certain. I believe they'll try persuasion of some kind to force a guarantee from me that I won't return to politics in any capacity whatsoever, king or otherwise. It seems the only reasonable explanation for keeping me preserved and alive. If I refuse to parley, of course it will be different."

"We can't refuse to parley. We must listen, and play them carefully. It's the only chance we have."

"Who are they sending, I wonder?"

Hadn't it crossed his mind even yet? It could only be Szados. "Whoever it is, he'll be picked for his cunning, sir." Szados was not cunning; he possessed his will, and that was his strength. He demanded without compromise. It was pointless to argue with Szados or to use cunning. The art of cunning was in tinting the picture, holding it at a different angle to change the opponent's view of it—to colour it and shade it, softening some parts and brightening others, to turn away from it and seem to forget it, until it was time to present it again, the same picture, to the dulled eye of the opponent for his acceptance. But Szados could see only black and white, and once he had formed his view it was etched deeply into his tin mechanical skull. One must accept or refuse, and take the consequences of the chosen course.

If he were to tell Nikolas that it could only be Szados who was coming, there'd be no parleying. He'd refuse to see him. But once closet them together with no way out, and he would have to meet the challenge. How much strength was there left in Nikolas II of Slavakia, after the years of bitter reflection and the slow dry-rot of idleness?

"Cunning? Who have they got that's cunning? I can't think of anyone, Petrik. They prefer the battering-ram to a clash of wits. They've learned it from Szados."

"I would advise, sir, that whatever their proposal is, we accept it, after a show of reluctance. We've no freedom here on the enemy's ground."

"Give our guarantee and then rescind it later?"

"The rules of open warfare——"

"I'll keep to my own rules. I shan't sell what honour I have left. We'll accept or refuse, and if they mean to kill me off we'll first try to fight our way out." His voice was level. He stared at the wall, at the unknown face of the enemy who was coming.

"We're not soldiers, sir——"

"Kings were soldiers once."

This was worse than a rage. "With your permission, sir, I'd like to talk to them first, as your adviser, and hear their terms——"

"And force a compromise of your own? These days when we give our brains a rub we raise a different genie. There's a throne there, down by the Duna, and it's mine." Suddenly he was facing Angelitri—"I made a good king, Petrik. We ran the country well and made it prosperous. You guided my father and you guided me. Slavakia claimed the respect of nations in peace-time, and won honour in war. It gave its sons freely and I gave two of mine. Now the people are giving again of all the little they have—there are children fighting in the streets, carrying guns. You say we're not soldiers. If children are soldiers, what are we?"

"Prisoners."

"There are no bars here."

"But guns."

"When they are ready to shoot me, I'll take my chance. You have your own choice to make. You have your wife, but I've no one. Whatever you do, Petrik, there won't be dishonour in it. Forget what I said; it's the same genie, but with two heads now, and it may be that yours is the wiser. It always has been."

He remembered his father standing at the window of the Palace, a few days before his death in the riding-park. He had spent all morning in audience with ministers and had forced them one by one to see the sense of his argument; but it had been hard work and there was no one to help him. He spoke, standing at the window, to himself perhaps but aloud; and the young Crown Prince had heard. "It's a lonely business, king."

The sheath dress was on the floor; her body had been drawn out of it and was now itself a sheath for Nikolas. Everything, it seemed now, led up to this: this was the pinnacle of days and happenings; but afterwards, she knew, it would take its place as a splendid incidental.

Bell had said nothing to her; there had been no manifest arrangement; it had appeared to happen by chance that when she went to the ex-King's room in the Residence, the guards were called away and they were alone.

Nikolas saw the key that was left in the door, and when he locked it and turned back to her she had an instant's cynical thought of Pavlov's dogs: Bell and the unknown experimenters knew that when this man was left alone with a young female of his species, he would look at once for the key and would lock the door.

"Louise . . ."

"The curtains?" she said. He searched them, and the dressing-room.

There would be guards outside, watching the window from the fire-escape; perhaps an eye at the keyhole of the door. She mustn't think about it. These were the freak conditions of a civilised society wherein love must be made while the blood was hot. In the war there must have been worse places: she had been going past the ruin of the little newsagent's shop with her mother, hand in hand after the first bad raid (the Monday Raid, as it came afterwards to be known), and had seen, startled, the two figures struggling together in the shadows where the beams slanted down from blackened bricks and the rain ran through; and she thought for a moment that they were fighting, but could say nothing to her mother because her adolescent instinct was aware in its own strange way that she was near the presence of It—the dirty whispered—of the exciting and mysterious It with so many fancy names and lowered glances, its long history still recounted by the modern animal on his midden walls. Her mother's hand had tightened. 'We must hurry, Louise.' So that she had known for sure. For nights she had gone to sleep sad, because of the black bricks and broken plaster and the drip of the rain through the holes that led to the clouds. Surely it wasn't so irresistible that it could happen anywhere, without comfort, even privacy?

An eye at a keyhole was nothing. But she hung a stocking over the key and asked him to draw the curtains. The light was grey, diffused, its scrutiny dulled.

"You must be careful with your poor hand."

"I could lift you with it."

"Nikolas, you know they want this to happen. It's by arrangement. They——"

His mouth stilled hers, but thought surfaced and gave her no peace. 'I don't imagine,' Major Bell had said, 'that you'll refuse to help us to persuade him.' So now she was on the other side, with them, against the King, worse than a courtesan, a poisoner. Then at times even thought was forced aside and the primitive ruled.

Her eyes closed, she saw his face more clearly, half its invisible colours brightened by her mind, so that he was more than Nikolas of this moment—he was the king-god of his palace and the memory on her hand down the great stone flight of steps; the young, aged face for an instant seen against the black cellulose of the car at the airport;

the stricken target of the little guard's gun; the photograph on her desk reflecting the window and the small church spire across the street in Aldersgrove. More than himself, he was what he meant to her.

Her body, now with his, was aware all the time of his wound and moved so that his hand should be rested and not involved; being with him, her body protected this painful extremity of itself as if it were her own, quite automatically and without thought until she ached with the unusual tension, and he in his turn felt her pain—

"Louise——"

"Your hand——"

"You've healed it now."

In the intervals, lying in the grey light with her senses singing, she savoured the mental pleasures of this experience, with among them the knowledge that the scandalisers were wrong: this man was no brute lecher who strummed a woman like a snatched-up instrument. The demands of his body swept beyond the confines of the flesh and touched the spirit, so that at one time she felt tears on her face and knew they were her own small evidence of the heart-break that was to come.

"Why are you crying?" He missed nothing; all that was herself had to do with him.

"I think too much."

"Am I too careless?"

"Too splendid."

His fingers touched her tears and stroked them away; it was the most he would ever be able to do for her, down the long stone flight of the years.

"I am Jezebel," she said. "They arranged for this to happen. They want me to help them persuade you to accept their terms, so that——"

"I accept your breasts and your soft eyes, and the shadows in your hair. Touch me here."

So that she had to think alone of the others, who would shoot him if he held out against them. An explosion, and this fine column of genesis would shrivel and be sterilised for ever by the cold and dark of death; the still-young father of so many scattered sons would die without their knowing it; without knowing it, they would lose their future brothers and never grieve. Already it seemed to her that he was separated from her, even now, a candidate for the last inquisition waiting alone, untouchable and with no more hope of rescue than a man alone in the midst of an ocean.

She held him against her, wanting to say that she was frightened. "I love you," she said. She wanted to say that she would never let him go, but nothing could make it true. When they cared to come for him they would come for him and take him away, and if he defied them there would be a shot, and there would never be an answer when she said his name. And of all his loves, she would have been the last. "If you weren't with me now, Nikolas, who would you rather be with?"

"Alone and thinking of you."

"I'm serious. La Contessa di Medici?" They had so many names for her, the Roman Tart, the Tart of Italy, names made up by the jealous and the envious who would give so much to be the King's mistress and must console themselves in calumny. "You needn't answer." He would think her stupid, a cool, passionless English girl with her mind running on, a thing apart, instead of engaged in the exaltation of the body. To ask a man what other woman he would rather be with . . . to force him into reluctant lies . . . it was the abyss of stupidity. But he had thought of it only because he might be, in a way, already dying. She said: "I want so much to make you happy."

"You give me pure delight."

"No. I'm inexperienced. But teach me everything, for my sake too. We'll go on and on."

"You must rest a little."

"I'll rest tomorrow." They were defeated, the others, in this one thing. Whether tomorrow found him dead—perhaps both of them—or both alive and never to meet again, this perfect deed was done, for him a pleasant memory, for her a thing of cherishment never to be lost. The others could do nothing now to change this day.

"You mustn't be sad for me, or afraid," he said.

"It's part of love. But make me stop thinking."

For a long time she let herself be swept wholly along by the ecstasies he inspired, surprised into a wild sensuality she had never dreamed herself to possess, meeting his passion with a freedom that surrendered her very identity so that she was no longer Louise but a part of something larger than a human being, a component of a universe, creative, deathless, indispensable. This was the whole and only world and she span among its airs and lights as predestined as a star.

"Nikolas . . . Nikolas . . ."

Everything had led to this, from the day she was born. The courses of two lives had crossed and touched and were for this short time caught together. Losing herself, losing Louise and all named things and documented memories, she had found what she was: a part of this.

He opened her fingers gently; their muscles burned; she had been hurting him, trying to bury her hand into him and weld flesh to flesh—"I'm sorry——" she caught her breath. "You mustn't ever go. Never go."

He said in his own tongue that he would never go, never leave her, while she thought: 'Shoot us now, together!' Yet a bullet would vanish in this fire like a drop of rain; they were immortal.

She lay sprawling on her side, cast up by the storm, the beat of her heart alive in the air. Immortal, because of the seed.

He murmured names to her in his own language, loved one, all beauty, his sweet Louise, while she lay listening, using his words for thoughts to fill her mind and keep the future out.

"Dearest," she said, so that he would know she was listening and not thinking away from him. And, though there were no others: "Dearest of all."

When she opened her eyes they saw immediately his face, watching hers as if he must remember it.

"How strong you are, Nikolas. Nothing tires you. Lie down against me." A bar of silver light crossed the ceiling from the gap of the curtains and her eyes used it for a path. "I once carried away the touch of your hand, Nikolas, all the way down those great steps you have outside your palace; I wasn't much more than a child, and I was on fire with just the touch of your hand, and now I'm a woman and there's all this, your whole fine body in my complete possession, for a little while. If I'd known it was going to happen, one day, and only five years later, I would probably have fainted, there on the steps. Your Majesty would perhaps have inquired about the untoward disturbance outside, and would have been told that it was only one of the English students who had eaten a surfeit of ice-cream; and you wouldn't have know it was I, fainting at the thought of you."

The silver path across the ceiling became hypnotic, so

that her eyes closed; yet the silver ran curving across the huge dome of the dark. Enclosed within herself and sightless, she was under the arch of the whole universe, floating between the earth and eternity. She listened to what someone was saying. "When I came in here, I nearly fainted anyway, although I'm not a child any more. When the men went out and I knew what was was going to happen, I couldn't breathe or move and the whole of my body was trembling—did it show? But even then I didn't know what it would be like, or I don't know what would have happened to me. Of course we've got a reputation, English girls, of fainting at the thought of sex, but some of us aren't really cold, just badly brought up, jolly good at hockey till we're found in the summer-house with the gardener's boy. It wasn't the thought of being made love to that made me shake; it was the thought of it with you."

A hand moved her hair and the silver path ran curving downwards so that she went falling with it, head-first in a beautiful curving dive, turning slowly as a child in the womb, and someone else said: "You're sleepy, Louise, lovely Louise . . ."

"Sleepy Lagoon . . . all the way down."

The wind moved her hair.

Whistling woke her. For a little while she was unaware that the dreams had floated down into the unconscious as her waking mind gained control, so that she lay listening to the whistler's tune until her naked body sensed the touch of the coverlet that had been drawn over her, and she remembered this room. It was in shadow; the curtains were still drawn.

"Nikolas."

When there was no answer she threw off the coverlet

and went to the window, pulling the curtains apart and turning, dazzled by the evening light. He had gone. The sudden wild beat of her heart was in her throat. They had come for him.

CHAPTER XXI

Under the sweep of leaves the light was green and the air had the stillness and greenness of aquarium water; the black iron railings stood in their hard cold row along the pavement, the bloom of the green light on their spikes.

"Where did you go?" asked Vaquier. His cigarette-end went bouncing into the gutter, quick as a squib.

"For a walk." Messiter watched the face of the Embassy building across the street, studying its windows and the door and portico where the constable stood.

"You have a good time," Vaquier asked, "on your walk?"

"Yes, very good."

Vaquier watched him in the green light of the evening. The more you asked Messiter things, the less he said. He was a difficult case, not really human. And he was busy in his mind with something, right now. He had gone along to the guy with the field-glasses, and borrowed them, taking them from him and staring through them for ten minutes before he gave them back. Then he had stood here for another five minutes to make you think he'd seen nothing through the field-glasses to exercise his mind about, before going for his walk. There were two ways you could walk, from here, round the square, and he had walked the way that would lead you past the telephone-box just by the corner: or to it.

A few starlings came dipping over the sand-bin and up again as fast and soundless as fish in the soft light. A taxi dropped someone off at the house next door to the Embassy, but Messiter didn't look down at it. He was fascinated by the windows of the Embassy.

"I'll have to phone my desk soon," Vaquier said. "Is that one working okay?"

"The G.P.O. telephones are all very efficient."

It must be killing to play chess with Messiter.

A black saloon pulled up at the corner; it had come in from Buckingham Palace Road; after a minute Vaquier said:

"What kind of car would you say that was, Tony?"

Messiter didn't look down from the Embassy building. "A police-car, possibly."

"Eyes like a fly."

Another car came in from the opposite end of the Square, and a man in a soft grey suit got out and walked down the pavement, taking his time. When he came to the Embassy steps he talked to the constable there, and then went back. The constable stood looking idly across at the trees.

"Cigarette?"

"No, thanks," said Messiter.

Vaquier turned round as he lit a cigarette for himself, and couldn't see any other cars arriving; but there was a bench among the trees just beyond the railings and whereas a little time ago it had been empty there were two men sitting on it now, admiring the white stucco of the Embassy building in the evening light.

"You got them along here pretty fast, Tony."

"M'm?"

"The boys. Police."

"What makes you so dramatic? Anyone would think you were on Spry-Photo instead of with A.P.A."

Vaquier looked along the railings and saw one of the press-scouts going across to the police-car; but they clearly weren't talking; he came back and stood in the same place. Two or three other scouts got out of their cars and began drifting along the pavement, worried. It was like watching dogs when the wind changed.

Messiter was moving off again.

"Hey, Tony."

He caught up with him. "You going for another walk?"

"I think so."

"You want company?"

"Not really."

He stood and watched Messiter go down the pavement to where the railings ran curving out of sight. Then he moved his position and saw him again, turning past the telephone-box. He wasn't going to make a call.

He set off after him and went a dozen yards before he stopped and came slowly back. You couldn't just follow the guy. You'd got your pride.

There was movement behind him and when he turned round he saw a man leaning against the railings, smoking a pipe, looking at nothing.

A car came out of the road leading down to the mews and stopped half-way round the Square with a faint squeal of tyres; but no one got out.

Wherever he looked, now, Vaquier saw small movements. The Square was becoming peopled, over the minutes, with figures that would never be noticed if you weren't standing here with cat's nerves cursing Messiter. There were the two men still on the bench reading papers, the man with the pipe, another man walking idly past one of the police-cars—you could even miss things by blinking:

the dark van hadn't been there a second ago, by the letterbox.

The evening air was calm, and only the haphazard darting flight of the starlings ruffled the stillness with a rush of wings. Traffic drummed, remote beyond the high windowed wall of the houses, the silence here the deeper for it. The leaves did not move.

Vaquier stood and listened to the tick of his watch.

Most of the windows of the Embassy were shut, and the air was close. Shoes made no sound on the carpets; the doors were opened and closed carefully as if there had been a death here.

"Where is Kosek?"

"I don't know," said the Baron. Every few minutes at regular intervals Sofi must ask a question, and he must answer. Every few minutes she must pace the room again and come back to him, her red hair catching the light from the windows, moving like a flame through the outer field of his vision. Once a guard had touched her arm, saying nothing, but guiding her towards the middle of the room, away from the windows.

Angelitri chain-smoked and looked at no one. The door had not opened for an hour. Kosek had gone out with the excuse of 'attending His Majesty', but the Baron was uncertain whether Kosek even knew where His Majesty was. The old servant had seemed to ingratiate himself with the Embassy staff, and was permitted by the guards to move about the house with his own pet escort, a peasant with an assassin's face and dull eyes.

"Should we demand to see Nikolas?"

Sofi was back again, chilling the air with the aura of her nerves, her child lost to her.

"We would be refused."

"How apathetic you are, Petrik! Have they drugged you again?"

"Resignation to the inevitable conserves one's nervous resources. The time will come when we shall need to call upon them."

She was content with any answer. The guards watched her pacing. The mute homosexual was not here, nor Antiquis; they would be with the ex-King, his faithful retinue. These men in here were strangers again; neither Sofi nor the Baron had seen them at the house in Richmond. This place was full of strange new faces in the room and along the passages, some of them members of the staff, others in Major Bell's pocket-command.

"God knows what she's advising him."

Baron Angelitri studied her white face and burning eyes. Poor Sofi. He said: "I don't think she is important, Sofi. We have no grounds for believing that she is against the King——"

"You told me it was she who used the hypodermic——"

"It was open knowledge, and for that reason I believe she used it in all innocence."

"We can trust no one."

"We have to. There's nothing else we can do. If we thought she was poisoning him at this moment, we could do nothing. We must keep patience."

"You don't understand, Petrik."

"Yes, I understand."

When Szados had come to the Palace, leaving his men in the grounds and half a regiment of traitors drawn up in the barrack square, Sofi had been magnificent, a strength to Nikolas and to them all. But he had been free then to face the enemy; now he was a prisoner and could be smudged out when they chose, meeting a fly's death.

"We have imposed one condition, Sofi, on the meeting that has been arranged. The Ambassador has been told that Nikolas will participate in no discussion with any arriving mission unless you and I are present as his advisers. Therefore we shall be summoned to attend."

"You have faith in the word of a man like the Ambassador?"

"I've faith in his intelligence. Until a deadlock is reached the meeting will proceed according to the traditions of conclave between statesmen; and beyond that point it will be appreciated even by these blunt gentlemen that statesmanship can ease a deadlock more usefully than a firing-squad."

Sofi smoothed her long white hands, washing them together, cleansing the dread away. "You are patient and sanguine," she said, "just as you were in Drovnik."

"We still survive."

She was not listening. "They must be together alone all this time, or she would be sent in here with us."

"You were always complacent before, when Nikolas was sporting with women——"

"If it were only that! The English chit wasn't brought to us for sport—she's no voluptuary."

"Perhaps with a lesson or two from the master . . ."

"Your wit's coarse, Petrik." She stood listening for seconds. "I can hear a car outside. Someone's arriving."

"People arrive and leave all the time. The normal business of the Embassy goes on."

"When will he arrive, this delegate? Can't you find out?"

"He's been here more than an hour already——"

"How do you know?"

"I learned it from the Counsellor. There was no reason

why he shouldn't tell me."

"Who is he?"

"I've not seen him."

She stared at him with suspicion. She suspected everyone of lying and deceiving. "But you know who he is."

The Baron turned his head and she looked round to see Major Bell standing in the doorway. The men in the corners of the room and by the windows shaped themselves for his inspection.

Sofi Mikayan moved towards him and his glance swung to meet her, as uncompromising as an aimed gun. She said: "We are impatient, Major. Has something gone wrong?"

"Nothing, Ma'm'selle Mikayan. I understand that you and Baron Angelitri are to attend the conference. We would have liked to introduce the delegate beforehand, over cocktails, but unfortunately he must return to Slavakia as soon as possible, and time is short."

Whenever this man is afraid, thought Angelitri, he turns his mind to urbanity and calms himself with the false picture of sociality. He wears the hangman's domino.

"Then the delegate has arrived?" asked Sofi Mikayan.

"Oh yes."

The fear in the yellow eyes was the fear of the delegate. Angelitri could see, in these eyes whose gaze was at flinching point, the hard stone shape of the man who was stronger than Major Bell as a rock is stronger than a reed, the delegate.

"If you'll accompany me," said Bell, and stood aside from the doorway.

CHAPTER XXII

Baroque encrustations of plaster ran the length of the ceiling in the Conference Room, but their gilt had been whitened over and some attempt had been made to chip away the more lavish ornamentation in the corners. Similarly the hearth and doors had been stripped and blanched as a more fitting background for the few plain pieces of Empire furniture that stood against the walls. The Embassy, once an office of the Slavakian monarchy, was now the property of a different régime; and the Baroque style had been rubbed out wherever possible, as if a priest in feverish zeal had blotted out chalked blasphemies along the walls. The conference table was a narrow oblong of mahogany, quiet as a coffin.

Nikolas stood at the far end of the room, so that when Louise was allowed through the doors she saw him immediately, and paused a moment to contain her relief. He was alone here except for the guards. He had not heard her come in, and she was half-way down the long room before he lifted his head. How different he looked now! His image in her eyes when she had fallen asleep had been of a sated animal, naked, beautiful, still in the thrall of lust, his eyes loving her; now he stood stiffly in a dark neat suit and his face was pale and even when he recognised her there was no softness in his eyes, no memory of anything more than her identity. He was part of the silence of this hushed place and she was afraid to approach him.

"Louise . . ." He made a step towards her, but she could see that it was no real welcome. She had drawn him away from unimaginable thoughts, and if she could have turned back and gone unseen out of the room she would have gladly done so.

"I—I fell alseep."

"Yes. I left you sleeping." His memory must reach back over centuries.

"I came to be sure that you were all right. Now I'll go."

He raised his head again and she heard Baron Angelitri's voice by the doors. Sofi Mikayan was with him. "We were anxious about Your Majesty," she said, gazing at him, wanting to touch him and assure herself that in the last few hours the world had not spun away into the regions of the loved dead, the last oblivion.

"I'm touched by your anxieties." He looked at each of them. "But I'm quite well."

"Your wound doesn't trouble you, sir?"

"I have forgotten it, Petrik."

Sofi turned to face Louise and spoke as if they were alone. "How long have you been here?"

"A few minutes. I fell asleep. Has anything happened?"

The brown eyes were bright, freezing against her, so that Louise looked away. Angelitri stood so that he could address the ex-King without losing sight of the doors where Antiquis stood. "We are told that the delegate has arrived, sir."

"Yes."

In the hush of the room they could hear Major Bell on the far side of the doors, calling an order to one of his men. In a moment he came in alone.

Nikolas focused his stare on him. "Is this a chance delay or must we wait till nightfall?"

"I felt that you might wish to consult for a few minutes with your advisers, sir. Otherwise we can convene at once."

"The sooner the better."

"Very well. Perhaps you'll come with me, Miss Cameron."

"No, Major, I'll remain here."

Sofi Mikayan began speaking slowly and did not once look at Louise as she delivered her attack. "Your Majesty, as your adviser I must point out the extreme unwisdom of allowing this stranger to remain here during the discussion of such profound matters, the outcome of which will affect the political and even the military situation throughout the world. It has been a great pleasure to us to observe that Your Majesty has taken the opportunity of light diversion during this period of strain and uncertainty, but now that matters of grave significance are to be approached in secret conference it would be less than reasonable that your close ministers should be expected to countenance the presence of a person completely unknown to them two days ago. In the event of——"

"I think," said Baron Angelitri gently, "that the point's made quite clearly." He touched her long white hand, and found it cold. The poor woman would make herself ill with hate; it had happened before. Better that both women should go outside and spend a happy hour scratching each other's eyes out while the conference proceeded in peace.

"I've all faith in her loyalty," said Nikolas briefly.

Sofi closed her eyes for a few seconds before she said with frozen calm: "Then I'm reassured, and will have no qualms in withdrawing." She made a step backwards. "With Your Majesty's permission."

Nikolas had a cold voice. "Not granted." He looked at the Baron, who did not fail him.

257

"If I might suggest a compromise, sir——" but Louise was moving away and paused only for a moment.

"Outside, I'll pray for the King."

Major Bell went with her to the doors, and soon voices could be heard beyond them. Angelitri stood close to Nikolas. "I need to know one thing sir, before they come. Supposing the people can carry their revolution to success, how far will you go to regain the throne?"

"As far as life allows."

Angelitri studied the lined resolute face. "Then I can only hope that God's with us in this."

Nikolas looked down the length of the conference table, where the light shone across the polished wood as brightly as across still water. Here ran the Danube or the Styx.

"I'm tired, Petrik, of being an exile. If my people can hazard their lives for freedom, then I'll risk mine to share it with them. I'll do what I can to win this day, and if I fail I'll fare no worse than my father."

Reflections of moving faces formed in the bright surface of the table. Major Bell stood near the doors as the Ambassador came in with his Counsellor and First Secretary and three members of the Embassy secretarial staff. The only greeting offered to the ex-King was one glance from the Ambassador, quite without gesture.

Two guards followed and Bell indicated their posts along the walls; there were now six of them present and the nearest to Nikolas was the thin pervert who looked at no one.

Szados came in alone.

The Ambassador and his team had taken their places behind the chairs and stood dutifully to civilian attention as the President stopped within a yard of the door and stood looking down the length of the table at the ex-King.

Angelitri, watching his face, knew that the decision Nikolas had made was now sealed. The mere presence of Imgrir Szados was a challenge and Nikolas would not refuse it. His face was a stone weathered by bitter seasons and now its lines were frozen in the light of this winter hour. To see this face, closed-eyed in the coffin, would be to know that here was a man who died resolute, for death would not alter its look. There was not even surprise in the eyes; and Angelitri realised that Nikolas must have guessed. They had sent Szados, the highest, as their delegate. It was a compliment.

Angelitri stared at the man with a surprise of his own. His memory of Szados fell away like a dropped photograph. In five years he had grown old and his square blank face had shrunk, its eyes receding into the skull for shelter, its mouth tightened to a clamp for fear of its own speech. The few steps the man had taken from the doorway to the table were less those of a ruthless automaton than of a puppet jerking beneath slack strings.

Szados was broken. By what? The revolution. He had failed to prevent it and the blame was his. Angelitri's head was busy with calculation: he must remember the leaders of the Szados régime and what their reaction would be towards this inhuman figurehead if he failed. To the merciless, mercy was a gibberish word—they would not have forgiven him. They would have shot him. Then why was he here? To make his redemption. To contain the revolution and then to put it down, with Nikolas his secret weapon.

The Baron watched him, measured him with the rule of experience. Szados looked broken, but you could never break a man like Szados and leave life in him. A dangerous animal, he would grow more dangerous the nearer he moved to death. This was his corner and here he must make his last stand.

Angelitri realised that the two enemies shared this in common: defeat would entail death; and each had accepted the terms.

The face had withered and the body shrunk, but the voice was obscenely the same as President Szados addressed the ex-King without preamble of any kind.

"We are here to parley. Have you any objection to the presence of any person at this table?"

"None."

"Let us be seated."

People walked through the Square.

Sometimes a car pulled in and found space to park. Often it would have a Press label inside the windscreen, and people noticed this, and noticed the group of men who stood opposite the Embassy, one or two of them with flash-equipment slung round their shoulders. Along the curve of the railings where the basement gates opened, residents came out of their flats and stood on the porches; those living in the basements came to the top of the steps and peered through the railings at the group of newspaper-men. In a little while the people stopped watching the group and instead watched the house that so obviously interested them. There had already been a disturbance to-day outside the Slavakian Embassy; was there going to be another one? Was it worth risking missing a good pro-grame on the TV? Which would be more exciting tonight, real life or the substitute? It was a vexing choice.

At Unic House in Aldersgrove, Miss Thorne had told no one of Mr. Messiter's phone call. He had asked her to keep it to herself after she had passed it on to the Yard.

But the girl at P.B.X. had heard most of the conversation, and had kept the line audible while Miss Thorne was talking to Whitehall. This girl had a boy friend who was an amateur photographer and who took his camera wherever he went. Sometimes he was paid as much as five pounds for a good picture, if one of the papers wanted it. Last year, just after they'd first met, he had made his biggest scoop—fifty guineas for one picture! She hadn't believed him until he showed her the cheque. And all the picture showed was Dolores del Mar falling down the steps of Compton's Hotel. People must be mad, to pay that much for the picture of an ordinary little accident. What would they pay for one of ex-King Nikolas coming down the steps of the Embassy? Oodles! She rang up her boy friend.

Her boy friend never told a soul, but splashed out and took a taxi—you'd miss a scoop if you piddled about on buses, and this one was going to be the Picture of the Year! He asked the taxi-driver to pull the stops out, and tumbled out of the taxi without waiting for change, his camera at the ready. Ten minutes later the driver, dipping his moustache into a cup of tea round the corner at Victoria, said to his mates: "What's on at the Embassy, then?" No one, these days, called it the Slavakian Embassy. You knew which one they meant—the one in the news. Only this morning they'd smashed a window there.

One of the taxi-driver's mates had a brother who was a caretaker in the Square; so when he began cruising round again for fares he stopped for a minute to talk to his brother, who was standing on the basement steps watching the small crowd of people round the group of cameramen.

Within an hour of the telephone call to Unic House a couple of hundred people stood in the Square, along the pavement opposite the Embassy, and special police were being drafted in, to keep order. Just before eight o'clock a mounted policeman walked his horse round the square, and as he came past the crowd of people one of the cameras flashed, because a crowd always makes a good picture especially with a mountie there to give it focus and drama.

A few minutes later the first pickpocket turned up, and started work.

Louise had not stopped shivering since the doors of the Conference Room had been closed twenty minutes ago. There was nothing she could have done to help if she had been allowed to remain in the room, but she would not have suffered the merciless torture of her own imagination that now gave her no peace.

The Conference Room was at the top of the main stairs, and near-by was a small mezzanine alcove with a table and two little chairs. Here she waited. Two of the Embassy staff were in the hall below, resident footmen with emergency orders from Major Bell. Another stood at the top of the next flight, and she was constantly within sight of all three.

Kosek had brought her brandy and hot milk, seeing how pale she was and knowing her love for the King. With Kosek came his personal guard, the dull-eyed country soldier with the bulge of a revolver in his jacket. He had the mien of a born poacher, his innocence feigned by habit. The cloth of his pocket was worn on the outside, where his hand had brushed so often to reassure him of his power.

"He is my friend," Kosek told Louise in the man's hearing. "He has me for a pet monkey and takes me about." He tapped the man's pocket. "Here is the string." Then he said in French, which he knew the man did not understand: "They are still in conference?"

"Yes, Kosek. It is only twenty minutes yet." Twenty-one, really, by her watch. She knew the face of her watch better than her own, now. At this hour last night she had been taken by Praggart to the house in Richmond, and had there met the King. In the last twenty-four hours time had become meaningless in the stifling vacuum of captivity; now the seconds spoke, each voicing a threat.

"We must wait, Ma'm'selle. We can only wait." He stood with the empty tray hanging from his hand, keeping vigil with her. It had been like this in the Palace when he had waited on the music gallery, looking down through the marble pilasters at Imgrir Szados. But then Szados had been kept outside the door by young Captain Vralmar's revolver; now Szados was inside and the King's men were all disarmed. What chance was there now? You developed a quicker nose for death in a palace than a cottage; it was an intimate visitor. This house had the smell; but you could do nothing; it was the place of execution and the time to cry a protest was gone.

The lady was shivering, still. A child, no older than Elsina would be now.

"We must not lose hope, *Duenaczina*. Perhaps they will reach an agreement."

"Perhaps they will." She looked into the kind brown eyes and tried to see what was there. Pity, and patience. Was there more? What would this old man do if there were a chance to save the King? He had thrown himself across the path of the bullet, or tried to, when Nikolas had been wounded; but there were so many bullets lying cold in the dark metallic wombs, ready for birth and the quick dazzling flight of the mayfly. If the old man got in the way of one there were others and he would die on the floor already valueless to the living when the King's turn came. There would be nothing anyone could do.

"If you should need me, *Duenaczina*, I shall be near. Now my master is impatient to take me for another walk." He smiled to the dull-eyed assassin. "He keeps monkeys in his native land, he tells me. He misses them now. He tried to bring two of them to England, but there was an argument at the Customs because they had not been cleared for medical inspection. A steward on the ship had to take charge of them, and my friend is very sad—but I give him great pleasure. Watch, *Duenaczina*." He made a realistic show of scratching himself for fleas, and the guard grinned at him, nodding, his hand ready at his pocket so that if his delight should leave him unwary his hand would work for him by habit.

Louise watched them go down the stairs, Kosek first with her empty glass on the tray, his friend after him, calling softly to him: *"Puchintsi, puchintsi mei!"*—calling him Monkey, my monkey . . .

Their footsteps faded. The three footmen did not move. The doors of the Conference Room did not open. The long stone flight of the stairs crumbled and the dust flew in clouds while her father shouted; then they were whole again, but the ground trembled with her body while the watch on her wrist ticked out its threats.

Pray the doors will open . . . but when they do . . . Pray they'll be closed for ever . . . but then this agony will never end . . .

She and the three footmen made no sound; they were enclosed in the intimacy of shared silence, until the doors of the Conference Room suddenly opened.

CHAPTER XXIII

Ex-King Nikolas sat at one end of the long table, President Szados at the other. To the right of Nikolas sat Baron Angelitri, to the left Sofi Mikayan. Then there was a gap between the chairs. Beyond the gap were the three Embassy clerks, the Secretary, Counsellor and Ambassador. President Szados had more pieces on the chequer-board, while only two defended the King's position. He was in check. These were the thoughts of Angelitri as he listened to the President.

"It is plain that our position is inviolable and yours indefensible. We are however able, because of our strength, to make concessions and a proposal. This proposal is that you should resume the throne of Slavakia and the title of King."

Angelitri felt a muscle twitch in his face. It was as much as he had ever shown of his thoughts even during the most tumultuous sessions of Parliament in Drovnik. He knew that Sofi Mikayan was staring across at him but he would not meet her eyes. He prayed she would say nothing.

Szados said: "At the outset we should like to hear whether this basic proposal would be agreeable to you."

Angelitri didn't look at the King. Nikolas was not, first, a diplomatist, for all his kingcraft; but his answer was admirably calm and the Baron delighted in each word.

"It is in any case my intention to resume the throne, should God spare my life."

"Then it augurs well." There was no expression, ever, on the face of Szados. It had been said in the Palace, during the days when his rise to Minister pointed the future and sounded the first soft alarms, that he had been born with paralysed face muscles. Other and more colourful theories were that since he possessed no heart there was nothing to show in his face; and that he had been delivered by breach-birth with his face inside out, so that only he could ever know when he smiled or frowned.

Watching him, Angelitri could learn nothing, though he had learned a little even from the many poker faces among his opponents. Szados was a broken man, a victim of the revolution he had failed to prevent even by the bloody purges and the ruthless massacres he had launched on the second day. But he could not have been sent here expressly to offer Nikolas the throne. He would have refused such a mission.

"There would be certain attendant conditions."

Of course. Conditions. But acceptable? Would he and Sofi really live to see Nikolas walk out of this house with pride left, and a future? It was an odd thought, because Angelitri had already added a few codicils to his will and asked Major Bell to dispatch them as an act of courtesy to the dead.

"The situation," Szados went on in his mechanical tones, "is that the world is at the edge of total war. It has been brought to this point by the Slavakian rebellion, which is still being fought out. The Union, whose interests are strongly involved in the affairs of my country, and who is prepared to stamp out these insurgents before they bring worse harm to the people, is in a position to overwhelm these hostile fascist elements by superior force of arms. But it would prolong the bloodshed and bring suffering upon the innocent population whose loyalty to the Government is unbroken."

You are a fool, Angelitri said with his eyes to Szados. Double-talk was for Press conferences, not private parley.

"It may be that the capitalist West would consider such a step on the part of the Union as sufficient excuse for the launching of the nuclear war that occupies so much of its thought. Hence the world is in grave danger. The Union is quite prepared to countenance such an effect of its peaceful determination to restore order in Slavakia, and to defend itself, and to out-obliterate the instigators. But we know what this will mean to mankind."

The small eyes looked out of the shrunken head, surveying the fate of mankind with no pity in them, no horror, no expression at all. It is worse, thought Sofi Mikayan, that this pig should show nothing than show hate.

"Under the friendly guidance of the Union, I have therefore evolved a compromise. If you choose to reject it, you will also choose to ignore the danger to which all people of the earth are now exposed. You will be party to their condemnation. We do not envy you your responsibility, yet we should not have approached you if we felt that you were incapable of safeguarding world peace by a willingness to make concessions, as we are doing."

Through one of the windows, Angelitri could see a street-lamp beginning to glow; but he wasn't a man for symbols and portents. There were lamps glowing in Drovnik now, with bodies swinging beneath. A light could lead kindly; it could also be a candle for the dead.

"Our proposal in more detail takes this form: you are invited to bring the revolution to an immediate end by broadcasting a message from London to the Slavakian People. You would inform them that after conference with me, as head of the present Government, it has been decided that a form of monarchy is to be reinstituted in your name and that you will return to the throne as soon as order is restored in the country. This is our concession, freely granted in the cause of peace. For your part, you would be required to accept the terms of a limited rule."

Angelitri leaned back an inch in his chair. So the lamp outside meant nothing; it was a gibbet for mankind. Nikolas would never accept the status of puppet.

"Your rule would be limited as follows. You would appoint as Head of the Army the present Minister of War and would have no authority over him in any state of emergency. You would leave undisturbed the right of the Treasury to issue money and to order estimates. You would be required to consult your Prime Minister before exercising the right of pardon, amnesty and the reduction of sentences. The modification of the Organic Laws, the appointment of ministers and under-secretaries of State would be made by royal decrees, but countersigned by the President of the Council of Ministers, who will have complete authority to regulate the affairs of the State." He laid a hand gently on the table. "There are no other conditions."

A minute went by. In the street outside, voices could be heard, the quiet murmur of many voices; and Angelitri was for an instant startled to think that his mind was slipping ito the spheres of illusion: these were the distant voices of the Slavakian people, gathered to plead with Nikolas for their salvation. Then above the voices came the brittle clop of hooves, and he saw the ghost of Starita, the white mare ridden to death on the steps of the Palace. He was wakened to reality by the King's answer.

"I cannot accept your proposal."

As if the President had not heard, he said: "It is held by some that although the fanaticism of the revolutionaries has been increased by your journey to London and your seeming intention of supporting their endeavours, they would continue to wage their misguided battle with undiminished fervour if by some chance you were to die. But we do not believe that these people need a martyr. We believe that the news of your death would halt them through loss of heart. If therefore our proposal is unacceptable to you, it would be necessary in the interests of world peace to arrange this incident and send immediate news of it."

Nikolas sat with one hand resting on the table. Sofi could not look in his direction. Much of her anxiety was spared by a decision she had taken a long time ago: rather than submit to insupportable grief she intended to prolong her life no further than it was required to find the means to end it, once Nikolas was dead. This was reasonable, since it was grief she feared, more than his death.

"Murder is essential to martyrdom," said Nikolas. "You stand the risk of misjudging whether or not my people need a martyr. If they do, you'll make one."

"We stand that risk. For you there is certainty."

"I cannot accept the terms."

On the ceiling came a faint white flash of light and the Baron looked upwards. He could not think what had made it. Perhaps the lights of a car in the Square; but it had been a very white flash. He could still hear the voices and now they seemed louder. Could it be that a lioness had whelped in the market-place? He watched Sofi's face for a moment. Poor Sofi; she looked already dead. He had not told her what Major Bell had confessed to him. 'If unhappily it becomes necessary to prevent the ex-King from making an attempt to return to Slavakia without agreeing to our terms, it would be arranged as suicide. He will be known to have taken his life, distressed by his inability to rise to the call of his people. It would therefore be necessary also that you, Miss Mikayan and the servant should naturally choose to accompany him, in all loyalty. Otherwise you may later try to ferment the people again by accusations of murder against the Government. I am sorry, but you know better than I that political warfare also claims its casualities.' It was then that the Baron had written his few codicils and entrusted their dispatch to the Major.

Angelitri did not lack stamina; he loved life; he had a loving wife; their two daughters were achieving brilliant success in music now in Paris. But as soon as he had known that terms were to be offered to Nikolas he had suspected those terms to be acceptable only to a weak man. Being strong, Nikolas would be likely to condemn them all. The Baron accepted this, and could wish for no more dear an executioner.

But Sofi didn't know. Perhaps she would not mind.

President Szados spoke to one of the clerks, who began placing copies of the memorandum along the table. It was the written proposal outlined by Szados. When the clerk returned to his chair the President said to no one:

"Tell me what is happening outside the building."

One of the guards came away from the window.

"There is a crowd forming, sir."

"How big is it?"

"A large one, sir, with a police cordon."

Again a faint white flash touched the ceiling and was reflected in the polished table.

"There are photographs being taken. Of what?"

"The building, sir, I think."

"Go down and find out why the crowd is there and then report to me." Before the man had left the room, Szados went on without the slightest change of tone: "I am surprised that you are willing to accept death so easily, when by living and working for your people under our guidance you could be of such worth to them and could remove from the whole world the immediate danger of atomic war."

"I am not as confident as you that the Union is prepared to instigate total war for the sake of crushing a single revolution——"

"It would not require nuclear assault. The West could not, however, oppose our aims militarily without the use of nuclear weapons. Hence the danger."

"Nor am I prepared," the ex-King went on deliberately, "to betray my people by acting as a figurehead while sanctioning foreign rule. Since this is your proposal and since I and my advisers are sitting here at the gun-point there is no question of compromise or bargaining. I cannot accept the terms and therefore I must abstain from further parley. I have no confidence in your respect for courtesies to the dead, but formally request that my remains be buried in the soil of Slavakia."

He stood up. Sofi Mikayan uttered a sound and then Baron Angelitri rose. He did not make the mistake of addressing either Szados or Nikolas.

One of the Embassy clerks pushed his chair back nervously and apparently in deference to the ex-King but was motioned to remain seated by the Counsellor.

The Ambassador gazed sadly along the table.

Outside, a man in the crowd was shouting something but the words were not clear. The feet of a horse clattered suddenly and there were flashes again on the ceiling.

These, thought Angelitri, must make do for the thunders and lightnings of a dying king, perhaps of a dying world.

Traffic through the Square had been diverted through Elton Street. Taxi left their fares in the side-turnings and then had difficulty in making their way out again.

A man had been arrested for causing a disturbance by brandishing a twelve-bore at the doors of the Embassy and striking a policeman with the butt; he was carried into a Black Maria sober but infuriated and still loudly demanding that 'Szados and his rabble of Red bastards' should be brought out and shot.

The crowd was estimated at three thousand by a quarter to nine, and the police cordon was now doubled. It was proof of faith in mere rumour that no one doubted that the ex-King of Slavakia was inside the Embassy building, for no one could have said with any confidence that they had learned of this from reliable sources. Yet of the few faces to have appeared at the Embassy windows during the last half an hour none was recognisable as that of the ex-King's. Had he appeared even for an instant he would have been recognised, for his likeness had been the subject of newspaper pictures since he landed in London.

Many in the crowd were Slavakian-born refugees from the last war. They had besieged Unic House all day for news of the revolution and the ex-King's whereabouts; when the word came by its devious routes that Nikolas was at the Embassy they hurried to the Square. But no one knew in what exact circumstances the ex-King was now placed. Only the most embittered believed that he was entering into some kind of negotiation with President Szados, who had arrived only a few hours ago.

Nothing was known at Unic House. During the afternoon an emergency conference was held by programme chiefs under the authority of the Top Directive. After consultation with officials of the Foreign Office it had been decided to extend the bare announcements in Slavakian and to move into line with Foreign Office spokesmen. If any of the Unic organisers knew exactly how much or how little pressure was applied by the Foreign Office to the broadcasting policies, not even their close friends knew their names. The fact was simply that Unic Radio began putting out theory instead of news. A broadcast went out soon after four o'clock to the effect that it was known by certain members of the British Government that ex-King Nikolas was 'quite safe' and 'under no form of duress', and that it 'would appear that private treaty between the ex-King and the Slavakian Government, prior to international talks, was not out of the question'.

Slavakian-born staff at Unic House asked for the exact source of these items and were left unsatisfied. Following the first such broadcast, when the announcers had time in which to question their content, Dr. Krosmitolf and Nadreanu declared their intention of refusing scripts whose content was without official source. They both remained in the canteen when asked to carry out their routine duties in the studios, and were joined by several others.

Soon afterwards Kristov Czinitri resigned his post and was joined by Andrey Turocz, who left his script on the studio table and quietly switched off the microphone before a substitute could be prepared. He said to Miss Thorne in her office afterwards: "Are the Democracies for or against our revolution? Do they want the King to be free or remain a prisoner while the revolution runs its course?"

"I've no information from anywhere, Mr. Turocz——"

"But we are still asked to read scripts that pretend to convey information!"

"We receive them from Chief Editors, who——"

"And who are the Chief Editors? The people we know, or the policy-makers at the Foreign Office? I tell you, Miss Thorne——" He leaned over her desk until she had one shoulder pressed against the wall behind her—"when we were fighting the Panzer divisions and the Luftwaffe, confused and deafened and blinded by the explosions around us, we used our secret radio sets whenever we could find one or steal one or make one—even in the prison camps, even while we waited for transportation and the firing-squads—and we were able to hear the B.B.C. transmissions, and believe in them. And I have never been told, since then, that those broadcasts were inaccurate, deceitful or distorted, or that they cost a single life when a word of information could save it!"

He took up a pile of programme layouts from Miss Thorne's desk and ripped them down the middle. "But this stuff? We are no longer a free voice in the world, but an instrument of policy." His eyes were bright with his excitement and Miss Thorne thought: 'Never expect control from a foreigner. They lack our training.' Her whole being revolted against excitement, the disorder of the torn papers now on the floor, these bright foreign eyes of the man who had slipped from his pigeon-hole and was at large in the regulated air-conditioned and cubicalised edifice of offices, the human building named Beatrice Thorne. "An instrument of policy," said Andrey Turocz, "controlled by propaganda experts whose aim it is to feed the ill-informed with the correct mental drug for the day! Unic Radio, Miss Thorne, has turned from a valuable ally of freedom into a bloody liar!"

He joined his friends in the canteen and repeated most of this in Slavakian. They remained drinking coffee until the service went on strike against the noise; and when the rumour came that ex-King Nikolas was in the Embassy they piled into taxis and drove to the Square.

They were here now. Bjelik Turocz had been collected on the way and stood with his brother looking up at the building that had once sheltered the representative of their King, and now imprisoned the King himself.

"We will storm the doors!" shouted Mr. Turocz, and was already trying to force his way through the police cordon before his brother dragged him back.

"You are not in Slavakia, Bjelik! For God's sake——"

"My King is here! Then I am in Slavakia!"

They pulled him to the rear fringe of the crowd so that he should not be arrested.

The man came back to the Conference Room, passing Louise in the mezzanine alcove. She stopped him and asked: "Why has the crowd gathered outside?"

He darted a glance at the footmen and then said softly and quickly: "They have heard Nikolas is here." He went into the room and closed the doors against her.

It was only a few minutes before they opened for the second time. President Szados came out immediately and was followed by the Ambassador and his staff. She saw Major Bell and went to the doorway.

"What has happened?"

He seemed to take a moment's pleasure in hesitating, his yellow eyes regarding her in a kind of secrecy as if he were invisible to her and looking out from hiding.

"The conference is over, Miss Cameron." Again he waited, forcing her to ask:

"What's been decided?"

"The ex-King has decided to reject the President's terms."

His eyes savoured her shock.

She realised she had stopped shivering. The waiting was over. "May I see him?"

"You may."

Nikolas was listening to Baron Angelitri and did not look up. She stood behind his chair so that she shouldn't cause an interruption. Sofi Mikayan sat rigidly with the calm of a nun.

"If they really believed the news of your death would halt the revolution then they would have turned to assassination before now. They need your co-operation. They sent the President himself to beg for it. Your decision has not been accepted, or he wouldn't have granted this quarter-hour in which to reconsider. When he returns he'll still oppose your decision."

Nikolas stared down the long bright table. "Yes, Petrik. He can threaten to shoot me, if I persist in my decision to be shot." He turned his head and looked into Angelitri's eyes. "Don't you see that we are equally powerless, Szados and I? But he came here to force my hand, and he's failed, and I've won. You mustn't worry too much. Life's not serious when it nears the end."

"I wish Your Majesty were more in the mood to raise a genie. There's time left."

"Fifteen minutes. Less. Time isn't enough to break open a deadlock." He looked at Sofi and would have given her a word of comfort, but she stared into the air, quite lost in her desolation. He said to Angelitri, "If I accept the throne on these terms I compromise my honour and betray my people. If I accept the throne on these terms and later try to reject them I shall invite immediate assassination and the good will be undone; let's not pretend that my every act as king won't be rigorously disciplined by the foreign rule behind the throne. If I refuse the throne on these terms, the news of my death is to be used as a weapon against my people in their struggle. Whether this will sway the wind, we can't say; but since my death is certain anyway—because as a free exile I would be a constant danger now that it's known my people need me and that I'm willing—it might as well come now. If they need a martyr I shan't die in vain. So my proposal, Petrik, is much more workable than theirs."

Angelitri sat with his great shoulders hunched. The King must out-match him in this argument, simply because there was no real answer to these truths. But given a little time . . . even these few minutes.

"If by your decision to let the revolution run its course the Union is forced to throw in an army of actual invasion it could raise an issue between East and West to be settled only by global war. If I were the keeper of the King's conscience, I would advise——"

"Petrik, your wits are failing! Is that an argument? That the people of a small Balkan kingdom should remain slaves for ever so that the rest of the world shouldn't blow itself up? If that's the stage mankind has reached it's ready for extinction." He looked up as Kosek came into the room. The old man was grey of face and there was sweat beading his brow.

"Does Your Majesty require anything?"

How many times had this man come to him with this same question. . . . It was asked out of love as much as duty.

"Only your blessing, Kosi."

"Then is it all——" He had to draw breath into his chest; the few words had exhausted him; the word 'finished' was too grievous to say aloud.

Louise touched the ex-King's shoulder and he turned his head with a jerk, startled, prepared to receive whatever death he must. His face softened. "Louise . . . I didn't know you were here."

"I'll always be here."

A flicker of light crossed the ceiling. For a few minutes there had been voices singing quietly, and now Angelitri turned his face to the windows.

"What is it, Petrik?"

"The Anthem, sir."

They listened to the singing. Sofi sat with her eyes closed and her hands clasped together on the table, both tears and prayers soundless. These voices were coming from across the years, and it was not easy to bear them.

"Where are you going, Kosi?"

"To bring cheer for Your Majesty." He left them.

"Louise, go with him."

"No, please let——"

"When we have talked again with the President, I shall come to find you. Be close." He released her hand. "Petrik, go and inform the President that I await his return."

Sofi did not move while the Baron was away. Nikolas did not wish to speak to her, knowing that she was in prayer.

There would be other tears, for a while; but he had no mother, and his son was too busy farming his orange-groves to spare more time than dutiful grief required. La Contessa . . . she would miss him, perhaps console herself in a convent until her blood stirred again. Others, and others, but he was indispensable to none of them. His people . . . if they could be told that he had died for them

278

it might give them the added strength of rage and turn the tide. It would be a thought for the journey.

The doors opened again and Petrik came back. Behind him were the others. Nikolas had time to murmur: "They look like defeated men, and so they are."

Szados sat down and the Ambassador and his staff followed. The singing in the Square had stopped.

"You have been given the chance of reconsidering your decision. We trust you have taken full advantage."

"The advantage was already mine. By my decision the object of your mission has failed, and I abide by it. I reject your proposal upon every point, and that is my final word."

In a moment Szados said in his toneless voice: "You realise that by this you forfeit your life?"

"I do."

Szados sat without moving, his small eyes focused on the table a foot in front of him. The Ambassador looked sadly at the window through his spectacles and merely turned his head when Sofi Mikayan collapsed. One of the secretaries went to her and Angelitri helped him.

"Take the woman out," Szados intoned.

Two of the guards lifted her and Bell opened the doors. Angelitri sat down again, saying: "She'll be spared the rest, Your Majesty."

When the doors were closed again Szados called Major Bell to his side and asked him: "You have made certain provision against the failure of this parley?"

"I have, sir."

"You will allow the ex-King a few minutes in which to speak with his companions and then have him taken to whatever place has been decided upon, and there conclude the matter."

CHAPTER XXIV

The singing voices died away against the windows of the mezzanine alcove where Louise waited. There must be many Slavakians down there; but the entrance doors of the house were shut and the two footmen were on guard.

Kosek had passed them and they had not stopped him. She wondered what had happened to his guard, the little dull-eyed assassin. Kosek looked ill, or just stricken in his poor mind; he had gone down the stairs slowly like a sleep-walker.

When he came back to the hall she saw him show something to the two footmen, and then one of them tried to throw himself upon him, but the gun fired, shocking the silence, and the man fell. She didn't believe what she saw, but went to the head of the stairs, drawn closer to the mirage. Kosek ordered the other footman to open the doors, and he was obeying. Kosek hurried him, pointing down at the body of the one who had tried to attack him, and the doors swung open.

She could see part of the roadway and the pavement, the feet of standing people, the legs of a horse, a sudden flicker of white light as Kosek prodded the man outside.

The crowd was silent; the people did not know what was happening—some of them had heard the shot and now they saw the gun in the old man's hand. He kept his aim on the footman and began calling to the crowd in Slavakian while she listened. The doors of the Conference Room opened and she saw Bell coming out.

Kosek was shouting: "Slavakians! Our King is here! He is in great danger! Who will save him?"

She could see their feet, motionless. The square was quiet. Bell stared down to the doorway and took out his revolver as Kosek kept on shouting.

"Slavakians! The doors are open to you! The King is——"

"Kosek!" she screamed.

Bell fired three times and the old man pitched against the doorpost.

A sound came from the crowd, a kind of grunt. An old man had been butchered in front of them and they must react; but they voiced only acknowledgement, not knowing whether he had died for the things they loved or the things they hated, not knowing even who he was. Then as their shock receded they remembered what he had said: that their King was here, and these doors were open.

On the edge of the crowd Mr. Turocz was shouting and there were people trying to get out of his way as he plunged through them. *"Salvinji Nikolas! Salvinji en Ryincz!"* He fought his way through them, shouting for them to save his king. Someone tried to hold him, simply because he was disorderly and they feared disorder; but he pushed them over and the others were caught off their balance; a woman became frightened and began a fluttering scream that brought a pocket of silence among all the other voices until people grew angry and shouted at Mr. Turocz. Once he fell, but sprang up again to scramble under the belly of a police horse while the rider tried to use his truncheon. *"Salvinji Nikolas!"* He broke free and was running across the open space towards the Embassy.

Part of the crowd had made a gap in the police cordon and its edge became ragged, breaking and surging between the uniformed constables who were striking with their truncheons when there was room to swing them; they fell back, driven and shouldered by the groups of Slavakians who now came together in a body and ran forward, their own massed momentum pitching some of them down and tripping those behind. As their vanguard reached the steps of the building, the few constables stationed there joined hands and moved forward to meet them; but even if they had carried machine-guns instead of truncheons they would not have halted the stampede. Many were shouting with Turocz, bearing along the King's name as an invisible banner above their heads.

Vaquier, a few moments ago standing quietly beside Messiter in the evening calm of the Square, was tugging at his arm and shouting: "That guy—the guy they shot—who's the old guy they shot?" But he lost hold of Messiter's arm and had to follow him through the break in the cordon as the people behind them closed in and widened the gap, their jostle quickening to a run across the roadway. They tripped against fallen men, but kept their feet.

A dog ran yelping among the legs.

"Messiter! Who was the guy they——"

Hooves rang, iron on flint, sparking as horses wheeled. A blue police-van was nosing forward and trying to block the pavement below the steps until men clambered on to the front wings; an elbow went through the windscreen and it shattered and turned to snow; constables dropped from the rear doors but were pressed back before they could find their footing.

"*Salvinji Nikolas!*"

A man waded through the mob with a child on his shoulders, unable to force his passage with his arms; the child stared across the heads of the crowd, too frightened to cry, its small white face a ball to be tossed along the tide of people and its eyes committing to memory this day it would never forget. Its father did not shout, but saved his breath for the long journey of a dozen yards against the living barricade. He reached the swaying police-van and perched the child on its roof—"Stay there . . . you'll be all right . . . you just stay there while I go and find Mum. . . ."

The child clung with small hooked hands, crying at last as it saw the biggest man in the world turn away to be lost in the sea of strangers.

"*Salvinji en Ryincz!*"

A cloud of starlings drifted upwards towards the Embassy roof as if borne there by the rising shout. Its echo circled the Square.

"Hey, Messiter! Wait for me!"

Messiter could not hear. He was struggling up the steps of the Embassy. The doors were still open. The first few Slavakians to reach them had knocked aside the footman before he could swing them shut, and now the tiled hall was filled with their voices and the storm of feet.

Shots came into the throng from above them, a flicker of bullets from the top of the stairs. Men went on climbing, a few dropping, their hands dragging at the banisters and the shoulders of their friends. Pressed against the wall, Messiter saw a face spin across his field of vision as a man toppled and was buried among them—Dr. Krosmitolf, his big-brimmed hat sailing off upside down, a sun-boat for his departing soul. Plaster flew from the wall and the deflected bullet picked a green diamond out of the coloured glass above the doors. Then Messiter saw Louise.

She was at the top of the stairs. Bell's revolver was empty and she was clinging on to him, trying to stop him going for the safety of the Conference Room. Two guards had come out and were sending down a fan of calculated fire from their guns, so that the press on the stairs began thinning as men were hit and others sank down for shelter. The Major threw Louise against the wall of the mezzanine alcove and lurched into the Conference Room.

"Louise! Get out of sight!" Messiter shouted.

She wouldn't be able to identify him among the human débris on the stairs; he was part of it, his living face close to Krosmitolf's dead one; but she might be warned by his voice.

Something hit him on the shoulder and paralysed his arm—a man's fist or a butting head from the direction of the main doors where men were surging inwards as thick and close as a forest on the march. They would not be halted by the few revolvers at the stair-head or the heaping bodies on the stairs; they would make this march with their own dead for a road, and at the end meet the outnumbered enemy. Messiter was already going down under the weight of shoulders, so that when a bullet dropped a man beside him he found his feet and took the chance, lifting the body of Dr. Krosmitolf and using it as a shield as he climbed the stairs, treading on stone and the soft uncertain steps of the dead, reeling sometimes against the banisters, but keeping his shield always in front of him. There was no danger of falling back: the men behind him were a hundred thick from the doors to the head of the stairs.

Sometimes he shouted: "Louise! Get somewhere safe!" He could no longer see her and there was no answer.

A crash came and for a moment he thought the staircase was collapsing, but there were no shouts. His feet were still on firm stone, and now they carried him stumbling across the flat of the mezzanine floor. The shooting had stopped. The leaders had forced the doors of the room on the right where the enemy had been making their stand; splintered timber fell across his head; he dropped Krosmitolf's body and went through the doorway and was halted among the pack of standing men.

Louise was pressed against the wall inside the doors, but he didn't see her. She was watching the King, but could not get to him.

Two of the remaining guards were reloading their revolvers by the windows. Angelitri was on his feet; the Ambassador and his staff had thrown back their chairs and stood as if frozen in the silence that was drawing through the room and across the stair-head. Without a voice or any signal the throng of men sensed that their assault had been halted of its own volition, and they were together in the presence of a kind of victory. The only sound came from the wounded and dying.

Nikolas had not moved, nor Szados; they were still facing across the length of the table.

The two guards were leaving the windows and Bell shouted to them: *"The King first!"* But the pale dumb boy was already behind Nikolas, and the blade sprang in the air. It struck the chair-back, deflecting as Angelitri's arms went out from their great shoulders. In his rage he broke the boy like a stick and flung him down. The guards began firing, but there was no room in which to draw back; the weight of men crushed them to the wall and there were no more shots.

Voices broke out from the staircase, asking to know what was happening. They were answered by those in the room.

Men jammed the doorway, their eyes bright. They had come a long way to this house, from political prisons and concentration-camps, from burned homes and their children's grave-sides; and they had thought that the years had staled this blood of theirs that was suddenly singing.

Those in the room grew silent, seeing the King; and soon the voices of those on the stairs and in the hallway below died away.

"I thank you all."

They made way for Nikolas as he moved from his chair. Angelitri asked them: "Who is your leader?" They did not know. A man was shot, they said, on the steps outside, and he had told them the King was here, and so they had come into the house.

"First see to your friends who are wounded. Take them down and ask for ambulances."

Szados got up and looked about him, his eyes shrunk into his face. Seeing one of the men holding a revolver, he made towards him, and when he was facing him he straightened his body and stood erect, and then raised his arm with the fist clenched and seemed about to strike the man; so the man fired into him, and the range was so short that a ring of black powder appeared on the silk shirt.

The faces were startled. A man moved, but Baron Angelitri said: "Leave him. See to your friends first."

People stood in groups on the staircase and along the hall. Camera-men still flashed a bulb now and then, shooting through the open entrance doors. The earlier pictures of what was already called the Embassy Revolution had been raced back to Fleet Street an hour ago and were nearing print; but so far no one had got the picture of the day: Nikolas.

Louise had pushed her way through the crowd to the far end of the Conference Room. When she had seen Nikolas sitting there, unharmed, she had just leaned with her back to the wall and closed her eyes, numb with relief. Messiter had found her there. He had come in while the dead and wounded were being taken down the stairs and into the packed street.

"Hello, Louise . . ."

She opened her eyes.

It was such a calm face to see, a quiet voice to hear. "Tony. . . ."

"You all right?" He didn't touch her.

"Yes. Oh, God, it's wonderful to see you!"

"It is?"

"There've been so many strangers—strange faces and strange languages. How did the news get out?"

"News?"

"That we were in the Embassy."

"Someone saw the Mikayan woman's red hair at a window, and took the hint. Is Nikolas badly hurt?"

"A bullet in his hand."

"We want him to broadcast. Kristov and some others have gone back to U.H. to plan the programme."

"A message to his people?"

"To all people. You may not know the situation. The revolutionaries are forcing the pace out there. Half Drovnik's in their hands and there's a Union armoured division coming in from the Carpathian Command with special orders to break it up. It's deliberate invasion now. But there's a chance, if the people can hear the King's own voice. They can still show us all that they have a future and mean to fight for it, not just that they're desperate for freedom and mean to die for it." He was looking across

287

at the ex-King, who was talking rapidly with Angelitri. "There's Slavakia's future. The people have got to be told. They think he's dead, or helpless, or not interested."

She led him through the groups of people. Angelitri was still talking quietly. ". . . And then one of the Embassy chauffeurs told me they'd found the body of one of the guards in a pantry not far from the main passage to the kitchens. He had been run through with a meat-knife from behind."

"That was Kosi's guard—the small one?"

"Yes."

Nikolas nodded. It had been the first thing Kosi had ever harmed in his life, man or animal. It must have gone against all his instincts, violating the gentleness that was his whole personality. No wonder he had looked ill, knowing what he had just done, and what he would have to do before the doors could be opened. "We will find out where they've taken his body. If we go back to our country, he will go with us. We owe that old man our lives, Petrik."

He turned to see Louise. Her face was pale, but her eyes shone. For a moment he held his hand against hers. She would see so little of this man, the father of her first child, before he went away. She would not want to follow; he could belong to no one person.

She introduced Tony Messiter, who said: "I've arranged for a police car to drive you to Unic House. We think it's urgent that this news should reach your people in your own words and your own voice. It may be that if you delay, certain political factions in London representing the Western Democracies would try to dissuade you from going back to Slavakia or even speaking to your people. At Unic House itself there's a division of thought, but a group of loyal Slavakian-born readers and technicians are waiting for you and will see that the broadcast is transmitted, if you decide to speak." He watched the pale contemplative face. "I hope, sir, that you will."

Just after eleven o'clock the ex-King came down the main staircase of the Embassy and was facing a barrage of flashlight before reaching the doors. At the request of the newly-appointed temporary chargé d'affaires, Baron Angelitri, policemen had formed a double cordon reaching from the interior hall to the roadway where the police car was waiting.

Behind Nikolas came Angelitri, Louise and Messiter. Sofi Mikayan was not yet well, but had been told the news.

As Nikolas appeared on the steps a sound came from the crowd. It was a cheer, but it was not loud, and did not last long. Not long ago a man had been shot down before their eyes, and since that time, ambulances had taken away some twenty casualties, seven of whom were known to be dead. And in the crowd were people who felt unsure of what would happen now that the Embassy had been seized from the Union. It would hearten the Slavakians who were fighting now in their cities along the Duna; but it would also provoke their enemies into blatant slaughter. If the West were forced to send an ultimatum, its warning backed by nuclear arms, and if it were ignored, these could be the last few days of peace that anyone now living would know.

Nikolas paused on the steps and looked up at the flag that had been put there in place of the other, which had been dragged down by people in the crowd and burned in the centre of the Square. Seeing the ex-King raise his eyes to it, the men in the roadway sent up another cheer—a short, fierce sound of satisfaction—and single voices called out to him as the police cordon struggled to keep its un-broken line.

Among the faces, Louise recognised only one. He was a short man in an overcoat. He saw her and smiled. He was Mr. Turocz.

There was gunfire on the hills along the south side of the Duna. Shells had been falling on the outskirts of the city since early afternoon, and many buildings were on fire. Tanks crawled through the rubble, trying to rejoin their units, but in the tide of smoke that was billowing in from the oil refinery they were lost and blind.

A party of youths marched by the ruins of the Radio Building on their way to join in the hunt for ammunition. Bullets were scarce; food was hard to find; in the south section of the city, typhus had broken out.

In a cellar near the barracks a group of people had gathered, and a man at the top of the steps was calling into the street, telling others to come. He could still hear the faint voice as it spoke to those in the cellar below him.

"... And will be brought back to Slavakia for trial before you all. President Imgrir Szados is dead by his own hand. His mission has failed. Above the Embassy in London, the true flag of Slavakia hangs, as it does, I well know, from so many of the buildings of Drovnik, where you are in hard battle with the enemy."

A messenger went past, dodging a patter of shot that was coming from the top of the telephone exchange. The man called to him, telling him to come and listen to the radio, but the runner said that he had no time.

"But it's the King! Nikolas!"

The runner halted among the debris and stared at him with bloodshot eyes.

Across the main railway track, men were mounting an anti-tank gun. Rumours had come that seven hundred tanks were rolling over the frontier at Dus Harkrevinj and were heading for the city with infantry divisions. Most of the ammunition-crates near the gun were empty, and the crew had started to pile them against the gun to help the camouflage.

A child was running from the shelter of a signal-box on the railway, calling to the gun-crew, her small voice shrilling in the dark. Many children ran crying in these streets, their mothers lost, their fathers turned into unrecognisable shapes that meant nothing any more. The gun-crew called a few words of comfort, saying that they had food for her, biscuits.

"It's Nikolas! Nikolas!"

They quietened her. "What Nikolas? Your brother?"

"The King! King Nikolas!" A name she knew, of a man she had never seen. They asked her what she meant. "On the radio set! Talking to us! In the big hole under my signal-box!"

They took her hand. She led them to the dug-out, where men were crouched, listening, the light of burning buildings flickering over them.

". . . *I cannot believe that our enemies will choose to lay waste all the civilisations of the world, rather than accept defeat in our small country. I cannot believe that the idea of one nation's freedom to live in peace is so intolerable that the whole world must suffer and become extinct. I cannot believe that any man, either friend or enemy, will deny that we have the right to drive out the foreigner from our dear soil, now that we have the strength and the will to do it.*"

Ex-King Nikolas had been speaking for only a few minutes before radio systems began picking up the broadcast all over the world. Monitoring staffs broke off in the middle of a sentence and began work on the speech that was coming from Unic Radio, London.

Press and radio comment followed within the hour, from quoted official sources, government spokesmen, and free-lance political prophets.

"The entire free world is dazed by this miracle, and it will be a little time before we can appreciate the brilliant fortune of the Slavakian nation and its resolute young king."

"It should be borne in mind that since the degree of international tension can only be described as hair-trigger, an incident of this kind can touch off the mechanism, and extinguish life on this planet by precipitating nuclear global war."

"Telegrams are already pouring in to Unic House and the Slavakian Embassy in London. Kings, queens, presidents and chiefs of state are showering Nikolas the Second with their congratulations and messages of goodwill."

"It will be obvious from the events of the past few days that since Nikolas has wilfully chosen to complicate an already dangerous situation by responding to the hysterical appeals of his suicidal people, he will be very lucky to leave London alive, and luckier still to reach Slavakia before a stray bomb or shell extinguishes this belated star."

"Viva Nikolas! Romance is not yet dead! The eyes of all the women in the world will shine tonight!"

"The machinery of the Distant Early Warning line must now be tightened to a pitch of superhuman alertness. If the Union decides to join issue with the Democracies, it will not wait for declarations. The polar bomber-routes will suddenly be black with wings: the stratosphere will suddenly be alive with ballistic missiles: and only the sharpest look-out will save us from surprise attack and inevitable annihilation."

"It is, of course, evident that, in the event of nuclear attack, nuclear defence can do nothing but double the intensification of the lethal content of the earth's atmosphere by atomic explosion. And since such 'safeguards' as the American Dew Line and other radar defences are fully alerted, it is just as evident that any attack will be followed by immediate counter-attack, so that there is no question of an advantage of surprise, when the end-result can only be a waste of radio-active terrain and water within a matter of days."

"*Now* will the United Nations make a stand? *Now* will the West take inspiration and courage from the example of this one small country and its phœnix king?"

"Reports are reaching us that American air squadrons are standing by for take-off from European bases, but whether they will carry nuclear bombs to the Danube, or 'pre-war' explosives, no one can say. It is clear that only strong military support can now enable the Slavakians to beat back the Union invasion from the north against Drovnik and the other cities under siege."

"The fact that King Nikolas is free, alive, and in a position to accept the throne from which he was driven only a few years ago, makes little enough difference in physical terms to the fighting in Drovnik. Short though his speech on Unic Radio has been, he would have helped his people more if each word had been a bullet for the guns of his soldiers. But in moral terms the value of his speech cannot be estimated yet. Slavakia now has a leader. He is a leader once recognised throughout the world as a powerful influence in the affairs of nations. He is a man who won millions to his side, despite—or was it because of?—a private life more in keeping with a Ruritanian vagabond prince than a vital and shrewd descendant of an historic monarchy. The bare fact that he is alive and ready to play his part in this tragic conflict could well be instrumental in turning the enemy back to its dark frontiers and striking a blow for peace and freedom that would change the whole balance of opposed world factions, so that even the cold war would terminate and leave the civilised nations secure at the conference tables."

"Nikolas must now ask the United Nations what they are going to do for Slavakia. They will be forced to answer and their answer will be public. Have they the courage to make their stand with him and with his cause, or must the threat of the mushroom cloud debar the peoples of this world for ever from using their tongues in forthright debate, before resorting to murder and counter-murder in the name of 'peace'?"

"It will be interesting to see how far the West is prepared to oppose the East on this now major issue, and whether we shall have the nerve, in years to come, to place our wreaths on the tomb of the Unknown Slavakian Hero if we have today been content to stand and watch him die."

"Even now, a few minutes after Nikolas finished speaking, tape-recorders that were running in the studios in Austria are being sent into Slavakian territory across the frontier where the roads are still open, so that those who did not hear him can listen to the echo of his voice, and warm their hearts."

"Reports that an ultimatum is already being prepared by an emergency committee of the United Nations have not yet been confirmed."

"At the moment, one voice alone among all the voices to be heard across the radio networks of the world is more true and may prove to be more powerful than any other. Whether its message brings hope or disaster, we listen with all our attention."

The long red pointer swung across the figures of the clock on the wall, counting the seconds in silence. The man sat alone at the table where the microphone hung. He spoke without a script.

Faces filled the glass panel in the sound-proof ante-room. They heard the voice on the producer's speaker. Baron Angelitri was in a chair, his chin resting on his knuckles, his eyes brooding. Czinitri was there, and Segrave, Nadreanu, others, watching. Behind Louise, Messiter, Andrey Turocz, listening. The air was stifling, despite the steady suck of the conditioner at the back of the room. The needle flickered on the amplifier dial as the tone of the speaker rose and fell. A red light glowed above the door, another in the studio.

"While you are fighting, you will know this: that by the grace of God I am now granted the honour of fighting with you. There is little time, and I shall not rest. We shall remind the nations that in the Slavakian people there is still the strength and determination to claim the most sacred of rights among men, which is freedom. We shall remind them that it was this same ideal that prompted our country to offer its services and the lives of its sons to the cause that was fought out in the last war.

"It may not be too late to remind the nations that it is not the size of a country that is important, but the quality of its people, and that in breaking the domination of an alien creed we seek to do no more than insist upon our birthright: that a man, in the company of his fellows, must have the right to live on his own soil, employ his hands in his own work, guide the steps of his children in the graces of his own choosing, and within the laws of his own making remain his own master. May God be your great leader in your great crusade."

The evening sky was grey. The rain had stopped an hour ago, but puddles shone across the tarmac aprons, reflecting the cathedral shapes of the hangars.

Two cars had left the doors of the Commandant Suite and were alongside the Viscount aircraft. Camera-men stood in a group, their bulbs already flickering and casting a white unnatural light across the faces of the passengers.

Sofi Mikayan had gone on board, and now Baron Angelitri went up the steps. He exchanged a word with the stewardess and the cameras caught her smile.

Sir Edmond Stross moved his polished shoes with care, avoiding the puddles, smoothing the scene with his urbane presence.

Messiter spoke to him, and for a moment they discussed the weather, the aeroplane, the fit appearance of the ex-King. They chose each word carefully, and therefore, to all intents and purposes, said nothing whatsoever to each other.

Nikolas was the last to go on board, since it was his wish. He had looked at the evening sky and the silhouetted frieze of London's roofs and towers and chimneys, and then had moved to the steps below the aircraft, where Louise was standing.

They were frozen in the sudden blizzard of flashlight, two unreal figures, their faces turned to each other, their voices unheard. His hand reached out to touch hers.

"We have a saying in our country. 'Those who part sadly take their first step towards return.'"

Her hand was cold. It was not easy to smile. "Then I shall get very giddy, going in circles. You must go now."

"I may never reach Slavakia. We don't know what will happen. I can only wait, in Vienna, and hold myself ready. There would be no danger for you if you came to see me in Vienna."

"There would be great danger to my heart."

The lightning of the cameras flickered about them and made her uneasy. She took her hand from his. "You must go now."

He nodded, looking down into her eyes and saying nothing. He turned away and climbed the steps, and in a moment the cabin doorway was vacant. The stewardess closed it and the lightning beat against the blank metal.

The aircraft took off when permission was received: there was no schedule since it was a charter flight. When it appeared in the distance, rising gently above the stationary shapes on the ground, the undercarriage was already withdrawing; the thin sound of the engines washed along the ground and sent echoes ebbing among the buildings.

The shape grew smaller and Louise did not move. It was reflected in her watching eyes, so that there was still a fragile contact between herself and the people on board, until the aircraft was out of sight and the last thread broken.